Somebody Pick Up My Pieces

Somebody Pick Up My Pieces

J. D. MASON

St. Martin's Press ❧ New York

SOMEBODY PICK UP MY PIECES. Copyright © 2011 by J. D. Mason. All rights reserved. Printed in the United States of America. For information address St. Martin's Press, 175 Fifth Avenue, New York, N.Y. 10010.

www.stmartins.com

ISBN 978-0-312-36887-6

First Edition: February 2011

10 9 8 7 6 5 4 3 2 1

Dedicated to:

John King

Connie Rodgers

Adam Tate

Mattie King

Roberta Brooks

Uncle

Charlotte

Cammy Rodgers

Justin & Clarice Braxton

And all the kids, especially Jade

I will miss you all!

SAY UNCLE

Twenty-seven years is a lifetime. And he'd spent a lifetime locked up. Uncle was an old man now, sitting outside in the prison courtyard across from some cat young enough to be his grandson, whipping his ass at another game of chess.

"Checkmate, son," he chided indifferently.

The young blood shook his head, rolled his eyes, and left without so much as a sportsmanlike handshake.

"Anytime, mothafucka," Uncle muttered. The sucka wore a blue rag on his head, representing the Bloods or the Crips or the Stumps or Bumps, shit. Uncle couldn't remember what color went with what gang these days. All he knew was that every damn body had a color and that fools lived and died for that nonsense, which was just ridiculous to an old-head like him.

He was his own kind of badass back in his day, and it didn't matter what color he wore. Everybody knew not to fuck with Uncle, and those that did, well . . . he'd said a silent prayer for each and every one of them before he sent them on their way. That last one got him, though. Even with a bullet put through his head, young, and scared shitless—half of Zoo's face was missing and that fool, unlike all the fools before him, had been the one to get Uncle sent up for time. Uncle had killed many men in his day. How ironic that the one who he had believed to be the most inconsequential turned out to be the one who had done him in.

A tall, lanky, dark-skinned kid, quiet and polite to a fault, in many ways Zoo was more like his own son than the ones who'd really belonged to him. Zoo wasn't a gangster, and never would be. But he'd always looked up to Uncle, wanted to go everywhere he went, and do what he did, only Zoo never had the stomach for the kind of life Uncle lived. The boy wasn't hard enough. He was soft, and that's probably what she saw in him.

Charlotte Rodgers was a high-yellow, lovely woman with a round behind and thick legs. Uncle held that image of her sacred in his memories. While everything else had faded, the vivid picture of her never did. Sandy brown hair, shimmering eyes, compact and curved in all the right places, she set his heart on fire the moment he first laid eyes on her that night in the club. She danced less than ten feet away from her man, Black Sam, who'd damned near turned white at the sight of Uncle walking into the place dressed to the nines with his entourage. Sam owed him money, but that night, the two men struck a deal, and he handed over that pretty little thing to Uncle on a silver platter.

"Don't street her, Uncle," Sam begged before leaving.

Uncle reassured him that he didn't have to worry about that. He had a stable full of hos, and this one had no business lying up with any other man but him. She was Uncle's pride and joy and he showered her with everything her heart desired. He had come as close to loving her as it was possible for him to love any woman, including his brawny-ass wife. Uncle took good care of that broad, until she crossed the line. She had an itch that needed scratching, and apparently, Uncle's rod hadn't been long enough to reach it. She did the wrong thing and went after Zoo when she thought Uncle wasn't looking. But Uncle was always watching. Even when he wasn't anywhere around—he was around.

When Uncle found the two of them together, laid up in his bed, in the apartment he'd been paying for, getting fat from the food he'd put on the damn table . . . Well, he lost all tenderness for that woman, put a bullet through that boy's skull, and had seriously considered putting one in hers too, had he not been so inclined to clean up after himself.

"Wrap him up in that bedspread, and get his ass down to the car!" he had commanded Dante and Leon, who had been busy taking liberties with pretty Charlie bleeding, crying, and snotting all over the bed. Looking at her, he'd almost felt sorry for her and it dawned on him, briefly, that most women would probably rather be dead than have a train pulled on them. He looked down again at the mess that was left of Zoo. What the hell was that boy's real name, he wondered, agitated. "Got brains and shit all over that new TV I just bought!"

The mistake he'd made in that moment was one he'd spend damn near thirty years of his life paying for. Uncle stared at that chessboard, scratched his scalp, and then ran his hands across the crop of silver hair capping his head, thinking back to the decision he'd made to get rid of that body, right then and there. Every now and then, he was still tortured over it. What if he'd gone ahead and broken her little neck like he'd planned on doing, and then taken them both out together and saved himself a trip back? To this day he didn't know what he'd been thinking or why it had been so important to get Zoo out of that apartment—divine intervention. Couldn't have been anything else, he'd concluded. The Lord always did work in mysterious ways and the Good Lord must've had it in for Uncle that night, and He'd gone ahead and set his ass up.

"Get rid of that shit, Leon, man," Dante said, glancing in the rearview mirror. "We got whitey on us."

Leon threw his weed out of the window and blew out the smoke in his mouth along with it, then quickly sprayed air freshener all over himself. Red and blue lights flashed in the distance, and Uncle slowly opened his eyes as the sound of the siren screamed to his soul that his life was about to change forever.

The Lincoln Continental gradually drifted over to the side of the road and finally stopped. The state trooper approached the car cautiously on the driver's side, shined his flashlight in Dante's eyes, then he put it on Leon, and, finally, rested it on Uncle.

"License and registration," he said in his thick, Southern, redneck accent.

Dante pulled out his license. Leon handed him the registration from the glove compartment.

The cop studied both documents entirely too long. "Well now, this don't look right." He sniffed. "Says here, right here on this registration that you go by the name of Uncle, boy. But uh . . . that ain't the name on your license."

Dante sighed his frustration. "Nah, man. Uncle's in the back. This is his car. I'm just the driver."

The patrolman put his flashlight on Uncle again, and then laughed. "Oh, so you just the driver? And what the hell are you?" he directed his question to Leon. "The bodyguard?"

Leon didn't respond.

He shined his light back on Uncle. "You famous or something, boy? You got drivers and bodyguards and shit. You some kind of singer or basketball player or something?" He laughed again. "Hell! Maybe you the president of the goddamned United States of America. Is that it?"

Uncle didn't say a word.

"Why you pulling us over?" Dante finally asked.

The patrolman suddenly stopped laughing and flashed his light into Dante's eyes.

"You were driving recklessly, boy. Swerving back and forth, all over the goddamned road. If I didn't know better, I'd say you fellas had been drinking or something." He sniffed again.

Out of nowhere, another patrolman appeared, but on Leon's side of the car. "This one here smells like weeds and lilacs."

"You boys need to get out of the car," the first patrolman commanded. When no one moved, he put his hand on the handle of his pistol in his hip holster. "Do I need to say it again?"

Those mothafuckas weren't as bad as they thought they were, Uncle remembered thinking, sitting in the back of the patrol car, with his hands cuffed behind his back, laughing under his breath at the looks on their faces when they found Zoo's ass in the trunk. That one fool threw up all over his partner's shoes, and both of them turned as white as the sheets they probably wore over their heads when they thought no one was looking.

Uncle wasn't surprised that they'd found Zoo with half his head gone. He wasn't surprised that he was going to prison either. He'd been fortunate longer than most men in his line of work. Good luck had been on his side for too long. What had surprised him was how much time he'd spent thinking about her, nearly every minute of every day that he'd been locked up. And ever since he first laid eyes on that pretty little thing's fine, honey gold behind, he knew that she'd be his demise. Uncle was just a man, after all, and men have a tendency to lose the best of themselves when it comes to beautiful women.

Through the years, he'd only memorized one phone number, and it was the only one he ever dialed, because he knew that these people were the only people in the world who would ever take a call from him.

Uncle waited patiently in line for his turn to use the phone. It was one of those inconveniences he'd become accustomed to through the years, being told when to make a phone call, when to wake up in the morning, when to go to bed at night, even when to take a piss.

"I didn't call to talk to Arnel," he said, matter-of-factly. "I called to talk to you, darlin'."

Uncle Lamont Williams had been locked up for twenty-seven years, and in less than four months, they were going to open up that gate out front and set him loose. He didn't know how to feel about that.

Arnel, his half-brother, had been with that white girl, Lynn Randall, for more than thirty years, and had never seen fit to marry her. But then, why buy the cow . . . Arnel was a shell of his half-assed attempt to be a man. He was a junkie before he was a man. He was a thief and a low-down dirty piece of shit before he'd ever been a man, and that dumb-ass Lynn Randall worshipped the ground he walked on. Uncle never understood it, but she tried to explain it to him once.

"Where I come from, don't no man talk to a woman the way Arnel talks to me. He says things to me, sweet things, that even though I don't know where it comes from, I love it. He ain't never hit me, Uncle. He ain't never done nothing but make me feel like I'm beautiful, and I can't help but love him for that."

Some people were too damn easy to please, Uncle concluded,

staring back at her that day. Poor white trash was pitiful, especially when she put all of her faith into a black-ass junkie mothafucka like Arnel. Obviously, they deserved each other.

"I hear you getting out soon," she said.

"Soon—I am," Uncle responded, sounding almost cavalier. "You gonna be glad to see me?" He chuckled, knowing that the next word out of her mouth would be a lie.

"Sure, Uncle. Of course I am."

He'd had that woman too many times to count, and too many different ways to remember, sometimes right under Arnel's nose—literally. She wasn't the prettiest woman he'd seen, but she was accommodating to a fault, and creative. Uncle smiled warmly. Miss Randall had an imagination that was downright sinful, and if it meant saving Arnel's dumb ass from a beat down, or worse, she'd gladly shared her illustrious talents with the masses.

"I hear he got the virus," Uncle said, solemnly. Dumb or not, Arnel was family.

Lynn sighed. "He does. And I do too."

Uncle had managed to escape the virus. He'd gotten caught for murder, but he hadn't gotten caught by AIDS, and for that, he said a silent "Thank you, Jesus." Back in his day, condoms were for suckers and VD could be cured by a shot at the clinic. It was easy back then, and only fools died from that shit. He didn't hear anything about the AIDS until the eighties, but by then he was locked up in here, all safe and sound, in a manner of speaking. No sucka had ever tried bending him over for no backdoor shit, either. Hell, he'd pinch a dick clean off at the quick like a turd if any of them ever tried. Of course, now he was just old, and thankfully Uncle wasn't anybody's type these days.

"He ain't doing so well, Uncle," Lynn continued. "It's hard having to watch him waste away to nothing."

Uncle sighed. "I can imagine, sugah. I can only imagine."

For the last twenty-seven years, though, Uncle had been wasting away his damn self. He'd come in here like he was cock-of-the-roost, chest all stuck out, dressed to the nines, looking like the super pimp he'd been, a gangster. Uncle had walked through those doors like a goddamned hero, to damn near cheers and shouts from prisoners who knew who he was as soon as he set foot in this joint. He had been a king back then, even in here. Time faded his ass to black, though, and eventually Uncle was nothing more than an OG to these young boys coming up in here—an Old Gangster and a joke when they thought he wasn't listening.

"Watch out, y'all! Here come Big Pimpin', looking like a yellow-ass Huggy Bear! Got them old hos—old as my grandmomma!" And then they'd laugh.

He left them fools alone, because they didn't deserve his time or attention. Sissy punks who needed to dress alike, wearing the same colors, and hanging out in packs like fuckin' rats instead of men. They didn't know shit about Uncle. They didn't know that he didn't need his crew to help him kill a man. He'd killed plenty on his own, with his own hands, until he decided he was tired of getting blood on his Stacy Adamses. He let other people get their hands dirty for him. Mothafuckas killed because he said so. It really was that simple.

Uncle was a shadow of his former self now, though. He could admit that, and he was cool with it, because what else could he be? His wife, Sherrell, had left his ass two weeks after he'd been locked up. Took all his shit, his kids, then came to see him one last time to cuss him out before she took off to Mississippi, following after some niggah.

"If you ever get out of this place, mothafucka!" she screamed into the phone on the other side of the glass separating them.

"Don't you ever call me, don't call my kids, don't even say my goddamned name! You hear me?"

He missed the hell out of that woman.

"You know why I'm calling," he said to Lynn, waiting patiently on the other end.

Lynn nervously cleared her throat before responding. "I think so."

He closed his eyes, and held his breath while the image of that pretty little woman materialized behind his eyelids as if she were being drawn. "Even after all these years," he said, quietly, "I still dream of that woman, Lynn Randall."

"You love her, Uncle?" Lynn asked, surprised.

Uncle laughed. "I love the notion of her, sweetheart. That's all it is. And Charlotte Rodgers ain't never been more than a notion."

"You tried to kill her, Uncle," Lynn blurted out.

"Says who?" He laughed.

Uncle was a complicated man. He always had been, and from the way the conversation was going, time in prison hadn't changed that fact at all. But Lynn had been there. She'd seen what he'd done to Charlotte, and knew good and damn well what else he'd planned on doing to her as soon as he came back to that apartment. Lynn had waited in her car outside of Charlotte's apartment, scared to death, and knowing that she was about to put her own ass on the line for that girl, but somebody had to do something. She never did understand why she felt it had to be her. But something inside of Lynn needed to try and do something before it was too late, because on any given day, and at Uncle's whim, Charlotte could've just as easily have been Lynn.

"Come on!" Her memories drifted back to that night, when

she found Charlotte naked and bleeding. Her face had been split wide open from the corner of her mouth to her ear. Uncle's pretty honey-colored girl had been violated in the worst way, and Lynn knew that it was only a matter of minutes before the man came back to finish the job. "Charlotte! Get up! Hurry!" Lynn pulled that girl up, and practically dragged her out of that door and down the stairs, then poured her limp and broken body into the backseat of her old car. Lynn hauled ass out of Kansas City that night and drove like a bat out of hell to anywhere. And she regretted it as soon as she did. Uncle wasn't dumb. He knew that Lynn had been the one to get Charlotte out of that apartment. He'd never come right out and said it, but he knew.

"She—she ain't the same as you remember her, Uncle," Lynn quietly confessed. "She don't look the same after you—"

"After I what, sugah?"

She didn't respond.

"Don't none of us look the same, darlin'. We done all got old, and I ain't expecting to find that woman looking the way she did thirty years ago. But that don't mean I wouldn't like to see her. Know what I mean?"

Lynn shuddered. Uncle had a tone to his voice that had always been unmistakably sinister, especially when he called himself being reassuring or even kind. She knew better than to argue or challenge him when she heard it.

Lynn almost felt herself start to smile. Uncle had to be inching up on seventy now. He was an old man who'd been locked away in prison for nearly three decades. Even his shadow wouldn't recognize him once he got out on the streets, because he was no longer that slick-talking, -walking, -dressing villain he'd once been. But even still, he was Uncle. He might as well have been the devil himself, as far as Lynn was concerned, and the last thing she wanted was to piss off the devil.

"She lives in Murphy now," she volunteered. Charlotte had been her friend. They talked on the phone nearly every day, and Lynn had thought enough of the woman at one time to risk her own life to save Charlotte from Uncle's wrath. But Uncle had been right about one thing. They were all old now. Lynn had other matters to tend to, like Arnel's virus, and her own. And it was about time that Charlotte stood face-to-face with her own demon and dealt with him herself.

"You got something to write with? I'll tell you where she lives."

One of these days he was going to have to come on out and thank Lynn for pulling Charlotte out of harm's way. Years ago, he'd thought about snapping Lynn's neck in place of Charlotte's for getting involved in his business the way she'd done—no harm, no foul. By the time she pulled that woman from that apartment that night, Uncle was on his way to prison. But as time passed, he began to realize that Lynn had actually done him a favor. She'd given him something to look forward to for the day when he was finally set free.

One Thin Dime

ONE

"Miss Rodgers?"

There was a cop standing at her door. Charlotte eyed him wearily through the screen. "Yes?"

"Miss Rodgers, your daughter, Clarice Braxton? Called the station saying that she hadn't heard from you and was worried. She asked us to check on you."

Charlotte didn't say a word.

"Are you alright, ma'am?" he eventually asked.

"I'm fine," she said tersely.

The officer didn't look convinced. "Are you sure?"

No, she wasn't sure. Her children had turned on her and left her here all alone. How in the world could she be alright after her children had dismissed her the way the three of them had done?

"I'm fine," she said, more convincingly.

He shook his head. "Call your children, ma'am," he said, annoyed, before leaving. "They're obviously worried about you."

Charlotte slammed the door shut, sat down in her recliner, put her feet up, and stared at the television screen. The volume was turned down so low she could barely hear it. That was how she preferred it. After Camille, her youngest daughter, had moved out and left with Connie and Reesy, that house had felt like a tomb, cold, empty, and too quiet. Always quiet. Charlotte had learned to live with it, and to wallow in it as a reminder to herself that nobody gave a damn about her. They never did.

Less than ten minutes after that cop had left her front porch, the phone rang.

"Mom?" It was Clarice. "Mom, it's me, Reesy. I know you're there. The policeman said he saw you." She sighed, irritably. "Mom, please. Don't be like this. We're worried about you. You haven't spoken to me or Cammy since we left. You're being silly."

Silly? Charlotte was being silly? She angrily snatched up the receiver. "I'm being silly," she huffed. "Silly is putting your nose in where it doesn't belong, Reesy! Silly is making somebody believe with all their heart that you care about them when deep down, you know it's not true!"

"Mom . . ."

"Silly is beating on your own mother, Clarice!" she said, letting go of bitter tears. "You're never supposed to hit your mother! God saves a special place in hell for children who beat their mothers!"

"I didn't beat you, Mom," Reesy said, defensively, "and you know why I did it," Reesy responded sheepishly. "I'm sorry, Mom. I am so sorry."

Charlotte's lip quivered. "I'm sorry too! Sorry I ever laid eyes on you again!" Charlotte hung up as abruptly as she'd answered.

She had loved Reesy more than the other two put together, until Connie, Charlotte's oldest, finally managed to turn Reesy and Cammy against her with her lies and her ugly ways.

"You're the one, Connie! Why the hell did you bring your black ass into my house?" Charlotte screamed.

"Momma!" Reesy tried stepping between Charlotte and Connie, standing toe-to-toe like two boxers.

"I always hated you!" Charlotte glared at Connie.

"I always hated you too, so that makes us even!" Connie shot back.

"You ain't better than me, Connie!"

"Shit, Momma!" Connie smirked. *"Who the hell isn't better than you?"*

Charlotte closed her eyes, recalling the rage she felt surging through her whole body as she swung her arm in the air, bracing herself to knock the shit out of that girl. And all of a sudden, she felt the sting and the heat from the slap across her face, not from Connie, but from Reesy.

Those girls had all expected for Charlotte to be perfect, but of course, she wasn't. No mother is ever perfect. She'd only been fifteen years old when she'd had Connie, and what she learned about taking care of children, she learned on her own. She'd made mistakes with all of them. Charlotte could admit it to herself and to them. Charlotte had thought too much of herself when she was young, and had put her needs before the needs of her girls, but she had atoned for her selfishness. Charlotte had atoned for everything she'd done from taking off with Sam and leaving her two oldest girls behind to maybe being a little too hard on Cammy. She had paid for the things she'd done a hundred times over in ways they could never imagine. And she was still paying for it.

Hell is living twenty-seven years and not knowing if your children are alive or dead. She had had Cammy in that time, but there was no replacing her golden girls, Connie and Reesy, who she'd left behind in Denver. Charlotte had come to terms with the fact that she'd never see her girls again, until she got a letter in the mail from Reesy. Her baby had hired someone to find Charlotte, and for the first time in nearly three decades, she had finally had a prayer answered and a chance to go home again. But just as quickly as it had been given to her, those girls had brutally snatched it away from her. Lynn Randall had brought Charlotte to Murphy, Kansas, to save her life. Lynn had saved her, but she'd condemned her to this place, and Charlotte's children had taken the key and left her here, like garbage, to rot.

TWO

For the first time in her life, Cammy lived on her own. She had lived with Reesy when she first moved here to Denver, but after a few months, Reesy's husband, Justin, helped to get her a job as a receptionist at the accounting firm where he worked, and Cammy quickly found a place of her own. Reesy and Justin had their own problems to deal with, and besides, she needed to be alone and away from Reesy watching her all the time, constantly urging her to talk about something she couldn't put into words.

"You just need time. You'll be fine before you know it."

How much time?

"You're young. You can have more children, Cammy."

But what should she do about the child she'd lost?

"If Tyrell really loves you, and if it's meant to be, the two of you will get through this together."

And what if . . . she didn't love him anymore?

It was easier for Cammy not to think about these things. Inside, she was quietly falling apart, but outside, Cammy smiled, and worked, and did what she'd always done better than anyone else. She pretended to be fine.

She'd lost her baby in a car accident six months ago, and there were times when she wondered why she hadn't died too. Cammy moved to Denver, with her sisters, Connie and Reesy. She had never even known her sisters until just before her accident. Charlotte had talked about them, but they'd never been more than fantasies to Cammy until Reesy's letter came in the mail and turned Cammy and Charlotte's small, intimate world upside down.

"My babies found me, Cammy. After all this time, they found me."

She had never seen her mother so happy and Cammy had never felt more nervous and unsettled than when she had first met Reesy.

Charlotte always had a knack for being able to flip the switch on Cammy at a moment's notice. One minute her mother loved her with all the passion a mother could feel for a daughter, and the next, Cammy might as well have been some stranger off the street. But until Reesy showed up, Cammy had been able to make excuses for her mother's unpredictable behavior. When Reesy came, Cammy could've been swept up in a tornado, and Charlotte wouldn't have even noticed she was gone. It was painful facing the truth that she'd loved her mother as much as she did, only to find out that Charlotte never loved her back.

When Cammy found out she was pregnant it was the happiest day in her life, and in Tyrell's life too.

"Shit," he said, grinning from ear to ear. "Ain't no reason you can't move in with me now, Cam. We can be a family, and get married, and have even more kids, girl."

"You wanna go be with that fool, then go!" Charlotte had said when Cammy told her about the baby, and that Tyrell wanted to get married. "But don't come crawling back here when he gets sick of you, Cammy, and dumps your ass when you get round and fat. I know his kind. He's

fine as long as he's getting his, but after that baby comes and you too tired to throw you legs up in the air for him, he'll send you packing! Ain't no revolving doors around here. You leave, you stay gone. I mean it."

Charlotte played tricks with her mind, the way she had since Cammy was small. One minute she was pissed, and the next, she cried, begged, and convinced Cammy that her place was with her mother, because the truth was that all they had was each other, and nobody should ever get in the way of that.

"We can take care of the baby together." The softness in her mother's eyes and voice was like a siren to Cammy, pulling her in to that warm place in her mother's heart that always felt so good. "I'm your momma, baby. You're all I have, and without you here, what will I do, Camille? I live for you. I always have."

Reesy had her babies. She didn't know what it was like to lose one. She had her man too, even though she wasn't really speaking to him. Reesy had a home, and people who loved her, who had always loved her, and she knew exactly where she fit in the world.

"We're sisters, Cammy," she kept reminding her. "Connie and I are here for you now. You're not alone anymore, sweetie."

It wasn't as simple as that, and Cammy wanted to tell her that, but all she did was smile and nod. "I know, Reesy."

She sat on the small sofa in her quiet apartment. All day long, she'd been surrounded by the noise of phones ringing and people constantly asking her questions at work. Cammy savored the quiet and dulled the noise in her head with glass after glass of wine. People from work would ask her to lunch or happy hour, but she always declined. Reesy found any excuse for "the sisters" to get together once a month, and Cammy would begrudgingly oblige.

Connie, the oldest of the three, just had a way of looking at Cammy that made her feel uneasy, because Connie looked at her as if she could see everything that was going on inside Cammy. She wasn't sure how to feel about that. Cammy was more comfortable with keeping her feelings to herself, and with trying to sort them out for herself, or justify them. Connie had no place being in her head like that, and neither did Reesy, because neither one of them could ever understand what it was like to be Camille, and, sisters or not, they were strangers.

THREE

"I keep telling myself that I'm here because of what he did." Never in a million years did she ever dream she'd be the kind of woman to have an affair. Avery Stallings held her in his arms, and listened quietly as she spoke. "Justin cheated," she continued explaining, "so why shouldn't I?"

He sighed, contentedly, squeezed her closer, and then kissed her exposed shoulder. "That's not why you're here, and you know it, Reesy."

Even if she'd wanted to argue with him, she couldn't, because he was right. Her being here now, in his arms, in his bed, had nothing to do with her husband. "I need for that to be the reason, Avery," she said softly.

"Would that make it easier for you? Make you feel justified for being here with me like this?"

She let her eyes close. Yes.

Avery Stallings was the detective she'd hired two years ago to find her mother, Charlotte. And while everyone else condemned her, and told her that she was crazy for even bothering to look for that woman, he was the one person who understood her need to find the woman who she'd loved more than anything when she was a child. Avery understood what Justin never even tried to understand, as far as Reesy was concerned.

"You're becoming obsessed with this, Reesy," he'd argued. "It's all you think about, morning, noon, and night, and the kids and I are becoming more of an afterthought to you. Not to mention, it's costing us a fortune to find this woman, who by all accounts isn't even worth finding."

Justin felt slighted and left out and abandoned, and found solace with someone else, a stripper who he paid money to for sex. Good money. Hard-earned money, and money that took away from his beloved family. He had no room to complain to her about what finding Charlotte was costing them.

Avery had been the one to reveal Justin's affair to Reesy. For her husband to betray her like that was unforgivable, and for six months the two of them lived apart, and she couldn't even look him in the eyes without seeing images of him and that prostitute together in the photos that Avery had taken and shown her. They separated, and Reesy even went as far as to hire a divorce lawyer, before finally giving in to the pressure from Justin, her parents, his parents, and the lost and confused expressions on her children's faces to try and work through their problems. He'd only been back home for a few weeks, suggesting counseling and prayer to help heal the wounds of their marriage. Reesy agreed, reluctantly, to talking to someone about their marital problems, but it hadn't happened yet. At least, not the way Justin had probably intended. She did talk to someone, and she'd lied to her husband tonight, telling him that she was going to see a movie with friends, so that she could spend time with that someone.

She'd showed up at the door of Avery's apartment with every intention of telling him that the two of them couldn't see each other anymore, and that she and Justin were going to work on their marriage for the sake of their children. As soon as he swung open the door, Reesy knew she'd lied to herself and that if she set foot inside his apartment they'd end up making love.

"I shouldn't be here," she whispered.

He reached out to her, took hold of her hand, coaxed her inside, and closed the door behind her. Avery pulled her closer, into his arms, closed his eyes, and grazed his lips against the side of her face. She closed her eyes too. Her heart raced. She wrapped her arms around his waist. Her fingers traveled up the length of his spine, and she pressed her body deeper into his.

Avery's lips pressed against hers, and he slowly parted her lips with his tongue. And she welcomed him. Reesy drank in his kisses. She let her mind drift from her husband's face until it vanished, but only for a moment. Justin's image flashed behind her eyes, and abruptly, she pulled away from Avery. He saw the panic in her face, and before she could utter a word, he held her tighter, and shook his head. "Don't, Reesy," he said, calmly, reasonably. "It's alright." Coming from him, it sounded like truth. A small voice inside her whispered that it wasn't alright, and warned her to leave. But Avery kissed her again. His anticipation for her swelled against her hip and that small voice disappeared in the deafening sound of the desire building between them.

Avery filled her with more than just his body. Easing slowly and meticulously in and out of her, Reesy welcomed each thrust with the sad realization that once this was over, it would always be over. But before it was, she wanted her fill of him. He seemed to sense what she was thinking and slowed his stroke, then lay motionless on top of her, planting soft kisses on her lips and neck. She resisted the urge to move, knowing that it would be too much for both of them.

Reesy closed her eyes and willed away images of her husband's face. She erased the sound of his voice whispering in her heart. Yes, she loved Justin, and she would always love him and she'd come here believing that she wanted her marriage to work. Lying here with him, she was ashamed to admit to herself that she didn't regret one moment of her encounter with Avery.

"What are you thinking?" he asked softly.

Reesy hesitated for a moment before answering. "You don't want to know." Tears threatened to fall from her eyes, but she wouldn't let them. Not tonight.

He rose up and gazed deeply into her eyes. "Then let me believe that you're thinking about me." He tried to smile.

She raised her hand to his face and touched his cheek. "That's not so far from the truth, Avery."

"How was the movie?" Justin asked groggily, as Reesy climbed into bed. He turned over on his side, kissed her cheek, and draped his arm across her waist.

She hated him touching her, and being so close to her. Could he tell she'd been with someone else? And even though she'd showered before coming to bed, could he smell him on her? Reesy took a deep breath to calm her nerves and ease her guilt.

"It was good," she lied. "Not the best, but good."

"Mmmmmm," he moaned. It wasn't long before he'd drifted back off to sleep, much to Reesy's relief. As much as she wanted to, Reesy couldn't sleep, and she couldn't stop feeling ashamed for thinking about Avery.

FOUR

If she didn't know any better, Connie would swear that what she was watching was a scene straight out of one of those corny G-rated family shows. For the first time in months she'd been able to sleep through the night, and it scared the shit out of her. Connie leapt out of bed and bolted like a bullet from the bedroom to the baby's room, only to find him missing from his crib. She took the steps three at a time downstairs until she discovered both men in her life asleep on the sofa.

It was a sight for sore and unbelieving eyes, to be sure, and something she never thought she'd ever see in her life, but there it was, big, bold, black, and absolutely beautiful. And right and good. John, a giant figure of a man, lay on his back, his arms and legs hanging off one side of the couch, with his mouth open, snoring softly. On his chest was a tiny version of himself, sleeping contentedly to the rhythms of his father's breath.

She went over and knelt down next to both of them. Waking them would be a crime, so she didn't bother. Connie was cool just watching them, both exquisite and hers. Damn! This shit was magic, and so much better than anything she could've ever dreamed up. Between the two of them, Connie and John had both survived some jacked-up lives, but they had survived for this moment right here. Jonathon was three months old and bigger than anything the two of them had ever experienced. He was the right to all her wrongs, and John's too, for that matter.

Connie gazed at John's bold, dark features and licked her lips. He'd had that effect on her since the beginning, but she was too cool to let on. She played it cool with him. Men like him had women falling at his feet, and if she'd have done the same thing, then she would've been one of the masses that he'd have probably just stepped over when he was through, ready to move on to the next one.

"Is that what you think?" he told her once, when she admitted her theory to him. John laughed. "I mean . . . I didn't have it like that," he said, trying to sound humble.

She rolled her eyes. "Well, I wasn't going to let you have it like that with me," she said smugly.

"Shame on me, if I'd have let you go, Connie." The look in his eyes when he said it struck a chord deep inside her. For once, he wasn't joking or trying to make light of his feelings, and he didn't want her to make light of them either.

John stirred and started to wake up. Connie braced herself, thinking that the man would stretch those long arms and legs, take a deep breath, and blast that infant off of his chest like a small missile, but he caught himself before she had a chance to fully panic. John realized that he had his son sleeping on his chest and looked over at Connie and smiled. "Why you looking at me like I was going to crush him?" he said in a low voice.

She smiled too. "Mother mode."

"Yeah, well . . . Daddy mode kicked in just in time, otherwise he'd have been a hamburger patty." He raised his lips to hers. "Morning."

Connie kissed him. "Morning, baby."

Connie had talked him into starting his own construction company. Actually, it hadn't been hard to do, since he'd been doing odd jobs here and there for some years, but she'd talked him into setting it up and taking it seriously. He put a name on the side of his truck, bought some business cards, and all of a sudden, he had more work than he could handle. J & A Construction was the name she'd come up with.

"John and Adam," she said, dancing around in circles. "Oooh! Doesn't that sound good? J & A Construction! Yeah, boy!"

Adam was his father's name. Leave it to Connie to know how to pay homage to somebody. In the blink of an eye John's whole life had changed, and for the first time John felt like he was connected to something. She blamed it on the boy, and she was partly right. Hell, it was a trip watching someone come into the world, brand new, and looking just like you. That counted for something. And it meant that John wasn't just a fool passing through time with nothing to leave behind besides an old beat-up car.

She'd wanted to name him John Jr., but he wasn't having it. His son deserved his own name because one day, he'd be a big, strong man in his own right, John had explained, and the last thing he'd need to be called was Junior. Connie came up with an alternative, though. She named him Jonathon, and he was cool with that. Jonathon Adam King. "Yeah," he said, smiling as soon as he heard it. "That shit's tight."

These days, he drove to work with purpose. After all, he had a family to take care of. Every now and then, though, doubt would creep in and remind him that nothing in life was guaranteed and just as easily as everything had fallen into place, it could fall out of place. She didn't have to say it out loud to know that Connie felt the same warning in her bones. They'd both had more than their share of disappointment in their lives. They'd both disappointed themselves more than anybody else ever could. But these days, they both fought to let those kinds of thoughts go, and to go ahead and feel good right where they were standing. She blamed that on the boy too. But Connie wasn't giving herself enough credit. John turned his attitude around for her, long before the kid ever made his way into the world. She'd given him something he never thought he'd ever be able to have: a reason to step up and be a better man than he believed he could be.

Love was crazy like that.

FIVE

Some ties could never be broken, like the one between Cammy and her mother. Charlotte understood this better than Cammy ever could. There would be days when Charlotte would see Cammy's number show up in her caller ID and Charlotte would refuse to answer. And other days, like today, when she couldn't pick up the phone fast enough.

"Momma?" Cammy said, breathing a desperate sigh of relief. "I'm so glad you—are you alright? Did you get my messages?"

Charlotte rolled her eyes, annoyed by the nasally, high-pitched, little-girl voice that Cammy used when she wanted to get on Charlotte's good side.

"I got them," Charlotte replied indifferently. "And yes, Camille. I'm fine."

"Oh, good," she said, relieved. "I was so worried about you."

"Worried about me?" Charlotte retorted. "Well, how worried can you be, Cammy? You took off and left me here all by myself. That doesn't sound like something a worried person would do."

Cammy didn't respond right away. Charlotte imagined all kinds of little sheepish thoughts running through that girl's mind at the moment. Guilt and shame should've been Cammy's middle names because the girl had spent her whole life damn near drowning in that mess for one reason or another. Cammy was a twenty-seven-, almost twenty-eight-year-old woman with the mind of a ten-year-old, and most of the time she wouldn't know her ass from an eyeball, if Charlotte hadn't been there pointing and telling her which was which.

"I do worry about you, Momma," she finally said in a tone that Charlotte had to strain to hear. "We all do. Reesy said she's been calling, but . . ."

"Reesy can kiss my ass like the rest of you. Tell her I said that."

"Momma, now you know that's not right. You know how much you mean to her."

"Oh, I know exactly how much I mean to all y'all, Camille. It's painfully obvious, which is why for the life of me I can't figure out how come y'all keep calling me. I'm right where you left me. I'm always going to be right where you left me."

"It wasn't meant to be for forever," she said softly.

Charlotte huffed. "I don't give a damn how long it was meant to be for. I'm here by myself, while all my children are happy and hootin' in my hometown, where I was born. You know better than any of them how badly I wanted to go home, Cammy." Charlotte's voice cracked. "How you think I feel knowing you're there and I'm here? It should be the other way around! You should be the one stuck here with that little fool you call a boyfriend! And I should be home. I should be home, Cammy!"

Cammy held the receiver to her ear long after her mother hung up on her. It was Saturday, and the sun was shining brightly outside her window. Cammy had the shades drawn. She was still in bed, even though it was past noon, and she had no desire to get out of the house at all. Finally, she put the receiver back on the cradle on the nightstand, lay back down, and pulled the sheets to her chin. She shouldn't have called, but Cammy couldn't help herself. She'd dreamed of seeing her mother laying facedown on the floor of that old house, with her eyes wide and bulging. Charlotte wasn't breathing in the dream. Cammy walked around her in circles, looking for some sign of life in her mother's body, crying and screaming for Charlotte to get up. Thinking about that dream now sent shivers down her spine.

There were days when she wished her mother dead. Leaving Charlotte was supposed to have been a dream come true. How many times had she imagined what it would be like to not have to live under her mother's rule? Growing up, she'd imagined the peace of having her own place, decorating it the way she wanted, making up her own rules, and having the freedom to come and go as she pleased. Cammy had that now, and no matter how hard she looked for it, happiness was nowhere to be found.

Her phone rang, and she suspected she knew who was calling even before he said anything. "Cam, it's Ty. Call me. Please. I need to hear from you."

She hardly spoke to him anymore. Tyrell had said he loved her, and back then she believed him. These days, however, Cammy couldn't bring herself to believe in much of anything.

SIX

"I'm not a perfect man, Reesy. I never have been. If you want to punish me for the rest of my life for what I did, then fine. I deserve it, but just don't make me pay for it like this. Don't take my family away from me."

The night he said those words to her, Justin was prepared to walk through hot coals to get his family back. He and Reesy had been separated for more than six months, and he'd counted every second of every one of those months, tormented over the fact that he'd risked everything he ever loved for an affair with another woman. Cookie—it wasn't even her real name. She was a stripper and somehow he'd convinced himself that she was the answer to the problems he was having in his marriage. He found comfort in her lap when he believed that his wife didn't give a damn about him. Justin bought Cookie's services, time and time again, simply because he felt ignored at home, and not a day had gone by when he didn't feel like an idiot for doing it.

"J. J.," Justin called to his oldest son playing video games in the den. "Turn it off. It's time to eat."

Some rituals were mandatory in their home, like sitting down together at the table and eating dinner as a family. Justin had recently moved back into the house and fell back, effortlessly, into a routine that was second nature to them all. The kids all seemed shell-shocked by the disruption of their father's absence. And both Justin and Reesy had worked double-time to try and shield them from the truth. His children were careful not to probe too deeply into why he hadn't been living with them or why he'd come home again so suddenly. The best thing Justin could do for all of them, though, was to be that foundation they needed, that rock he'd always been for his family. He came home, acting much the same way he did before he left. He came home as daddy, and they needed to know that he was and would always be there for them, no matter what.

Justin went into the kitchen, where Reesy was finishing preparing dinner. "Are we out of salad dressing?" he asked, searching the counter for the bottle.

"Check the refrigerator," she answered.

She'd cut her hair short. In all the years that he'd known her, she'd always worn it long, down past her shoulders, and he'd always loved it. He'd loved running his fingers through it. Reesy had gotten it cropped short a few days after he'd moved back home, and he couldn't help but wonder sometimes if she'd done it out of spite, or if she'd done it for the reasons she'd said. "I needed a change." But even he had to admit, it was flattering on her. The shorter length drew more attention to her eyes, and the shape of her face. His wife was a beautiful woman. For a moment in their lives, though, he'd forgotten that.

After dinner, the kids took their baths, and then all three of them disappeared into their rooms. The boys were no doubt immersed in video games, but Jade, who'd been unusually quiet lately, was sitting on her bed, playing with her dolls when he went in to check on her. Justin stretched out across her bed. All the pink in her room made him feel as if he were lost in a pillow of cotton candy sometimes.

He stared mesmerized at his little girl, awed by the fact that she looked like the perfect mixture of Connie and Reesy. She had Reesy's round face and Connie's light eyes, and she had both of their smiles. Looking at her reminded him that he was going to have to invest in a shotgun for the string of boys who would no doubt be showing up at his door in the near future.

"You ready for bed, baby girl?" he asked tenderly.

She smiled and nodded. "Yes, Daddy."

Jade was his princess. She wasn't his daughter biologically, but he'd fight any man tooth and nail for even thinking of trying to take her from him. Of course, she didn't know the truth about him, Reesy, and Connie, and the decision they'd made on her behalf when she was a baby. He used to believe that they needed to make sure she knew that she was adopted, but the older she got, the more possessive he and Reesy became over her, and the truth mattered less and less.

Justin stared at her long and hard enough to see the wheels spinning inside her eight-year-old head. She had something on her mind, and of all the people in the house, Jade was the one least likely to just let it pass.

"Are you going to move away again?" she asked, quietly.

God! He hoped not. But that's not what she needed to hear. "Nope. I'm staying."

She batted her soft eyes at him, looking for reassurance. "Promise?"

Justin leaned over to her and kissed her forehead. "You're not getting rid of me, little girl, until you're old enough to get married and move out of this house with your husband, and that's not going to happen until you turn thirty-four," he teased.

Jade wrinkled her nose. "Thirty-four?" she screeched. "That old?"

Justin stood up to leave. "Yep. I'm afraid so."

"Well." Those wheels started spinning again. "When can I have a boyfriend?"

He thought for a moment before responding. "When you're thirty-three and a half."

By the time he left, she was giggling hysterically.

Justin made it to the bedroom in time to see Reesy naked and coming out of the shower. For a moment, their gazes locked, but she quickly turned away and slipped into her robe. The two of them were like strangers now, with an uneasy truce between them. Justin could walk on eggshells all he wanted, the truth was that getting her to trust him again was going to take much longer than a few weeks.

He cleared his throat and started to undress. Reesy sat on the edge of the bed, rubbing lotion on her hands and feet. Justin couldn't remember the last time they'd made love. He wanted her so badly he ached. "I'll be home early tomorrow to take J. J. to basketball practice," he said, sitting on the opposite side of the bed.

"You don't have to, Justin. I'd planned on dropping him off on my way over to the gym."

"I know I don't have to," he said, trying to hide feeling offended. "I want to."

"Fine," she responded quickly.

Reesy went over to the closet and pulled her nightgown off the hook. She hesitated for a moment, and then went into the bathroom and closed the door behind her to put it on.

Justin shook his head in disgust for what his marriage had become, and before he knew it, he bolted to his feet and pushed open the bathroom door. Reesy had barely gotten the gown over her head, when he burst in. She let the material fall past her shoulders and down to the floor, and stared stunned at him.

"You don't have to do this," he said, gritting his teeth, fighting hard to control his anger. "I'm your husband, Reesy. It's alright for me to see you naked."

Reesy brushed past him, not saying a word.

"I'm trying, baby," he said, woefully. "Can you just give me—"

She spun around to him. "Give you what, Justin? You know, I'm trying too. It's not easy for me to—to act like nothing ever happened. To get the image out of my mind of you and that stripper."

He sighed, and then ran his hand over his head. For months he'd had to live with the wedge of the other woman between them, and it was exhausting trying to push past her to get to his wife. The battle was long and constant, and sometimes he wondered if they'd ever get back to what they once were. "How many times do I have to say I'm sorry, Reese?" he said, exasperated.

Reesy stared at him, appalled. "*Say* you're sorry?" She walked over to him, and dared him to look her in the eyes. "You have to *be* sorry, Justin," she said, quietly, with tears filling her eyes. "You have to live sorry. And you have to know sorry, through and through, because what you did to us will never be fixed by just saying the word."

"Do you really want it fixed, Reesy?" He regretted asking the question as soon as the words fell from his lips. Justin looked away.

"I'm going to bed," she whispered. Reesy turned away and crawled into bed, pulling the covers up to her shoulders. Justin quietly left the room and went downstairs to watch the news. At least, that's what he told himself.

She shuddered and squeezed her eyes shut after he left. Dear God! What was happening? Reesy and Justin had agreed that he should move back into the house. They agreed that they should work on their marriage together, but every time he tried to get close, she felt repulsed and angry and betrayed. And convicted. Avery was never far enough away, and her own guilt rested just beneath the surface of the resentment she had for her husband.

Reesy could tell herself over and over again that she was having an affair to get back at Justin, but two wrongs certainly didn't make a right, especially at this delicate stage of their reconciliation. She thought about Avery constantly, and spent nearly every waking moment looking for ways to get away and spend time with him.

Reesy had wanted her family back together as much as Justin did, and she wanted things to be the way they had always been— balanced and right. But how could it ever be right if she wasn't? He was trying, and Reesy wasn't trying hard enough. Seeing Avery put her marriage at risk, and if she wasn't careful, she'd lose what mattered to her most.

It used to be so easy. Justin was the sun and the moon and there was nothing or no one in between. She'd never even fathomed being with anyone else. More and more now, she was getting to the point where she could hardly fathom Justin anymore.

SEVEN

He wasn't a sentimental man, but Uncle had to admit, standing in his motel room and staring down into a city that had once been his pulse, that even he couldn't help but feel a little choked up. It wasn't the same as it had been when he left; buildings were boarded up, or burned. Broken glass and dirty needles littered the streets. Carl Denny's butcher shop on the corner was long gone, and addicts and drunks slumped on the street corners. He'd even stopped by that old club of his a few blocks over, and what had once been a classy, soulful establishment that served some of the best barbeque in all of Kansas City was a strip joint now, filled with old-ass strippers with stretch marks and needle tracks running up and down their arms. Shit. Even the hos had gone downhill, he'd surmised. But then, it had been his own damn fault. Uncle had left the yard unattended for too long, and this was the result.

"How you want it?"

He turned around and stared at the young, used-up girl standing naked in the middle of the room.

"You gave me a fifty." She shrugged, staring at him with dull cow eyes. "So, you can have it any way you want it."

Talk about a bargain.

He hadn't had a woman in damn near thirty years. Had fantasized about quite a few of them, jerked off to images he still had stored up in his head, and even came close to having the actual thing pumping a few he-shes in the ass a few times.

She wasn't the prettiest thing, but she'd do.

"On your knees," he told her, and she obliged without hesitation.

Uncle sat down on the side of the bed and watched patiently while this girl unzipped his pants and went to work with gusto on his johnson. It took her awhile to get him going, but in time she got him up just fine. He was going to have to get himself some of that Viagra, first chance he got.

Uncle closed his eyes and drifted back to more desirable memories, of a time when he was king and she was his little honey-colored princess. Charlotte had always been his favorite. She couldn't suck a dick worth a damn, but he didn't need her for that. She was nice to look at, and she always smelled so damn good. She'd bat those pretty, light-brown eyes at him, spread those lovely lips into the prettiest smile, and when she did, Uncle didn't have the slightest inclination of what it would mean to tell her no.

"Love is bullshit, baby. Anybody in their right mind knows that," he told her late one night, with Charlotte laying on top of him in bed. *"But what we got here is better than love."*

"How you figure, Uncle?" she asked, sweetly.

"We got understanding, girl," he explained. *"You know what I need, and I know what you need. We meet in the middle and give each other what we need. It ain't complicated."*

"Then maybe that is love."

"Naw. Love just throws in a whole bunch of shit and nonsense and fucks everything up. Love makes you think too much on dumb shit.

Makes you question what ain't, and what should be, when all that matters is what is. Trust me, darlin'. You don't ever want to be in love with a man like me, and I ain't too sure I want to lose my mind over you either."

The sweet thing between his thighs worked some serious magic on his ass, and Uncle shot a wad in her mouth that would've drowned a less experienced ho. She swallowed like the pro she was, and then stared up at him with his cum still dripping off her chin. "You want something else?"

He sighed and shook his head. "Naw, sugah. That's plenty."

Lynn Randall had given Uncle Charlotte's address and phone number. She'd warned him that Charlotte wasn't the pretty woman she had been.

"Her face is all messed up, and she's fat now, Uncle."

He laughed out loud at the thought, but rested in the knowledge that underneath scars and a few extra pounds still lurked the woman of his dreams.

EIGHT

"Congratulations, sweetheart." Liz Brooks' publisher, Derek Anderson, greeted her with a kiss on the cheek. "Number one on the *New York Times* and *USA Today* bestseller lists—again! You're too good to us." He smiled.

"Oh, it's the least I can do, Derek," she chided with a wink. "Thanks for the party, by the way."

"You deserve it, Liz." He wrapped his arm around her shoulder and squeezed. "I mean that."

She'd never been one for swanky parties, or big, noisy, restless cities like New York. Liz Brooks might have been one of the most successful authors in the world, but she was a smidgen shy of being a recluse back in her modest Seattle bungalow. This party wasn't her idea, but she'd been summoned and flown first-class to attend the event, so she did her best to try and make the most of it.

"Here you go, sweetie." Her agent, Gloria, sidled up next to her in the crowded room and handed her a glass of champagne. "You look like you could use it."

"Is it that obvious?" Liz asked, relieved.

"Only to me, because I know how much you hate these things.

To everyone else in the room, darling, you look like you're having the time of your life."

The room was filled to capacity with everyone who was anyone in the publishing world, scattered with some celebrities and a ton of other folks who might as well have been from the moon as far as Liz was concerned, because she hardly knew any of them personally. But then, that's what happens when you live your life sitting behind a computer. Liz was a writer and writers wrote, which meant endless hours locked away in solitude pouring her thoughts into her laptop. Somewhere along the way, however, she'd become too comfortable alone, and one day it dawned on her that every important relationship she had with actual human beings took place by way of social networking sites, e-mails, and blogs. It also dawned on her that she actually preferred it that way, probably more than what was considered healthy or normal.

Liz was sixty-four years old and had never been married, nor had kids. Sometimes she'd hoped for marriage and children, but other times, she realized that she was better off without either. Her closest family member was her younger brother, CJ, who was retired from the navy and living in Hawaii with his wife. She'd been promising to visit him for years, but had just never followed through.

She scanned the room, amazed at the course her life had taken through the years. Liz hadn't designed a path to this kind of success. It had come to her as if by magic, and accidentally. All she'd ever wanted to do was to squeeze her eyes shut tight against the horrors she'd seen unfold in front of her as a child, and pretend that they'd never happened. Liz had taken every kind of tranquilizer and antidepressant created at one time or another. But nothing had worked for her the way writing had. With writing, Liz could blot out the things she didn't like and create new things, new people, and situations. She was the god of her characters, and in trying to erase real scenes from her own life, she'd somehow managed to become a bestselling author. Sometimes, the irony made her laugh entirely too hard, and cry a little too often.

To this day, Liz was a small-town girl at heart. Even the Seattle suburb that she lived in proved too much for her at times. She rarely ever went home anymore. Bueller, Texas, was barely more than a memory, until she went to New York and places like it. Then it was a cocoon she felt she'd left behind, and, for very brief moments, Liz would be surprised by how much she'd missed the intimacy of it.

NINE

This time, she'd called him, and Avery could hardly believe his good fortune, sitting on the leather sofa in his small apartment, watching this glorious woman dramatically undress in front of him. Reesy was what many would consider a full-figured woman, but to him, a woman should be nothing less.

She smiled at him, blushing but bold in her intentions. This wasn't like her at all. The Clarice Braxton he knew was a conservative woman, even uptight, proper and deliberate in all of her actions. But something had definitely gotten into her, and Avery nodded appreciatively, happy to conclude that maybe he was the reason behind her budding sensuality.

"You're trying not to laugh." She eyed him suspiciously. "Aren't you?"

She stood there with her blouse unbuttoned down to her navel, delicious cleavage spilling out over the tops of laced bra cups. Avery stared at her like she was the main course in a starving man's dream. "I don't see anything to laugh about, Reesy. Please, don't stop."

She slipped her jeans down past her round hips, wiggling out of them until they fell to her ankles and she stepped out of them and kicked them in his direction. Reesy stepped closer to him and allowed him the privilege of undoing the last two buttons of her blouse.

"I shouldn't be here, Avery," she whispered.

He nodded. "You keep saying that." He slid the blouse from her shoulders. "And yet, here you are."

Reesy started to step out of her high-heeled pumps.

"No," he said, stopping her. "Leave them on."

Reesy felt drunk in his arms. She straddled his lap and rode him with the slow, deliberate intention of making their lovemaking last for as long as she possibly could. Reesy kept telling herself that seeing Avery was a disaster waiting to happen for an already rocky marriage, but when she wasn't with him, she thought about being with him, and she spent far too much time trying to find an excuse to see him. It hadn't taken her long to realize that where Avery was concerned, the last thing she needed was an excuse. As soon as he answered the phone, he begged the question, "When can I see you?"

"I'll be there in half an hour," she'd told him, and there he was, waiting for her.

He wrapped both arms around her waist and buried his face in the folds of her breasts. Avery inhaled her, he nibbled on her, and drove himself deeper into her with every passionate thrust.

"Ahh," she moaned.

The woman perched on that man's lap wasn't somebody's wife. She wasn't a mother, a sister, or a daughter. She was just his and she belonged right where she was, and that time between them was all that mattered and all that was. Reesy felt more liberated than she'd ever felt in her life, and with Avery, being right or perfect or even reasonable didn't matter.

He raised his face to hers and pushed his tongue into her mouth. Reesy arched her back, raised her hips, and moaned again. He broke the seal of their kiss and stared long and deep into her eyes. He didn't need to say it, because she already knew. Avery was cumming, and Reesy wanted him to.

An hour later, she stood in the shower of her master bedroom, still feeling high from the remnants of her encounter with Avery Stallings. Reesy searched her soul for guilt but it wasn't there. It should've been, she wanted it to be, but it was nowhere to be found. What she did discover surprised her, though. Reesy felt satisfied for the first time in years. She felt more satisfaction than she'd felt even before she and Justin started having problems.

All of her life, she'd been the good girl. Reesy had bent over backward to do the right thing the right way and to live the kind of life other women envied. She'd married the man of her dreams, raised the kind of well-mannered and intelligent children that everyone praised, and she'd been the shining star in the dark and stormy lives of both her sisters.

Look at me, she'd tell her sisters in her mind. *Look at how I live my life. This is how you should live yours because it's the right way.*

She'd judged them both, perhaps too harshly, but always with the intent of making them see in themselves what she'd seen in them all along, particularly Connie, who could do so much more and could be so much more than she'd settled for all these years.

Reesy squeezed her eyes shut and let the water wash over her face. She'd dropped the kids off at school today, come home and loaded the dishwasher, watered the plants, washed a load of clothes, and then drove across town and fucked a man who wasn't her husband simply because she wanted to. Nothing good could come from it, or the fact that she couldn't wait to do it again.

TEN

"I didn't see Cammy's car outside," Reesy said breathlessly, as she breezed through Connie's front door. "I take it she's not here yet."

"Well hey, Reesy," Connie said sarcastically. "It's good to see you too."

Reesy ignored her, slipped off her sunglasses, and sat down on the sofa. "Where's my nephew?"

"He's asleep."

These sister-bonding gatherings were Reesy's idea and she was the only one who looked forward to them. Connie and Cammy could've easily lived without them, but she refused to give them the opportunity.

"I'm gonna go peek in on him," Reesy said, heading upstairs.

"Don't you dare wake him up," Connie warned.

"Just pour the tea, Connie. Oh, and call Cammy to see where she is."

Reesy still had a hard time being alone in a room with Connie. They'd barely spent any time alone together at all since they returned from seeing Charlotte for the last time. Between Connie's preoccupation with Jonathon, and Reesy's marital problems, the only time they were together was during these gatherings, and even then, Cammy was there, bringing her own bag of tricks into the mix.

Reesy tried not to talk about it, but her heart was broken. Charlotte's true colors had come to light and she had no idea what to do with what she'd learned about her mother. Any faith Connie had ever had in Charlotte had gone up in smoke before Connie finished kindergarten. Reesy's letdown had come much later in life, and that made it harder to take. Reesy hadn't ever come out and said that she blamed Connie for the rift between Connie and Charlotte, but until six months ago, she'd never come to Connie's defense either. Charlotte had still owned that mother honor in Reesy's mind, despite the fact that she'd walked out on the two of them when they were children. Before leaving, Charlotte had taken out her frustrations on Connie and poured out her love on Reesy. All these years, Reesy had had a one-sided perspective of their mother. Six months ago, she'd finally opened her eyes and saw the other side of that woman. Knowing how badly the truth had hurt Reesy hurt Connie, and she actually felt sorry for her sister.

Cammy showed up five minutes after Reesy arrived, looking far more uncomfortable than necessary. "Hey, Connie." She smiled unconvincingly as the two embraced. "I'm sorry I'm late."

"Not so late, Cammy. Reesy just got here too."

Reesy came downstairs at the sound of Cammy's voice. "You had me worried, baby sister." She went to hug Cammy. "Thought you might be a no-show."

Cammy suddenly looked on the verge of tears, but she managed to smile anyway.

This is going to be a long afternoon, Connie concluded.

Connie threw together some sandwiches and iced tea, and the

three of them sat around the kitchen table to bond. As usual, Reesy decided to take the lead and talk to everyone else like she was teaching grade school.

"So, have you spoken to Charlotte?" Reesy asked, staring at Cammy. She knew better than to ask Connie a dumb question like that.

Cammy shrugged. "Yeah. We spoke the other day, but just for a few minutes."

It was hard to miss the hurt in Reesy's eyes despite her best efforts to hide it. "How is she?"

"Fine." Cammy nodded.

Reesy waited for her to elaborate, but Cammy didn't.

Connie studied Cammy. That poor girl always looked like she was about to get in trouble for something, like she was teetering on the edge of disaster all the time, expecting to make a mistake.

"Justin's home?" Connie asked, directing her question at Reesy.

"Yes." She smiled. "I thought I told you that."

"Maybe you did. So, how's that going?"

"It's . . . challenging," Reesy responded. "We're a long way from where we once were, but we'll get there again, eventually."

"Oh, I'm sure," Connie said.

Once upon a time, Reesy's marriage had been perfect. She and Justin had been the poster children for what happily-ever-after was supposed to look like and anyone within spitting distance of the two of them was green with envy.

"How's John?" Reesy asked.

Reesy had never liked John, but she was really giving it a valiant attempt these days. It was strained, but Connie appreciated her effort. John didn't care one way or another, and that's what she appreciated about him.

Connie grinned, and then fanned herself.

Cammy snickered.

"I didn't need to know all that." Reesy smirked. "What about you, Cammy? Met anyone new?"

"Yeah, I've met some new people."

"Who?" Reesy probed.

Cammy seemed caught off guard. "Um, just some people from work."

"What are their names?" Reesy persisted. "Maybe I know them."

Connie watched the interchange and marveled at how much more uncomfortable Cammy visibly became. Reesy was being her usual pushy self, but Cammy was buckling entirely too easily and it was obvious this girl needed rescuing.

"Tell her to get her own friends, Cam, and to stop bugging you about yours."

Reesy shot Connie a look. "I'm not bugging her about anything, Constance. I'm just asking who her friends are."

"What difference does it make? You've never asked me who my friends are."

"Your friends don't work with my husband."

"I met a woman named Deana," Cammy blurted out, obviously trying to keep the peace. "She works in a different company in the building, but we met in the cafeteria."

"Well, that's nice," Reesy said, staring smugly at Connie.

Connie rolled her eyes and shook her head.

"Have you two hung out?"

"Not yet," Cammy said sheepishly. "But we've been talking about, you know, going out. She wants to show me some clubs."

Reesy reached across the table and took hold of Cammy's hand. "That's fantastic, Cammy," she said earnestly. "You need to get out and have some fun, and having a good friend will help."

The sound of the baby crying caught Connie's attention. "Excuse me," she said, heading upstairs.

Moments later, she returned with Jonathon, sat down at the table, and started breast-feeding him.

"He's beautiful." Cammy stared at him like he was an apparition.

Reesy smiled proudly at Connie. "You both are."

Connie looked embarrassed. "Don't get weird on me, Reese."

Reesy's expression turned serious. "You're the one who's gotten weird, Connie. And I'm proud of you. You're a good mom."

"Good enough for you and me to sit down and have that discussion with Jade?"

Now it was Reesy's turn to look uncomfortable. "Soon," she said quietly. "With everything going on between me and Justin . . . The timing sucks, Connie."

Jade was that last frontier between Reesy and Connie. They'd come to terms with Charlotte, in their own special way, but the subject of Jade was still hallowed ground. The little girl was eight, and Connie was her birth mother. But Connie had been in a bad place emotionally after Jade was born and Reesy and Justin had agreed to help take care of her until Connie came to her senses. Years passed and Jade grew close to her "parents." Connie signed over her parental rights to her sister and brother-in-law, and Connie's child legally became their child. It was an arrangement that had worked for everyone concerned until Connie blurted out the truth in Reesy's kitchen within earshot of Jade. The confusion on that child's face stung both women's hearts, and in that moment, they both knew they had to sit down with that little girl and have the conversation that would change her young life forever. Connie felt she was ready, but Reesy was still stalling. Connie understood, though. Staring down at her son, nursing and looking up at her, she definitely understood that protecting your child meant everything.

Jade was hers too, though. And rather than continue letting her spend another day living in doubt and confusion or questioning something she couldn't possibly understand on her own, Connie and Reesy owed that little girl an explanation.

ELEVEN

"The mailman changed his delivery time," Charlotte said to Lynn over the phone. She'd been sitting out on her front porch, waiting for him.

Talking to Lynn every day at noon was the only thing she had to look forward to, which was sad because Lynn didn't have shit to talk about except for sorry-ass Arnel. Charlotte had learned a long time ago, though, never to say anything bad about Arnel to Lynn. The last time she did, Lynn had hung up on her and didn't call her again for a month.

Arnel had AIDS. Charlotte thought she'd remembered Lynn telling her that she had it too, but she couldn't be sure, because most of the time she didn't pay attention to half the mess that came out of Lynn's mouth.

She waited while Lynn told her about how sick Arnel was getting, and about all the medicine the doctor had them on, and about how she wished they'd been smarter when they were younger, so they wouldn't have to be paying for it now. Charlotte let her talk without interruption. Until it was her turn.

"Cammy's been calling down here more and more," she said, irritably. Now it was Lynn's turn to listen quietly. "Half the time

I don't even answer the phone. As old as that girl is, she still acts like a child sometimes. Calling down here, talking about, '*I miss you, Momma. I wanna come home, Momma,*'" Charlotte mimicked in an exaggerated, shrill tone. "She can kiss my ass with the rest of them," she said indifferently. "If she missed me so much, she would've never left, or, better yet, she'd have stayed her ass down here and made them take me to Denver instead."

"You spoke to either of the other two?" Lynn asked unenthusiastically.

"You know Connie, the oldest, she ain't got shit to say to me, and I ain't got shit to say to her either. But Reesy calls, and I talk to her," she lied. "She said she's going to send for me soon as she gets me a room ready. I told her not to bother, that I didn't want to be any trouble, but she keeps insisting on bringing me back home," she said arrogantly. "I told her I'd think about it."

"You like that one. Right?"

Charlotte rolled her eyes. "I guess I like her good enough. Between them other two fools, she's the only one who seems like she's got any sense."

Lynn knew when Charlotte was bullshitting. Charlotte adored that one she called Reesy. She called her some silly name like Baby Bug or Love Bug or Hug Bug. Reesy had the big house and fancy husband. Reesy was the one who'd paid all that money for some detective to find Charlotte.

Lynn sat for another half an hour, listening to Charlotte go on and on about how they'd done her wrong. "I'm only human, Lynn, like they're human. I did the best I could for my girls. Truly, truly I did. You know that."

Lynn knew no such thing. When she first met Charlotte, she was laid up in Uncle's love shack, fucking the man for new furniture, fancy clothes, and a few groceries. She'd told Lynn that she'd left her kids with her mother, but through the years, different versions of the truth came up in conversation, and when pressed, Charlotte conveniently forgot the details. She left her children behind to look after themselves, chasing behind some dude named Sam who owed Uncle some money. She didn't give a damn about those kids. Even now, Lynn could hear it in her voice. Thirty years later, Charlotte was the same woman she'd been back in Kansas City. If it wasn't about her, then it wasn't about nothing. All of a sudden, Lynn didn't feel so bad about the conversation she'd had with Uncle.

"I'm glad to hear that you and Reesy made up, Charlotte."

Again, Charlotte didn't respond right away. "That sister of hers, Connie . . . she's the one that's got Reesy's mind all screwed up about me," she said snidely. "Connie's been doing that her whole life, telling Reesy things about me that ain't true."

"Like what?"

Like how Charlotte left them alone in that apartment. Like how she might've hit Connie, when Reesy wasn't around. Like how she never really loved them at all. "Like lies, Lynn," she said, coldly. "Connie was always a difficult and undermining child, and that's the kind of woman she is too. Reesy and Cammy buy into that mess, but I'm the only one who knows the truth about that heifer, and one of these days, they're going to know it too."

Lynn listened intently, thinking that Connie must've been the smart one in the family.

"I got to go," Charlotte hurriedly said. "My mail's here." Charlotte hung up before Lynn could say, "By the way, Charlotte. Uncle's on his way to see you." But that was fine. She'd find out soon enough.

TWELVE

"What's your name, baby?"

"Cammy."

"Can I dance with you, Cammy?"

He didn't wait for an answer. She'd seen him once or twice in that old neighborhood bar that wasn't much more than a hole in the wall. He smelled like the place, stale cigarette smoke, funk, and mildew, and he was old enough to be her father. But that didn't stop him from wrapping his arms around her waist and pulling her close to him. Cammy didn't stop him either. She was almost too drunk to stand up on her own, and welcomed his shoulder to rest her head on.

"Pretty girl like you don't have no business dancing by herself," he said. "Don't need to be drinking alone neither."

She sighed, satisfied at how easy she fell against him, resting all of her weight in his arms, and letting her eyelids fall shut. He talked, but the only thing Cammy heard was the bluesy sounds of a guitar and some horns.

"Whatchu drinking, sugar?"

"Rum and Coke," she muttered.

She'd stopped here right after leaving her job. Sitting alone in

that apartment night after night, the walls felt like they were closing in on her sometimes. There were better clubs in town, nicer
places filled with people closer to her own age, but Cammy didn't
have the energy to look for better or nicer. Places like this didn't
require effort. Cammy could come here, sit in the dark in the
corner of the room, drink all the rum and Cokes she wanted, and
walk home if she needed to.

If he ever told her his name, she didn't remember. But she did
remember sitting at the bar together, and watching his lips move
as he talked and laughed. She remembered how another drink
would magically appear after she thought she'd finished one. It felt
good not to think, to have to listen, or to do anything else besides
smile and let him kiss her neck, and it felt good to forget about
everything and everyone that had hurt her, losing her baby, losing
Ty, and Charlotte.

"Aaaaahhhh, girl! Yessss!"

She had the good sense not to let him kiss her, but she let him
do just about anything else.

"Be good to daddy," he said from behind her, grabbing hold
of her hips, while Cammy bent over the back of his car, her skirt
hiked up around her hips. The parking lot was nearly empty,
and he'd parked behind the building. Cammy was too drunk to
complain, or to care. "Shit, girl! Damn, it's good!"

Was it? Was it really?

"Cammy, I am expecting a client at eleven. Can you please buzz
me in conference room two when she arrives?"

"Yes, Tom," she responded quietly.

"You alright? You don't look so good," he asked, concerned.

"I'm fine." She forced a smile. "Just . . . long night."

Being at the office today was hard, but being alone with herself was harder. Cammy had been drunk off her ass last night, but not drunk enough. She'd let that old man do things to her that made her stomach turn, and yet it never occurred to her to stop him.

"You sho' is fine . . . and young. Probably too young for me." The sound of his voice haunted her.

He'd kept the drinks coming, the compliments flowing, and had made it so easy to put aside all of the emotions gnawing away at her.

"Oh, the things I could do to you." He laughed. "Thirty years ago, I was a good-looking man. I know you might not believe it, but back then, I had women coming at me from every direction."

"Maybe you did," she slurred. "Maybe you did."

Cammy had showered before coming to work, but she still smelled him on her. She could still hear him grunting in her ear, and she shuddered. Inside, she was a mangled mess, and just getting out of bed every day was becoming harder to do. Cammy had tumbled down a deep, black hole with no way of getting herself out, so she'd stopped trying or caring because there was nothing waiting for her even if she did manage to save herself.

THIRTEEN

"There you are, Adam."

His eyes fluttered open at the sound of the soft whisper of her voice. He nearly laughed out loud hearing it. She sounded like music, the sweetest song that he prayed would never come to an end.

Pain gripped his midsection, and Adam groaned low and deep in the back of his throat, muffling the noise and drawing his knees to his stomach. It came to him more and more now. Adam clenched his teeth, squeezed his body as tight as he could into a ball, and fought the urge to scream out loud, but not even the pain was enough to drown out the sound of her voice from his memories. And death couldn't do it, neither. No, Lawd. Not even death could quiet that beautiful sound. It was late, and he didn't want to wake up Moses and Sara, because he knew they were tired.

He held his breath, thinking that if he didn't breathe, it would go away, and for a moment it did. But not for long. Adam was an old man now, old like Moses. They both had white hair and slow-moving bodies, but Adam was the oldest. Sometimes old men had pains, but this one was different. It was hard and angry and choked his whole body from head to foot. He'd only remembered feeling this kind of pain once in his life: back when his friends Davis Phillips, Clyde Jones, and Walter Haskins got mad at him. Adam was a younger man back then with black hair and straight, strong arms and legs, and he loved Mattie up close, but they didn't like it when they found out.

"Don't tell nobody 'bout us, Adam," she'd warned him. "Won't nobody else understand 'bout you and me if you tell."

They took him in that old barn and asked him the same question over and over again. "Did you touch that gal, Fool? Did you put yo' hands on her?"

His momma had taught him not to lie, so he told them the truth. "I-I held her . . . in . . . my arms and k-kissed her mmmouth." He was careful with Mattie and he tried to make them understand that, but when he told them the truth, they beat him.

He missed her. Adam had lost track of time but he knew it still ticked by whenever he saw that boy of his. He was a big man, as big as Adam was once, but not as big as Moses. Mattie had made that boy right before she'd died. That's what his brother had told him. She'd made him for Adam, but years went by before John came to see him. Mattie had told him about that boy in his dreams. Nobody believed Adam's dreams, but he didn't care. He always believed them.

"He's grown, Adam," Mattie whispered in his ear every time his son came to the house. Adam never understood how she could know so much, when she wasn't even here anymore.

"Mattie died a long time ago, Adam." Moses had to remind him of that sometimes. But that didn't stop her from talking to him. It didn't stop him from hearing her when she did, and it sure didn't stop him from recalling the scent of her hair when the wind blew just right.

Lord, even after all the time he figured had passed, Adam missed and loved that girl like he had all those years back. Mattie was the best time in his life. She was the happiest thing he could recall, and when he was with her, nothing in the world was bad. All he had to do was close his eyes and think about her. Adam squeezed his eyes tight and found her face behind them. He couldn't help but smile, despite the pain stabbing in his belly. And Mattie saw him, and she smiled back.

"I love you," he heard himself utter out loud. He didn't stutter when he said it. Most words that came out of his mouth were stuttering and didn't make much sense. But when he spoke to her, Adam was like any other man in love. He was perfect. Not broken. Not old. Not ugly. Not a Fool. Perfect. "I love you, Mattie," he said again, sighing, relieved that just the memory of her was enough to take his pain away.

Her smile glistened like the sun bouncing off waves in the lake. She wore her hair back, away from her face, tied up real pretty with a pink bow. Her skin, dark and pretty, was as smooth and looked as soft as he'd remembered.

"I love you too, Adam."

The pain was gone, because she was the medicine he needed to make it disappear. And that's all he had to hear. She was all he needed.

Moses wasn't the kind of man who cried. He rested his hand on his wife Sara's shoulder while she did enough of that for both of them. They listened to the doctor's grim diagnosis of his older brother Adam, who lay sedated in intensive care. They'd heard him cry out and found him unconscious in his bed.

"The cancer probably started in his pancreas and has spread through his stomach and his liver," he said remorsefully. "There really is nothing more we can do for him, except to try and keep him as comfortable as possible. We'll move him to hospice in the morning."

The doctor left. Sara got up and excused herself to the ladies' room, and big, strong Moses, Adam's younger brother, suddenly felt his knees grow weak, and he had to sit down before he dropped to the floor. Moses wasn't the kind of man who cried, but this time, he went ahead and let the tears fill his eyes as he fixed his gaze on Adam.

Adam had always been the better of the two of them. He'd had the kinder heart, the warmer disposition, and the best intentions. Without even trying, Adam had been the one to teach Moses what it really meant to be a man, and in his own quiet way, he'd inspired Moses to put down his fists and his anger, which had ruled him when he was young, and pick up patience and tenderness and to let them rule instead.

"Y-y-you got to t-t-talk nice to p-people, Moses," Adam admonished him on more than one occasion. "And d-don't look-look so mmmmmean. You scare folks."

Being scary was easy, Moses always thought. But being Adam, well . . . being Adam was being right.

Sara composed herself and stood quietly in the doorway of Adam's hospital room. Moses had always told her that he married her because she had the same name as his mother, and that was partly true. He married her because she was lovely. Moses had been with a lot of girls when he was younger, but none of them drew him in the way she had. He wanted her, because she wasn't nearly as impressed with him as the others. Sara was quiet, spent most of her time in church, and eyed him suspiciously over the rumors she'd no doubt heard about him. She made him court her properly. He had to dress nice and pick her up at the house. He had to meet her parents, who never did like him, but had no choice but to reluctantly accept him, because she somehow managed to persuade them that he was the man for her.

"I had to convince Momma, first," she told him. "I knew that if I convinced her that you and me should be married, she'd work on Daddy."

"Yo' daddy hated my ass," he told her after her father's funeral. "All the way up to the day he died."

"Yes." She nodded in agreement. "He certainly did."

Sara's fine, gray hair was cut short now. But her eyes were as rich and bright as they'd been when he first gazed into them, even now, after all these years of being married to his big, mean ass, and after not being blessed to have all those children she'd wanted. She was still lovely.

"We'll need to call John," she said quietly, wrapping her arms around herself. Moses could see in her eyes that her heart broke for that boy. John and Adam hadn't known each other long. John was a grown man by the time he'd worked up the nerve to find out the kind of man his daddy really was and stopped listening to all of the nonsense he'd been told was the truth by everybody around him. Tears flooded her eyes again. "But not tonight." She stifled a sob. "In the morning. We'll call him in the morning." She turned and walked away.

Moses lifted himself up out of that chair, walked over to his brother's side, and placed a firm hand on his shoulder before leaving.

All he wanted to do was to look at her, and if he didn't have to blink, he didn't. Mattie and Adam didn't say anything else. They just stared and smiled, and held hands.

FOURTEEN

"He's dead, I take it."

"Cain't get much deader."

She had blood on the front of her gown and on her hands and on her face, like she'd wiped it on herself.

Her face was like stone, her eyes staring toward the room where he was, her lips moving, but without sound.

". . . a weapon? Where? You found it?"

The woman stood with bare feet, swaying like a tree in the wind. That house had always felt sad. Years would pass and the sadness that filled the space in that house still left a residue on skin and a stale scent of hopelessness behind. That night, it felt empty all of a sudden, probably because he wasn't a part of it anymore.

"You kill him? Answer me, and tell me why you did it."

"What did she . . . ?" The old woman rushed in, frantic and breathless. She stared at the younger woman covered in blood. "Where them babies?" she suddenly asked, staring horrified at the woman.

"Who're you?"

"They grandmomma! Where my babies?"

He looked like he was sleeping.

"Lawd, Jesus! That baby just hollerin'!"

His eyes were closed. One arm da
he looked like he was sleeping.
   "Li'l girl! Come on outta there
   "Hey! Come on now. You do
mother."
   "Is he sleepin'?"
   "Yeah. Yeah he is."

Some memories simmered like a pot of stew sitting on
burner. For the most part, you paid no mind to them, but every
now and then, they boiled over. Liz had too many memories that
were just fragments, small pieces of something bigger that would
never be fully completed. She'd used her imagination to fill in
the blanks, using small-town gossip as the glue. She supposed that
that was how she had fallen in love with the art of storytelling.
Stories were almost always more compelling than the truth, and
the parts you didn't know, you could always make up to suit your
needs.

Liz sat up in bed. Moments later, her wake-up call came from
the front desk, and she assured them that she was awake. It was
time to go home, thank goodness. She had work to do; a manu-
script to finish drafting and a lecture to prepare for a presentation
next week at Berkeley. Staring across the room at the blank wall,
she saw her again, standing in that dingy, white slip in her bare
feet, her eyes empty and longing.

Liz smiled. "Hello, Momma."

The woman was dead and gone but that never stopped her from
showing up every now and then to remind Liz that she wasn't just
a figment of her imagination. She never said a word, just stood
there with empty, longing eyes.

d to stare as the image gradually began to fade
If she didn't know any better, she'd have sworn she
eep, and that she had just had a dream, but Liz knew
tter. She had been seeing that woman for as long as she
remember, and she had loved her, and been frightened by
. But she most certainly knew her as intimately as any child
nows her mother.

FIFTEEN

Reesy had always been her favorite. Reesy had been her Love Bug, her sweetest baby, and the one Charlotte could never sweep clean from her heart. But she'd turned on her mother too, bought into the shit about Charlotte that Connie had filled her head with, and given in to that girl's lies. Even to this day, Charlotte still felt the sting of Reesy's slap across her mother's face, defending the mess Connie had started.

Charlotte sat on the front porch of her house and squeezed her eyes shut at the memory of being slapped by Reesy, as fresh as if it had happened yesterday. She was a grown woman and betrayal was nothing new to somebody her age, but Reesy had broken her heart in ways she never had thought possible. Charlotte had seen every hope for her future and any chance that she'd ever had to get back to Denver go up in smoke the day Reesy chose Connie over her own mother.

The sun had set hours ago, and a chill had moved in with the night. Charlotte had meant to go inside but had lost track of time thinking about all the things she'd lost in her life. She had always been a proud woman, but on nights like this, pride gave way to sorrow, and it was so much easier sitting here and feeling sorry for herself than it would've been to get up and go inside that lonely house.

Charlotte had been a greedy and ambitious woman when she was young. She could admit that now, because she'd paid dearly for her transgressions and because she lived the consequences of the things she'd done every single day of her life. She stared at them when she saw her reflection in the mirror and that ugly half-moon scar stretching from her earlobe to the corner of her mouth glaring back at her. Charlotte had wanted what every woman wanted. She wanted to be in love and loved. She was excited about the possibilities that life dangled in front of her just waiting for her to pick from and to experience. She'd wanted to stay beautiful and desirable to men and to shine like a brand-new penny in her children's eyes.

"Quit lyin', girl." She jumped, startled by the sound of his voice.

Uncle wasn't here. He couldn't have been here, and she knew instinctively that he had spoken to her from his soul to hers, haunting her the way he sometimes did.

He'd shot Zoo. Almost thirty years ago, she'd watched him put a bullet through that boy's head and seen the back of it splatter against the wall behind him, while Zoo's body fell in a heap at that monster's feet. And even though she'd never actually seen it in the papers or had anyone tell her, Charlotte knew that Uncle had killed Sam too, big, black, handsome Sam who she didn't love but could've loved had she been able to get to Memphis with him. Uncle would've killed her too that night, but, by God's grace, he didn't. In times like this, though, when she was alone and forgotten, she wished he had.

The sound of the phone ringing and the sound of Reesy's voice on Charlotte's answering machine reminded her of what time it was. Reesy called every night at seven, and she always listened with a heavy heart at the message Reesy would inevitably leave.

"Hi, Mom. I just wanted to say that I love you, and—I miss talking to you." Reesy paused. "One of these days I know that you'll miss talking to me enough that you'll take my call again, and we can have a nice conversation without all the arguing. Until then, good night."

Reesy had always loved her mother the most, even more than Cammy. She had always been the one who could bring an easy smile to Charlotte's face and joy to her heart, and if there was ever anybody who could get Charlotte home, back to Denver, it was Reesy. Charlotte didn't have money for a plane ticket or a hotel room, and she couldn't stay with Cammy because that dumb broad had a roommate. But Reesy would send for her, and she'd give her a nice place to stay in that pretty, big house of hers, and she'd take care of Charlotte the way those other two fools, Connie and Cammy, never could.

Charlotte sat back in her chair and sighed. She'd been mad at her baby Clarice long enough. Holding a grudge wasn't going to get her anything but more of what she already had. She smiled contentedly. The next time Reesy called, Charlotte would swallow her pride and answer the phone. And she'd make sure to tell Reesy that she'd missed her too and ask how her husband and kids were doing. She'd make sure to remind her that she was a diabetic and that her blood pressure had been higher than normal, and maybe she'd even mention that she was afraid being here all by herself like this. Oh, and she'd have to thank Reesy for the pictures she'd sent to Charlotte of the family portrait they'd all taken, but she'd leave out the part about how she'd scratched out Reesy's eyes with a Bic and scrawled the word BITCH in big, bold letters across her face.

SIXTEEN

Cammy met Deana Wilkins in the sandwich shop across the street from her office building. The two of them were about the same age, and Deana struck up a conversation with Cammy and wouldn't let up. A few weeks after meeting her, Cammy agreed to meet Deana and some of her friends out for happy hour Friday after work at a place called Club Reign.

Cammy sat quietly while the other three women sitting at the table with her laughed and gossiped, drank and devoured hot wings and fries.

"You ladies need another round?" the waitress asked.

"Yes," Cammy blurted out.

The other women looked at her, and then all burst out laughing.

"Uh . . . sure." Deana nodded. "I guess we're thirsty."

"Either that," one of her friends chimed in, glancing at Cammy, "or some of us had one hell of a week."

It wasn't long before Cammy lost count of how many drinks she'd had and before she'd lost track of her friends.

"What's your name, girl?"

Cammy danced with abandon until her head was spinning.

She felt herself smile, but she wasn't the least bit interested in holding a conversation with this fool on the dance floor. The music was too loud to talk, and the beat was too good to do anything else but groove.

She spun around, away from him, and set her mind free in that crowded room.

"Yeah!" she heard him say, as he inched up behind her.

That fool was all over her ass, but Cammy didn't give a damn. Their bodies blended together into one, bumping and grinding in full accord. He put his hands on her waist, bent his knees into the backs of hers, and ground his swelling dick into her ass. But Cammy didn't care.

"So, what you drinking, baby?" he asked, taking her by the hand and leading her to the bar.

"Gin and juice," she blurted out, slumping into him.

For the first time since he'd asked her to dance, Cammy had a good look at him. Sagging pants, an oversized shirt, thick gold chain . . . a quick glance around the room—he dressed like every other guy there.

"What's your name?" she slurred, looking into his eyes for the first time.

"Isaac."

Isaac's thin mustache added a hint of maturity to his full baby face. He was cute. Not manly handsome, but cute.

"You never told me your name, though," he said into her ear.

"Cammy."

He smiled. "Cammy. I like that. So, can I get your number?"

She shook head. "Nope. I ain't trying to give out no numbers."

"Aw, come on. I'm a good guy. I promise."

"Then be my friend if you're such a good guy."

"Fine. I'll be your friend, but friends give each other their phone numbers."

"Yeah, but . . ."

"It's just a number, baby. How else can I get to know you better if I ain't got a number?"

He made all the sense in the world, and Cammy jotted down her number in his palm.

"Cammy, girl." Deana came up behind her. "Dang, girl! You avoiding us or something?" She laughed.

"No. No, Deana." She turned and hugged Deana. "This is my friend . . ." She looked at Isaac, trying to remember his name.

"Isaac."

"Isaac. Isaac, this is Deana, my good friend from work."

Deana gave Isaac a weak smile. "We're getting ready to go, Cam. Come on. I'll give you a ride home."

"I can take her home," Isaac volunteered too quickly.

Cammy laughed. "Why don't y'all take each other home, then, 'cause I'm not leaving." She weeded her way through the crowd and sashayed herself back out onto the dance floor.

"Cammy!" Deana followed her. "Cammy, you are drunk off your ass. Let me take you home."

"I don't wanna go home, D," she protested. "Look, he can take me home." She nodded in Isaac's direction.

"Are you crazy? Girl, that's a date rape waiting to happen. Ain't no way I'd let that pervert drive you home."

"He's not a pervert."

"Really? Then how come he's looking at you like you're lunch?"

Cammy smiled. "He thinks I'm pretty."

Deana took hold of her arm and led her off of the floor. "Yeah, well, I think I need to get your pretty ass home safe and sound before you do something you'll regret and that I'll feel really guilty about."

"Can I finish my drink first?" Cammy started to take another sip, but Deana took it from her.

"You're done."

SEVENTEEN

"Is he down for the count?" John lay in bed.

Connie came into the room and nodded. "Sleeping like a baby."

Small talk wasn't necessary. She untied the front of her robe, let it slip off her shoulders and fall to the floor. He threw back the covers and welcomed her as she mounted him. Connie slid down the thickness of John, and stopped. Her lips met his; he cupped the back of her head and made love to her mouth with his.

She'd put on fifteen pounds since she'd had the baby, and the first time they made love afterward, she'd been so self-conscious that she'd insisted on doing it in the dark and underneath the covers.

"Why?" he'd asked.

"Because I'm fat," she'd said.

John shrugged. "P-H-A-T fat? Or F-A-T fat?"

"F-A-T," she responded, embarrassed.

He flipped on the light switch, pulled all the covers off the bed, tossed the pile into the corner of the room, stared down at her nakedness, and smiled. "F-A-T looks more like P-H-A-T to me." He crawled into bed next to her. "But then, I'm biased."

Connie resisted the natural urge to move her hips. Making love with John was a treat she relished because she was free to love him completely, inside and out, and time had shown her that he belonged to her.

He ran his hands down the length of her back to her hips and held her steady in place, and, suddenly, thrust himself deep inside her.

"Mmmmm!" she moaned, her lips still glued to his.

She opened her eyes and saw him staring at her. A thousand words were spoken in that moment, all of them exceptional and so was the sex.

After they made love, Connie lay behind John with her arm draped across his waist. Of course, he was asleep, but she was wide awake. The sun was just starting to rise and the baby would be up in an hour to nurse and she knew she was cheating herself out of precious time to get some rest, but this was one of those moments when she had to pinch herself to make sure she wasn't dreaming. Connie Rodgers, the little street urchin, who never believed she deserved a man like him, or a life like this, finally had it all, and as scary as that was, it was also about damn time.

She nearly jumped out of her skin at the sound of the phone ringing at that time of morning. "Hello?" Connie asked, her heart pounding. "Hi. Yes. Yes, he's right here. Hold on."

John turned over, still half-asleep, and took the phone. "Yeah."

Connie sat up in bed and waited anxiously, watching him open his eyes.

"What happened?"

She sat up and turned on the lamp on the nightstand.

"Yeah," he said gravely. "I'll be there. Tell him . . . tell him I'll be there."

He hung up the phone and stared up at the ceiling.

"What is it, baby?" she asked softly.

He turned toward her and placed his head in her lap. Connie held him, knowing that whatever it was, John had to process it and make it make sense on his own. He'd tell her when he could.

Jonathon started to cry at that moment. John rolled over on his back.

"John?"

"Go get him," he told her.

By the time she came downstairs with the baby, John was already up and packed.

"Adam's sick, Connie," he explained, sitting at the table, finishing a cup of coffee. "He's been sick for a while, but nobody knew it."

She sat down next to him. "Is he going to be alright?"

He looked away and shook his head. "Nah," he said simply.

"What's wrong with him, John?"

He swallowed. "Cancer," he said hoarsely. "Terminal." He picked up her hand and kissed it. "I don't know . . . I don't know how . . ."

John wasn't the kind of man who'd ever let anybody see him cry, but tears filled his eyes, and he quickly blinked them away. "I need to go," he said, finally looking at her.

Connie had no problem with crying and tears slid down her cheeks. "I know, baby." She reached out to him. "I can have me and Jonathon packed in a few minutes." She started to hurry from the table, but he held onto her hand.

"No, Connie," he said gently.

She stared at him, confused. "It won't take long."

He pulled her down onto his lap. "I got to go—alone."

"No, you don't. We're together. We can go together."

He shook his head, and started to stand up. "I'll call you when I get there," he said, heading for the door.

"John?"

He left without saying another word.

He could've driven to Bueller, Texas, in his sleep.

"Yo' daddy's dying, son. He got the cancer, and it ain't lettin' up on him. They say he ain't got much time."

Leave it to Moses to put it all into perspective in a few short sentences. Adam and John had been strangers to each other most of their lives. John had grown up hearing lies about Adam. He'd hated the man even before he'd ever laid eyes on him.

"Fool raped that girl," people around town whispered. They called him Fool because of his disability. Fool, Adam, was a grown man with the mind of a six-year-old.

"He raped her and got her pregnant with that boy. She was a small girl, even for fourteen, and she died havin' that baby. He look just like his daddy too. Talk about addin' insult to injury."

John grew up believing the lies, loathing his father and himself, and living with the guilt that he'd been the reason his mother had died. It took Moses, and decades of time passing in between, to set him straight. No one was more surprised than John when he discovered the truth two years ago, that Adam and Mattie had loved each other. He'd never hurt that girl. Mattie died for their love, but Adam paid a high price for it too, and for most of his life, even John had paid a price.

Adam loved her. Yeah, she'd been too young for him, and yeah, he'd made a kid with her. But he'd never have taken advantage of her, and knowing that old man the way he'd come to know him, John couldn't help but wonder if it really hadn't been the other way around.

"Y-you my b-boy!" Adam said it with pride every time John came to see him, and he couldn't help but admit he liked hearing it. He'd never known his mother, but he knew Adam. Adam was his connection to the planet. He solidified John's existence in a way that a father does for his son. All of a sudden, when he met Adam, when he found out that those two people, Mattie and Adam, got together and made him, it wasn't an evil union. It might've been fucked up, with a mentally challenged man on one side and a fourteen-year-old girl on the other, but it wasn't violent. And knowing that set his existence at ease.

A lump formed in his throat, but John swallowed it, rolled down his window, and inhaled deeply. He'd just found the old man. And now he was going to have to figure out how to let him go.

EIGHTEEN

"I can't get away tonight." Avery had called while Justin was getting the kids settled for the movie.

"What about tomorrow? It's been nearly a week, baby. I miss you."

Reesy sat on the edge of the bathtub, whispering. "I don't know when," she responded. She wanted to see him, and that was the problem. Reesy found herself thinking about being with Avery too much. She found herself missing him too, so much that her obsession with him was beginning to spill over into her family life.

"Where are you right now?"

"In my bathroom."

"What are you wearing?"

She chuckled. "What?"

He laughed too. "What are you wearing?"

"Sweats."

"Sexy sweats?"

"Not exactly."

"Well . . ."

"Well . . . what? Were you going to ask me to touch myself or something?" She blushed, hearing herself say that.

"It would be nice."

Reesy laughed out loud.

"Reesy?" Justin called from the other side of the door. "You alright?"

"I'm fine," she shouted back.

"What's so funny?" he asked.

"Nothing. I just . . . nothing."

Reesy's heart raced. She'd had no idea her husband had been that close, and she started to panic and hang up.

"Movie starts in five, babe," he told her. "We're counting on you for the popcorn." His voice faded, and she listened to the sound of him heading down the stairs.

"So?" Avery continued.

"I've got to go, Avery. This is . . . crazy."

"No, Reesy. It's not crazy. It's you and me, talking on the phone."

But it was crazy. She was crazy, and on the verge of losing her mind. Never in a million years did she ever expect to be sitting in her bathroom, talking to her lover while her husband and kids were downstairs getting prepped for movie night. Suddenly tears flooded her eyes. "I can't—this needs to stop."

"No," he said gently. "Not yet, Clarice. It just started."

"I can't lose my family," she said meekly. "Justin and I need to work through this and we can't do it with me doing . . ."

"Me?" His comment was in poor taste, and he knew it, and regretted it. "I'm sorry."

"So am I. Good-bye, Avery."

Reesy had been an idiot and a hypocrite. She'd condemned Justin a million times over for doing the same thing she was doing right now, and Reesy hated herself for it. What chance did he have, did their marriage have, if neither of them could be faithful? Jesus! What had happened to the two of them? They'd loved each other like their parents loved. Reesy's adoptive parents had been married for over forty years, and so had Justin's parents. The two of them looked to their parents as examples of what marriage should be, but now Justin and Reesy had made a mockery of everything their parents had taught them.

Tonight, however, Reesy made up her mind to get her act together and to focus her attention where it belonged. She splashed water on her face, took a deep breath, and made up her mind to start working on her marriage the way she should've been working on it all along. And she'd start with popcorn.

"Reesy," he shouted before she hung up and turned off her cell phone.

"Dad! Tell Jade we ain't watching no princess movies tonight," Justin's son DJ argued.

It was the third Saturday of the month, movie night in at the Braxton house, and that boy had been making that same statement every one of those nights ever since Jade was old enough to become the Disney groupie that she was.

"Shut up, DJ!" Eight-year-old Jade rolled her eyes and held on tight to her DVD.

"DJ," Reesy said, coming into the room carrying bowls of popcorn, cheese curls, and juice boxes. She handed Justin a beer. "We don't use the word 'ain't' in this house, and Jade—" She glared at the little girl. "We don't tell anybody to shut up."

"Daddy said we could watch it," she whined.

"Daaad?" the boy cried out.

Of course they'd watch it, because in that moment, he was the happiest man in the world, grateful beyond measure to be home with his family again. Reesy sat opposite Justin on the sofa, sipping on a hot cup of tea. She looked beautiful without even trying, wearing an old, faded pair of sweats, one of his old shirts, and a pair of his socks.

"Why don't you come over here?" he asked, smiling and holding out his hand.

Reluctantly, she took it, and slid closer to him, resting next to him as perfectly as a piece to a puzzle. He hadn't made love to his wife in over six months. Needless to say, that's all he'd been able to think about lately. He kissed the side of her head. "Love you," he whispered.

Reesy smiled. "I know," she whispered back.

It was a start.

Justin never set out to have an affair with Cookie. Thinking about it now, it seemed like someone else's life, and not his own. A friend from work was getting married and a group of them had taken him out the night before the big day. A few drinks later, Cookie was giving him a lap dance, and Justin's good sense went up like a puff of smoke. He was feeling sorry for himself back then, sorry because he felt he wasn't getting enough attention at home. Maybe he wasn't, but he could've at least been man enough to resist the temptation of risking everything that meant anything to him. He looked at each of his kids, and then gave Reesy an appreciative smile. No woman was worth losing everything. He knew that now.

NINETEEN

The last time Reesy had seen Charlotte, she'd hit her. She'd called her, time and time again, only to end up having to leave another message, beseeching Charlotte to return her call. But this time Charlotte surprised her, and, instead of Reesy having to leave a message, her mother picked up the phone.

"Mom?" Reesy was shocked.

"How are you?" Charlotte responded coolly.

"I'm f-fine." Oh goodness. Reesy had been calling her mother all this time hoping to speak to her but now, all of a sudden, her mind went blank and she was speechless. She had no idea what to say first, but one thought was clear. She needed to clear the air between them about what had happened the last time they were together. Reesy had relived that moment over and over again, stunned by how it had all come about, and even more shocked by the revelations she'd finally had about the woman her mother really was.

Cammy had just gotten out of the hospital after her car accident and losing the baby. Connie had come into town to show her support, and Charlotte gradually lost her mind and was about to lose it on Connie the way she used to do when Reesy and Connie were kids, when Reesy stepped in and delivered the blow to Charlotte's face that Charlotte had intended for Connie's.

"Don't you ever put your hands on her again, Momma! Connie took care of me! Not you! Connie combed my hair . . . bathed me . . . made sure I ate!"

Reesy had grown up believing what she wanted to believe about Charlotte. She'd wanted to believe that their mother was mother of the year, a woman who worshipped her daughters, and that Connie had just been a difficult, misunderstood child when Charlotte walked out on them. The reality was so much further from the truth, and it hurt. It still hurt, but Charlotte was still her mother, and, despite everything, Reesy still loved her.

"How are you, Charlotte?" Reesy asked reluctantly, fully expecting the woman to figure out who she was and hang up on her.

"Oh, I've been better, I suppose. You know."

Pain jabbed her heart. Charlotte was all alone out there in Kansas. Cammy had always been there to take care of her in the past, but now, there was no one, and the thought didn't sit well with Reesy. "Do you need anything? How's your health?"

Charlotte sighed. "I have most of what I need. My health is the same."

Charlotte was a diabetic and had high blood pressure, which she used to her advantage when and where she could.

"Have you spoken to Cammy lately?"

"I don't speak to Cammy very much," she said, sadly. "How is she?"

Charlotte was melodramatic, but Reesy couldn't tell if she was acting or if she really didn't know how Cammy was doing.

"She's okay, I guess," Reesy said, reluctantly. "But, you know how she can be."

"How is that?"

"Closed. Cammy keeps to herself a lot and she doesn't say much about what's going on with her. We've tried to get her to open up and talk about losing the baby and moving here, but—"

"She was never that way here," Charlotte interrupted. "I could never get that girl to shut up when she was here. Talked from sunup to sundown."

"I think she's been through so much. And she's having a hard time adjusting. She'll come around."

"Maybe that roommate of hers can help her."

"Maybe if she had a roommate they could help her," Reesy said absently.

Charlotte got quiet on the other end of the phone.

"I think she'll be fine eventually, though, maybe with some counseling."

Charlotte still didn't respond.

"Um . . . So, I was thinking of coming to see you. To check on you."

"I don't want you to come see me, Clarice," she responded sternly.

"Charlotte—Mom, don't be like that. I'm worried about you."

"Since when? Since when have any of you girls given a damn about me?"

"Since when haven't we?" Reesy let her own frustration come through. "You're being stubborn and you're being silly, and I'm not going to let you get away with that."

"You can't come here if I don't want you to."

"You can't stop me from coming, Mom."

"I won't let you in."

Reesy chuckled. "Then I'll bring the police with me and have them kick in your front door."

"Oh, no you wouldn't!"

"Oh yes I would!"

"You got no rights with me anymore, Clarice," she said indignantly. "Not after what you did to me."

"And what about what you were about to do?" Reesy blurted out.

Charlotte got quiet.

"Mom," she said, exasperated. "Look, I didn't call to argue. I called because I love you and I'm worried about you and I want to come check on you. Period. No matter what, you are still my mother and after all the time and money I put into finding you, I promise, I'm not letting you go."

Of course, Charlotte hung up the phone satisfied when she and Reesy finally said their good-byes. And of course, she wanted her baby to come see about her. Seeing Reesy was the first step to getting what she really wanted, which was a trip home and a nice room to live in once she got there, or her own small apartment. Charlotte didn't need much, just a small place to grow old in, with a pretty window that let in lots of sunshine. The thought spread a smile across her face, but then it vanished when she recalled what Reesy had said about Cammy. That little bitch had lied to her mother like she was some stranger on the street.

"Even if I could get you here, Momma," Cammy had said, *"you couldn't stay with me because I have a roommate."*

Charlotte huffed. "A roommate my ass!"

TWENTY

Who's making love to yo' old lady

While you were out making love

Uncle drove that stretch of highway bobbing his head to Johnnie Taylor wondering the same goddamned thing. Of course, he knew the answer to that already, and he'd taken care of that niggah with a bullet to the head without thinking twice about it.

Charlotte Rodgers had looked like a dream the first time he laid eyes on that woman, shaking her ass to Al Green on the dance floor, while Uncle and any man with a pulse watched, waited, and wished she'd just make eye contact with any of them. The first time he'd had her, she was damn near on the verge of tears when she found out Sam's ass had left her stranded in Kansas City. Uncle was right there to pick up the pieces though, just like he planned, and that silly girl became putty in his hands the first time he held her in his arms.

"That sho' was some good pussy," he muttered under his breath, tapping his fingers against the steering wheel.

Young and thick, pretty round ass, pretty brown eyes, and compact enough to fit in his pocket, she was his lovely little trinket, his pretty doll—landing a woman like Charlotte was like winning the lottery.

"You take such good care of me, Uncle." Charlotte rolled over on top of him, easing her hips against him.

He pretended to be annoyed, but he really wasn't. "Now, you know I just shot a wad, girl. Can't a man rest before you wanna get him all worked up again?"

She laughed. "I can't help it that I got it bad for you, daddy. You know I just can't get enough of you and that good loving you bring over here to me."

That girl could get a dead man hard. Charlotte's eyes were light brown, and when the sun reflected off of them, they looked gold. He called her Honey because of the color of her skin. Uncle had always been piss yellow, but all light-skinned black folk were not created equally and she proved his point.

"What am I gonna do witchu girl?" he asked sincerely, wondering how any woman could bewitch him the way this one had.

She lowered her lips down to his and squeezed juice from him like she was squeezing the juice from an orange. "I'm your girl, daddy," she said, sounding sexy as all get-out. "You can do whatever you want to do with me."

Uncle had been married back then, but he'd never felt the kind of tenderness toward his wife, Sherrell, that he did for Charlotte. He'd spent twenty-seven years in prison and not once did it ever occur to him to try and get that woman out of his system, because it just wasn't an option. He wouldn't have killed her that night. He'd have made her wish he had, but he knew deep down that he wouldn't have killed her. Uncle would've put her ass out there on the corner, he'd have made her life hell from then on, but he could never fathom what it would be like knowing she was gone from this earth and that he would have to be left here without her.

Lynn had warned him that Charlotte wasn't going to be happy

to see him, but what the hell did he care about that? He needed to lay eyes on her again. Uncle was an old man, and she was old too, but he needed to see her like he needed to breathe. He needed for her to see him too, and they both needed to be able to look at each other and see what was left of them both, and maybe have a few drinks and laugh and relive some of the good times they'd had. What happened after that was anybody's guess.

TWENTY-ONE

Deana talked a lot and Cammy loved hearing her talk. If Deana was busy talking, then that meant that Cammy didn't have to.

"Girl, I know I talk nonstop," she'd told Cammy when the two of them first met. "It's my momma's fault. She talks more than me, nonstop, in a weird combination of Spanish and English." Her mother was Mexican and her father was black. Deana wore her naturally wavy hair cut short, much to her mother's chagrin, and she had the biggest, brownest eyes Cammy had ever seen on a human being. "The only place I ever seen eyes that big, brown, and pretty was on a cow," Cammy had told her once. Deana wasn't too thrilled with the comparison, but Cammy assured her that it was a compliment.

The two of them were having a late breakfast at Dozens on Havana, and while Deana talked, Cammy played her role and nodded, grunted, rolled her eyes, and laughed on cue.

"Statistics is kicking my ass, girl." Deana cut into her slice of ham. She looked like she hadn't touched her food, because she'd been too busy talking to eat. Cammy, on the other hand, was nearly finished. "I shoulda majored in something different, like art history, or some shit," she joked. "I don't think you have to take statistics for art history."

Deana was a business major, whatever that meant. Cammy had asked her once what a business major does, but Deana never really told her anything that made sense.

"You signing up for next semester, like you promised?" Deana asked.

Cammy nearly choked on the potatoes she'd put into her mouth. "Did I tell you that?"

Deana rolled her eyes. "I knew you wouldn't do it."

"No, I just didn't remember saying that." Her voice trailed off. "But yeah. Yeah, I'm enrolling."

"And you could go at night, Cammy. Even online would be better than nothing, and you could do that on the weekends."

Cammy just shrugged. College was for people like Deana. Cammy had never liked school, and she sure as hell didn't want to get roped into doing something like statistics.

"You want to be a receptionist your whole life?"

Cammy shrugged. "I like my job, and the money's good."

"What do you make? Ten, twelve dollars an hour?"

"Fifteen," Cammy said proudly.

"Fifteen's nice, but thirty's better. If you want to make more paper then you've got to get that paper. Know what I'm saying?"

Cammy shook her head.

"A degree, girl. You need a college degree to even make a dent in corporate America these days."

Deana knew a few things about Cammy, like that Tyrell, who called constantly, had been someone she had loved and who had loved her. She knew that Cammy was close to her mother, and that Cammy's sisters, Connie and Reesy, hadn't always been in her life, and she'd admitted to Deana that she didn't always know how to feel around them because sometimes, and that was most of the time, she felt like they were strangers. And every now and then, she talked about "the car accident" she'd had before moving to Denver. Deana was more interested in what Cammy didn't tell her than in what she did. There was just something sad about her, even when she smiled.

"Ladies," a man said coolly, coming over to their table. "Good morning."

Isaac Tillman didn't wait to be invited to sit down at the table. He slid into the booth next to Cammy, draped his arm behind her, and kissed her on the cheek.

"Uh . . . hi," Cammy said, stunned.

He winked at Deana and shrugged. "How you doing?" he asked, smugly.

Deana hated him on sight. She instantly knew his type. The slick-talking, fast-moving type who believed that no woman could resist his irresistible ass.

Cammy looked downright uncomfortable with the brotha, and like she had no idea who he was, but Deana remembered him from the club the other night.

Five eight, stocky build, with diamonds shimmering in his ears, it didn't take much for Deana to figure out this fool was his own biggest fan. He looked too damn old to be sitting there in an over-size Sean John shirt, sagging jeans, and Tims, but while he basked in his own glory, Deana wrestled with the urge to call him out on his rudeness.

"How come you ain't called me back?"

That explained the strange number she kept seeing showing up on her cell phone.

"This is my friend Deana," Cammy said, clearing her throat. "Deana, this is . . ."

"Isaac. Nice to meet you again, Deana." He jutted his chin in her direction. "How you doing?" he asked, trying to sound too damn cool.

Deana smiled sarcastically and then sipped her coffee.

"How've you been?" Cammy asked.

"If you'd been answering your phone, you'd know how I been," he said too quickly.

"Did you leave any messages?" Deana asked.

He looked at her like she'd just asked him to jump off a ledge. "I don't leave messages."

"Then how's she supposed to know you called?"

"She got caller ID," he shot back.

Deana was about to say something smart, but Cammy stopped her.

Cammy grinned. "I didn't recognize the number."

Isaac stared deeply into her eyes. "Well, now you know that it's me calling. You gonna answer next time. Right?"

Cammy nodded uneasily. "Sure."

"You look nice this morning," he muttered, seductively running his thumb up and down Cammy's shoulder.

"Thank you," she said quietly.

The country mouse and the city rat. Deana stared at Cammy, amazed at just how naïve this girl really was to the ways of the world and the snakes of the world. He sat his ass down, claiming his piece as soon as he did, and she looked absolutely clueless.

"Whatchu doing later?" he asked.

"We're going shopping," Deana blurted out before Cammy had a chance to say something stupid, like *nothing.*

Isaac stared disapprovingly at her. Deana stared back as if to ask, *"What?"*

Cammy just looked dumb.

"How 'bout I call you later?" he asked her.

Cammy nodded. "That's fine."

"Maybe we can hook up tonight." It wasn't a question. Isaac picked up Cammy's glass of orange juice and finished off half of it. He glared at Deana. "Y'all take it easy."

Deana held his glare with her own. "You be easy too."

He got up to leave, but left Cammy with a memory of his presence and a promise of things to come with a kiss.

"See you later, baby girl."

Cammy couldn't help but notice the disdain on Deana's face after Isaac left. "What?" she asked.

Deana sighed, and went back to eating. "Nothing."

Cammy studied her for a moment, and then stated the obvious. "You don't like him."

"You do?" she responded shortly.

"I don't know," Cammy said impatiently.

Deana shrugged. "Then do you, Cam."

"What's that supposed to mean?"

"It means, I hope the sex is good," Deana said curtly.

Cammy looked confused. "You don't even know him."

"And you don't either. Look, I've met plenty of dudes like him, and I knew what he was about as soon as he stepped to you. What bothers me is that you have no clue."

Cammy was offended. "I'm not as dumb as you think I am, Deana," she said bitterly.

"No, girl. But you country as hell. You haven't been out of no-fucking-where Kansas two minutes, and you're already entertaining the riffraff." Deana didn't mean to offend Cammy, but that's how it came out.

"Don't worry about me, Deana," Cammy said, offended. "I really can take care of myself."

Despite the earnest look in Cammy's eyes, Deana just wasn't quite convinced.

TWENTY-TWO

The baby was sleeping and Connie was working in the back room of the house, soldering an intricate pattern on a silver bracelet she was making. She'd closed down her boutique right before Jonathon was born but still sold custom jewelry and artwork from her Web site. John had been gone for three days now, and he'd called to let her know that he'd made it okay but she hadn't heard much from him after that. She knew better than anybody what he was going through right now and the fact that he wasn't feeling very talkative at the moment was understandable.

He'd spent his whole life not knowing who his father was. John had heard about Adam, and he'd heard the rumors surrounding Adam, but just about everything he'd grown up knowing was lies. He was forty when he finally went back to Texas to see the woman who'd raised him—his grandmother, Agnes—and to finally face his father. Adam wasn't the monster everyone had made him out to be at all. John never came right out and said it, but she suspected that it was pretty much a love-at-first-sight kind of thing between the two of them. In finding Adam, John had managed to find a few missing pieces of himself, and he'd found peace.

Adam had only been in his life for two years, and now he was dying. That kind of knowledge had to hurt John deeply. Two years was better than nothing though. Now wasn't the time to tell him that, but she knew that he'd eventually see that it was true. There was a happy ending to his story the moment he found out that Adam wasn't the man he'd grown up thinking he was. Anything that happened after that, well . . . was just the natural way of things.

Connie turned off her soldering torch, sat back, and admired her work. She had mad skills when it came to manipulating metals. Connie loved making her art, because for so long it had been the one thing she'd always felt she could control in her life. The decision she'd made to have Jonathon had been hers to control too. She'd been a step away from another abortion when it dawned on her that she did have the right to choose, and so she chose and prepared herself to accept the consequences of that decision no matter the costs. She thought about her baby boy and smiled. She'd made the right choice for the first time in her life, and, months later, she still didn't have any regrets.

Jade's face never strayed too far from her thoughts, though. She hadn't seen much of that little girl since she'd had Jonathon, and the few times she had spent around her felt strained. Jade had come by with Reesy right after Jonathon was born. Jade, Connie, and Reesy were all upstairs in the nursery watching him sleep and Connie happened to glance down at Jade. Reesy looked at her too.

"Isn't he beautiful?" Reesy knelt down and whispered in Jade's ear.

Something like confusion shone on her small face as she bit down on her bottom lip and nodded.

Connie smoothed back Jade's hair, and suddenly the little girl turned and hurried out of the room. Connie looked at Reesy with tears in her eyes. "Maybe this wasn't a good idea."

Reesy stared back, helpless. "Maybe not."

John's situation with his father had suddenly shined a light on her situation with her daughter. Reesy and Justin were Jade's parents. No one on earth, especially Connie, would ever dispute that, and her intentions had never been to disrupt it. But the older Jade got, the more Connie sensed the urgency in telling her the truth. Until recently, Reesy had fought her tooth and nail on the subject, but circumstances had compelled them both to see eye to eye on the matter and to sit down together to explain what happened to Jade.

Connie heard Jonathon starting to cry on the baby monitor and she hurried upstairs to him. As she nursed him sitting in the chair next to the window, she couldn't take her eyes off of him. He looked so much like his father, but he saw some of Jade in him too. Connie had nursed her too. It was the only time in their brief mother-daughter relationship that she'd felt like that little girl belonged to her. The rest of the time, however, Connie felt herself choking on the pressure of insecurity and doubt, afraid that she'd let Jade down the way she'd been let down by her mother. Worried that she would fail Jade and make her suffer through Connie's poor sense of judgment and undeserving attitude. Jade deserved more than Connie had to give at the time and Reesy and Justin had plenty.

Jonathon stared up at her with dark eyes, as mesmerized by her as she was by him. Connie wasn't the same woman when she found out that she was pregnant with him that she'd been when she found out she was going to have Jade. She'd come to terms with herself and had forgiven herself her mistakes. Connie had become stronger and she'd learned to live without looking back all the time, because forward held a much nicer view.

She'd made some beautiful babies, and if God never gave her

another thing, he'd given her her children and the realization that she was not now, nor would she ever be, Charlotte.

She dialed her sister's number. "Reesy?" she said over the phone.

"Hey. I was just thinking about you," Reesy said cheerfully. "Whatcha doing?"

"We need to talk about Jade."

Reesy hesitated before responding, and Connie half-expected Reesy to come back at her with attitude. Reesy sighed. "We do."

"Thank you."

"For what, Connie? You're her mother."

"No. You're her mother. I'm the best auntie in the world, or at least, I used to be. I just think she deserves to know the truth."

"She does, Connie. We'll talk to her soon."

TWENTY-THREE

John's daddy was a rumor and an anomaly. Racine Cook stood next to Adam Tate's bed at the hospice, staring keenly at him, searching for traces of his son in his features. They weren't hard to find: the shape of his face, the curve of his mouth, his hands, and, even closed, his eyes. She'd grown up hearing the stories about him like everyone else in town, and, like everyone else in town, she believed them to be true.

Somebody say they saw him, trackin' after that girl on any given day.

He was sneakin' and lurkin' in them bushes behind her house when her momma ain't home.

He looked harmless, she thought, smiling down at Adam, sedated. At one time in his life, he might've been a much larger man, even handsome, but now he just looked old and frail and like he wouldn't hurt a fly. John King was fortunate in that he found out the truth about his father before it was too late. For the last two years, he'd had the privilege of having Adam in his life and, even though it could never be enough to make up for a lifetime of deceit, it had to count for something.

"Hello?" Moses' wife, Sara, stood in the doorway of Adam's

hospital room, carrying fresh flowers. "Can I help you?" she asked, uncertain of who this woman was visiting her brother-in-law.

Racine turned to her, smiled, and then crossed the room extending her hand to shake. "Hello." She smiled nervously. "I'm . . . My name is Racine Cook. I'm a friend of John's."

Sara was no rocket scientist, but looking at the woman, she easily surmised what kind of friendship John King had had with her. Of course, she'd seen her around town. Bueller wasn't big as a minute, so she had no doubt that she knew some of this woman's people. "I'm Sara. John's auntie."

Sara shook her hand, and then stepped around her to place the flowers on the table next to Adam.

Racine cleared her throat. "I assume John is here?"

Sara turned to her and smiled. "Not yet. He's on his way, though."

Racine nodded, and then shifted uncomfortably under the weight of Sara's unwavering gaze. "They look alike." She nodded in Adam's direction.

"Yes. And when Adam was younger, they looked even more alike." Sara turned to Racine. "Adam's the nice one, though." She smiled.

Racine couldn't help but smile too. Anyone who knew John King as well as Racine knew him understood what Sara meant. He was a magnet to any woman with two eyes and any semblance of a libido. John was that elusive fish that could never be hooked, the king of the jungle with his pick of any cat in the pride. No woman possessed the power to keep a man like John King, but that didn't stop them from trying.

"Well, when John gets into town, could you tell him I stopped by?"

Sara had never met Connie personally, but they'd spoken on

the phone. She liked Connie. She didn't care much for Racine, though.

John was already in town, but Sara didn't think that was any of this woman's business.

"Maybe I'll mention it."

The friendliness faded from Racine's expression, but something in Sara's warned her not to push the issue.

"Well, then, maybe I'll get a chance to tell him myself." She turned to leave.

"Anything's possible," Sara muttered under her breath.

Racine stepped onto the elevator, angrier at what that woman didn't say to her than what she did. She and John King were friends. They'd grown up together, and had been boyfriend and girlfriend when they were teenagers. Back then, John King had snuck in and out of her bedroom window too many times to count. She'd come by here hoping to see him. Racine had heard his daddy was sick and she knew that Adam's illness would bring him back again. John was going through a difficult time now, and he'd need someone to talk to. He knew he could talk to Racine. And he knew he could do other things with Racine too. She counted on him remembering that.

It was late when John finally arrived at the hospice. Sara had fallen asleep in the only chair in the room. Moses trailed behind John; he touched her shoulder to wake her. Sara wrapped her arms around John and squeezed him tight.

"How's he doing?" he asked, clearing his throat, staring between Moses and Sara.

She turned him to face Adam. "Why don't you try asking him yourself," she said quietly, stepping back into Moses' arms.

John reached over and pulled the chair next to the bed and sat down. Adam appeared to be sleeping, and John was apprehensive about waking him up, but he needn't have been.

He's here. Her voice filled him like a cool breeze. Adam's eyes fluttered open, and he turned his head slightly and saw his son. His smile was brilliant enough to light the darkest room.

"Hey boy," he said sluggishly. Adam raised his arm in the air and waited for John to take hold of his hand.

"Whatchu been up to, old man?" John teased him, swallowing any hint of sadness from his tone.

Adam didn't respond right away. He seemed to drift back off into sleep, but not for long. "I . . . been . . . resting." He sighed.

John turned to Sara and Moses, wondering where Adam's stutter had disappeared to.

"It's the morphine," Sara volunteered. She shrugged.

He turned back to his father. "I heard you weren't feeling too good."

Adam laughed. "Sssometimes I don't. Sometimes . . . I do. I always ffffeel good to see you, though."

John squeezed his hand.

"I wanna . . . to see the baby," Adam said. "And your . . . ggggirl. You bring 'em, thissss time?"

Adam suddenly winced, his face twisted in pain, and John watched as his father desperately dispensed morphine with the push of a button.

"No." He swallowed. "Not this time, Adam." For the first time since he'd been back, tears filled John's eyes, but he blinked them away before they could fall.

"Awww . . . I wishhhh you'da brought 'em." Adam sounded disappointed. "She wanted to see 'em."

John looked confused. "Who? Who wanted to see them?"

Adam smiled again. "Yo . . . mmmmmomma, son. She wanted to . . ."

And just like that, Adam drifted back off into a drug-induced sleep.

Sara and Moses wanted him to follow them home, but John needed a drink. He pulled into Marty's, which was nothing more than a hole in the wall, sidled up to the bar, and ordered gin with a beer chaser. Adam was a relic of a bygone era of John's sordid and screwed-up past, and here the old man was, on his death-bed, and he'd gone and resurrected little Mattie King. He shook his head in awe. That was some shit. That old-school, forbidden, sordid, crazy shit.

"Did your aunt tell you I was looking for you?" Racine slid into the seat next to him and draped both arms over his shoulder.

John grinned and inhaled Racine. She always did smell good. "No."

"I didn't think she would." She motioned to Leroy, the bar-tender. Racine didn't need to bother placing an order with the man. A few minutes later, he sat a rum and Coke down in front of her and winked.

"Come here often?" John teased.

"Where else is there to go in this town?" She nudged him with her shoulder. "I'm sorry to hear about your daddy," she said sincerely.

"Me too." John finished his gin, then motioned for another one.

"How long you staying?"

He shrugged. "As long as . . ." He was going to say as long as it takes, but changed his mind. It was an empty statement, and when Adam died, John would be empty too.

"And Connie?" she probed. "Is she here too?" Racine suspected that if the woman had come down, she'd have been sitting at that bar next to her man.

"Nah," was all he said.

She sipped her drink, relieved. John King was in her system, and nothing she could do seemed to be enough to purge him. The last time he'd come to town, the two of them had spent a lot of time together. Good times. And despite her best efforts to do the right thing and send him home to his woman, Racine's heart had skipped a couple of beats when she found out he was coming back. Maybe this time, she wouldn't be so eager to be so right.

"You staying at Moses'?"

John hesitated before answering. "I got a room."

"You want company?" she asked, unable to ignore the passion warming between her thighs.

John looked at her for the first time since she'd sat down. Racine was a fine woman, built, sweet to the taste, and accommodating to a fault, and temptation washed over him like a warm shower. The bartender set his drink down in front of him, and John finished it in one gulp, and then polished off the last of his beer. He pulled his wallet out from his pocket, dropped a twenty dollar bill on the counter, and kissed Racine on the cheek.

"Night," he said wearily.

TWENTY-FOUR

Cammy hadn't heard from her mother in over a week, and, despite her best efforts not to, she was starting to panic. She paced back and forth in her bedroom, holding the phone to her ear, growing more frustrated by the minute that the only answer she was getting from all her phone calls to Charlotte's was her mother's answering machine.

"We're not home right now." She rolled her eyes at the sound of her own voice on Charlotte's machine. "But leave a message and we'll call you back as soon as we can."

"Momma!" she blurted out. "I know you're there, Momma. Answer the phone," she demanded.

What if something had happened? What if Charlotte had fallen or someone had broken into the house? What if she'd had a car accident or what if she'd . . .

"Please, Momma," she said, pleading. A lump swelled in her throat, and tears of frustration filled her eyes. "Don't do this to me." Her voice trailed off pitifully. She waited until the machine disconnected her and hung up the phone.

Charlotte was punishing her. It's what she did, and she was doing it now because Cammy had left her alone. Cammy crawled into bed and curled up with one of her pillows clutched tightly to her chest. She was twenty-seven years old and she'd lived her whole life for Charlotte. She'd loathed every minute of it, but Charlotte had always been the only thing in her world that felt natural. Cammy couldn't wait to get away from her when she moved to Denver with Connie and Reesy. She thought that if she could just get away from Charlotte, finally, that she could know what it felt like to live her own life and make her own choices. But that was the problem. Even after all of these months, Cammy wasn't living her own life and making choices. She was a stranger in this place, in this city, and even in her own apartment. And despite the fact that Reesy and Connie were her sisters, they were strangers too. They didn't know anything about Cammy and she really didn't know anything about either of them. Denver was a big place, and no matter how hard she tried, Cammy felt out of place and alone. What the hell was wrong with her?

The phone rang and she couldn't answer it fast enough. "Momma?" she asked anxiously.

Charlotte hesitated before responding. "I got your messages," she said indifferently. "What is it, Cammy?"

Some things were automatic, like the ease with which Cammy could tune out her mother's callous tone and find comfort in the sound of her voice. She'd learned from when she was a little girl that it wasn't what Charlotte said, or even how she said it, that mattered. All that mattered was that she was speaking to Cammy, and every word that fell on her ears from her mother's lips was like gospel.

"I was worried about you," Cammy said quietly, comforted by the trap she'd let herself fall back into, and loathing herself for it at the same time.

Charlotte didn't say a word, but she didn't need to.

"You doing alright?" Cammy asked sweetly. "You need anything?"

You were wrong to leave her like that. Her own thoughts convicted her every day. When she left home, she was angry, and hurt, and no matter how hard she tried sometimes, she couldn't remember why or what had been so bad that she felt she needed to leave Kansas, especially when she knew how much Charlotte needed her.

"I'm doing 'bout as good as I can be," Charlotte said, dryly. "All things considered."

The implication wasn't lost on Cammy. *Considering that you left me here by myself. Considering that you knew how badly I wanted to move back home, and you left without me. Considering that I need you here—I need somebody here to help me.*

Cammy's conscience gnawed at her insides. "I bought you some things," she said quickly, trying to ease her guilt. "Whenever I go shopping I pick up some nice pretty things I think you'll like, and I have a whole box of stuff for you, Momma." She sounded like a little girl again. And she felt like one too. "I'll put it in the mail tomorrow. You should have it in a few days."

"Don't bother," Charlotte said indifferently. "Clarice is bringing me some nice presents when she comes to see me this weekend."

Cammy was stunned by the news. She had no idea that Reesy and Charlotte had even spoken. The last few times she'd spoken to her sister, Reesy had complained that Charlotte still hadn't returned her calls.

"Yes," Charlotte continued. "She said she was bringing me some new sheets and towels, oh, and when I mentioned that I'd like some new dishes, she promised that we'd go shopping for some nice china and crystal as soon as she got here," Charlotte lied.

The small gifts Cammy had bought couldn't compare with china and crystal. Listening to Charlotte go on and on about Reesy, Cammy began to find that emotional and familiar place that reminded her of how insignificant she really was. Charlotte had never loved Cammy the way she'd loved Reesy, and she never would.

"Well, I'm glad to hear that, Momma," she whispered. "Maybe I'll see if they'll let me off work for a few days and I can come to see you too," she said pitifully.

Charlotte sighed. "No need."

Desperation engulfed her. "Maybe I can come down with Reesy." Tears watered her eyes. Cammy hadn't thought about ever setting foot in Murphy again, but now all of a sudden, she felt like a homing pigeon that needed to get back to its base. All she'd ever wanted was Charlotte's approval, and for Charlotte to love her half as much as Cammy loved her. She had forgotten how much that had been until now.

"Oh, I don't know about all that." Charlotte added salt to her wound and sounded disappointed.

Cammy bit down on her lip. She knew this game. Charlotte wanted to hurt her, and Cammy conceded. It was the nature of their relationship. The heart of it, in fact, and the two of them needed each other in a way no one else would ever understand.

"It's no problem, Momma," she said, hopeful. "I'll call Reesy and let her know I'm coming too."

"Well, you do what you wanna do. That's just how you are, Camille. How you've always been."

After saying good-bye to Charlotte, Cammy pressed her hand to her mouth to stifle a sob. She felt herself losing footing in Charlotte's life and it scared her. Coming here had been a mistake. She knew that now more than she'd ever known it.

Cammy's lying ass thinks she's slick, Charlotte thought smugly after hanging up the phone with her daughter. But Charlotte had her number, and if Cammy thought she was going to keep on playing Charlotte for a fool, she had another think coming.

"You can't stay with me, Momma," she had lied. *"Ain't no room in this small apartment with me and my roommate, and I'd want you to be comfortable. Besides, you wouldn't like her anyway."*

The bitch didn't have a roommate. Charlotte was livid when she first found out Cammy lied, but lying was what that girl did best. She'd lied about marrying Tyrell's ass, and about being pregnant until her belly started pushing out through her clothes, and now she'd lied about having a roommate. Obviously she didn't want Charlotte around.

Cammy was an insecure girl, though, especially where her momma was concerned. A satisfied grin spread across her face, cocking Charlotte's crooked smile to the side. She wanted Charlotte to herself—always did—and always would too, and she turned flips making sure that she was always Charlotte's special girl. Cammy's ass was fine with Charlotte being all alone without a single soul to look after her, but the minute she'd heard Reesy was coming, all of a sudden that heifer could come up with some "vacation time."

Charlotte chuckled bitterly and shook her head. Cammy could bring her dumb behind down here if she wanted to, but she'd pay dearly for abandoning her mother. That girl had a whole lot of ugly buttons that could be pushed if you knew how, and nobody knew how better than Charlotte. Before it was all said and done, she'd bring that child to her knees—but shit—Cammy deserved it.

TWENTY-FIVE

The kids were in school, Justin was at work, and Reesy and Connie sat in Reesy's living room, drinking tea and eating cookies. Leave it to Reesy to conjure up something as bougie as tea and cookies. Reesy had taken the baby as soon as Connie had come inside and hadn't put him down since she'd served the damn tea and cookies.

"He's sleeping, Reese," Connie complained. "Put him down. You're going to spoil him."

Reesy rolled her eyes and stared lovingly at her nephew. "That's old-school thinking, Connie. He's a newborn. There's nothing you can do to spoil him."

Connie had told Reesy about John's father, and her response was surprisingly sympathetic. Reesy had never been a fan of John King, but more and more she had come to respect him.

"So, there's no chance Adam can come through this?" Reesy asked sincerely.

Connie shook her head. "They didn't catch it in time."

"Well, why'd they find out so late? Hadn't he been seeing a doctor for checkups?"

Connie shrugged. "Adam isn't like most people, Reesy. He's stubborn."

"Like John?"

Connie smirked. "He's never liked doctors, and I guess getting him out of the house is a huge commitment in and of itself."

"I imagine he had been in a lot of pain, though, Connie."

"I'm sure he probably was, but if he was, he didn't complain, which doesn't surprise anybody who knows him."

Reesy studied Connie. "So, how come you didn't go with him?"

Connie thought for a moment before answering. "I think he needed to be alone to process this. Know what I mean?"

Reesy didn't respond.

"You know how John is. He internalizes everything, especially when it really gets personal."

"It's not good to shut you out of stuff like this, Connie. He may have internalized things in the past, but things are different now. He has a family." Reesy hadn't offended her sister. A year ago, Connie would've jumped up defensively, ready to go to blows to defend her man. "Maybe you should think about taking a trip to Texas."

Connie stared back at Reesy. "Maybe I should."

Reesy sighed, and decided to walk through the door that had just opened up between them. "I'm going to see Momma," she blurted out.

If she expected Connie to say anything, she quickly realized she'd be waiting a long time. Her sister just sat there.

"I just think I should check on her."

"Really?"

Reesy cleared her throat. "She's alone now. She's older, Connie, and not in the best health."

"You don't owe me an explanation, Reesy," Connie said unemotionally.

"I know, but . . . You know, we've just found her, Connie."

"You found her, Reesy."

"I think that we need to keep moving forward," she continued quietly. "Our mother has made her share of mistakes."

Connie smiled.

"But I can't just pretend she's not there. And I can't turn my back on her no matter how horrible she's been."

"Is Justin alright with you leaving?"

Any other time she'd have argued that her decision to leave to go see her mother wasn't up for a vote or approval from Justin, but Connie asked the question because she knew all about the problems Reesy and Justin had been having.

"It's not the best time, but—"

"But you're trying to mend your marriage. Do you really want to risk any progress you may be making for Charlotte?"

Had they been making progress? Until recently, Reesy wasn't even sure she wanted to reconnect with her husband. Her doubt must've registered on her face, because all of a sudden Connie looked concerned.

"What's that look?"

Reesy shrugged. "What?"

Connie leaned forward and stared into Reesy's eyes. "I thought the two of you were doing better?"

"We are," she said quietly.

"How come I'm not convinced?"

Reesy became frustrated. "Maybe because I'm not? It's not easy getting our marriage back to where it was, Connie. I don't know if it can ever go back to what it was."

"Do you want to work things out?"

Reesy looked appalled. "How can you sit there and ask me that?"

Connie shrugged. "I'm asking. Do you?"

Uncertainty washed over her face, but Reesy pushed her response through it, hoping Connie hadn't noticed. "My family means everything to me. You know that."

"What does Justin mean to you?"

"I'm trying, Connie," she said disappointedly. "That's all I can do."

Connie sat back and sighed. "So, when are you leaving for Kansas, Dorothy?" Connie asked sarcastically.

Reesy rolled her eyes. "Friday, and no wicked witch jokes, Connie. I can see them dangling from your lips."

Connie grinned. "You don't want me to talk about your momma?"

"Please don't talk about my momma."

"Fine. I won't say a word about the heifer."

Reesy shook her head, and decided to change the subject. "I hate to say it, but this beautiful boy is the spitting image of his ugly daddy."

"That's childish, Reesy. I talk about your momma and you talk about my man? Childish."

Reesy laughed. "Speaking of children." Her expression suddenly turned serious. "Maybe we should wait to talk to Jade until after I get back."

Connie didn't like it. She had half-expected it, but she didn't like it. "There's never going to be a perfect time to tell her."

"I know," she said defensively.

"We put it off until after Jonathon was born, and then we waited until you and Justin figured out what you were going to do."

"I know, Connie. But this is huge."

"It needs to be done."

"Yes. Of course it does. But I can't drop a bomb like this on my daughter and then leave town for a week. She's not going to be able to process this on her own."

As much as she wanted to argue, Connie couldn't bring herself to dispute her reasoning.

"She's only eight, Connie."

"I know how old she is, Reesy," she said irritably. "I was there. Remember?"

"You know what I mean. She's going to need help with this."

Connie glared at her before responding. "As soon as you get back, we do this."

Reesy swallowed. "As soon as I get home. I promise."

TWENTY-SIX

Like a moth to a flame, Liz was always drawn to two places whenever she went back to her hometown. She pulled her rental car to the side of the road, got out, and stared at the empty space in an open field. There was nothing left here now except for a pile of rotting wood and weeds as tall as she was. She used to live here. She'd been a little girl in this place. Both she and CJ had actually been born in the house that used to stand here, and her father had built it.

She was sixty-four years old now and sometimes it was hard to believe she'd ever been a little girl, but coming here reminded her that she hadn't imagined her younger years. Images of her sitting between her mother's knees near the fireplace, cringing as that woman dragged that comb through her hair, almost brought a smile to her face.

"Turn yo' head, 'Lizabeth! Hold still, girl. Got nappy hair jus' like yo' daddy."

Even now, the notion that she'd had anything remotely similar to her father's attributes was comforting. Her memories of living here weren't all bad. She stared so hard at the place where that house had once stood that Liz could almost see the shadows of her small self sitting on her father's lap on the front porch as he told her stories that made her giggle. CJ had been cheated out of his memories, because he'd been so young when their father had died, but Liz still managed to cling to a few precious ones that she prayed would never fade away.

Eventually, she climbed back into the car and followed the roads leading to one other place. The place where she and her brother had come to live after their father had passed away, and the place where, ironically enough, her mother had died.

Granny Muh's house was still standing, although just barely. It had been ten years since she'd last visited her hometown and this house, and it looked even smaller than it did the last time. Liz stared at it, wondering if it was really shrinking, or if the world around it was just outgrowing it. She longed to go inside, but the steps leading up to the porch didn't look too safe. The old fence around it had decayed so badly most of it had fallen, but the front gate stood strong, like it had planned on being there forever.

"Yo' momma fell in the yard. She just fell and died."

The day she got the news, Liz didn't even remember crying. She didn't remember feeling anything at all, except the sense that a chapter in her life had come to an end. She and CJ never even went back for the funeral.

In Bueller, Liz Brooks was something from a past so old that anybody who knew the stories surrounding her life was more than likely already dead and gone. The few who remained, like Alice, no longer talked about it much, if at all. Bueller wasn't necessarily a fan of the bestselling author. Most of them had never even read any of her books. They stared at her because she was someone they didn't recognize. She was new to town, until someone mentioned that she wasn't, and then she became a curiosity more than anything.

"Who yo' people?"

She'd smile, and tell them the simplest answer. "The Samples."

After their father died, Liz and CJ went to live with their grandmother until she passed away. Liz was in high school, and CJ was just starting junior high. Larry and Joan Sample, from their grandmother's church, agreed to take them in after her death. The couple had four children of their own; two were grown and had moved out of the house by the time Liz and CJ came to live with them. The younger ones, Alice, who was a year younger than Liz, and Ben, who was nine, became like a brother and sister to Liz and CJ, and through the years, Liz and Alice had managed to keep in touch.

Alice had been the one to call her with the news. Nobody in the world knew Liz's secrets like Alice, not even CJ. No one knew her true feelings the way Alice did, and no one understood her doubts and fears, and accepted that they would always be a part of her the way Alice did.

"I heard that Adam is in the hospital," Alice had told her. "I heard that he ain't doing good, Liz. He ain't gonna make it."

Nobody but Alice knew who Adam was in Liz's life. Not even CJ.

Children grow up hearing things. Little girls, in particular, are better listeners than anyone in the world, with the uncanny ability to eavesdrop on conversations not fit for young ears. They can listen intently and play games at the same time, fooling grown-ups into thinking they hadn't heard a thing, when in fact they had heard and absorbed every word.

The word "Adam" was a ghost word, haunting her from the moment she'd heard his name, every single day of her life, even when she wasn't thinking of it.

"You know that boy was his. She found out, and that's when it all happened. That girl lost her damn mind."

Liz listened to enough gossip and innuendos to put together the pieces of a puzzle that tied her and CJ to this Adam, but she'd never had the courage to share what she'd known with her brother, thinking that he would just think she was making up one of her stories.

"Daddy wouldn't do that," she could hear him saying. *"Nosey-ass people ain't got nothing better to do than to make shit up, Liz. They're bored. They make it up because they ain't got nothing better to do."*

CJ always had a way of picking and choosing his notion of the truth, and Liz never disputed it.

Alice had insisted on Liz staying with her and her husband, but Liz decided to get a room instead. The last thing she needed was Alice buzzing around trying to pick her thoughts from her head and get her to talk openly about this Adam. She had talked about him all the time when she was a teenager, and Alice would listen, eyes wide and ears wider, taking in every word, every nuance and implication, like a drug addict. If she ever told anybody, it never got back to Liz that she did. But Liz stopped talking about Adam after she left and went away to college. She stopped talking about him, but she never forgot him.

A phone call from Alice had brought her back to this place. Since she'd graduated, Liz had only come back here for funerals. If what Alice said was true, then this would be the last opportunity she would have to finally come face-to-face with this man and to say the things she never thought she'd ever have the courage to say out loud. Maybe, he would have a chance to say some things to her too.

TWENTY-SEVEN

His daughter hated his guts, and with good reason. Avery had turned his back on her at a time when she needed him most, and she'd never forgiven him for it. He'd never forgiven himself either. She was eleven years old when the man her mother remarried first put his hands on her. Avery was too busy with his second marriage to notice, but by the time he'd found out, the damage had been done. The last time he'd seen Lisa, she was stripping in a club in west Denver, under the moniker of Cookie. Cookie was an exotic dancer, and made more money doing things he really didn't want to think about. Justin Braxton had been one of those things. Avery snapped pictures of Justin and Cookie together, then mailed them to Clarice and turned her world upside down. At the time, he thought he was doing her, and mostly himself, a favor. But it didn't quite work out that way. Hell, he wasn't sure how it was all working out to be honest. Reesy and Justin had gotten back together, but not before Reesy and Avery had taken their relationship to another level. It was anybody's guess how it all would pan out in the end.

Lisa lived in a small apartment in south Denver. She'd be pissed if she knew he was still keeping tabs on her, but he owed her. She might not think she needed him anymore, and maybe she didn't, but Avery counted on a *just in case* where his daughter was concerned. *Just in case* she ever did need him, he wanted to be there this time.

He waited a few minutes after he saw her pull into the parking lot of her building and then disappeared into the parking garage. Avery didn't expect a warm welcome, but he needed to see for himself how she was doing. He'd been given a second chance with Clarice; maybe, by some miracle, he'd be given another chance with his daughter.

"What are you doing here, Avery?" she asked, looking even more annoyed than she sounded.

Hey. At least she answered the door. As far as he was concerned, that was progress.

He resisted the urge to scoop her up in his arms and swing her around the way he used to when she was small. "I just wanted to see how you were, Lisa."

She looked so much like her mother, petite, caramel complexion, long, soft hair, full lips. Lisa wasn't wearing tons of makeup like she used to wear when she was stripping, and she looked even younger than twenty-five.

"Can I come in?"

She thought about it first before stepping aside to make room for him. "What? You dying or something?" she asked, callously.

He chuckled. "What?"

"I figure there must be something tragic going on for you to be reaching out to long-lost relatives and shit. Why else would you be here? What? You need a kidney or something?"

He stared apologetically at her. "I hardly consider you my long-lost anything, sweetheart, and my kidneys are fine." He smiled; she didn't.

"Then what do you want?"

He shrugged. "Just to see you. Make sure you're okay."

"Ah." She nodded. "Still working on that last-ditch effort to salvage our relationship, Daddy dearest. Gotcha."

Avery wasn't as amused by her sarcasm as she seemed to be, but he understood it.

"Well, if it's any consolation, Avery, I'm fine. I'm living, breathing, and taking care of myself the way I've done since you walked out on us. There." She smiled. "That make you feel better?"

"You still stripping?" he asked, bracing himself for the fallout about how that was none of his business and she was grown and could do whatever she wanted.

"No," she responded simply.

"No?"

"You deaf? I said no."

He wanted to ask, but how could he? As far as he knew, the only thing Lisa knew how to do was be a stripper.

She seemed to read his mind. "I'm going to school, Avery. College. And I work at an insurance company part-time. Is that what you were wondering?"

He shrugged. "I was. Good. That's good, Lisa." He stepped toward her, reaching out to hug her, but she backed away defensively.

"Whoa, cowboy!" She put her hands on her hips. "Please don't get it twisted and think that we've got a happy little family reunion going on here, 'cause it's not that kind of party and it never will be. I'm doing okay, Avery, but not so okay that I want you back in my life again. You missed that train a long time ago."

Avery couldn't find it in himself to blame her, but that didn't mean he'd ever stop trying to make up for his past mistakes with his daughter. "I understand how you feel," he said, choking back his guilt. "But in any case, I'm still happy to hear it."

"Yeah, well, I can't dance forever, and prostitution could get me locked up," she said smartly.

"You never had to do that, Lisa."

"You don't have a clue about what I had to do, Avery. I took care of myself the best way I could. Period. Right or wrong, I did what I felt I had to do because nobody else was going to, until a good friend of mine told me that I deserved better . . . believed that I could do better. That's all. He believed in me enough to convince me that he was right."

Justin Braxton had paid $1,500 for a weekend of her time once. She fucked him like it was nobody's business, and enjoyed doing it too. He treated her like a queen that weekend. No. He treated her like she was his lady, and she repaid him by trading in her old life for a new one. A better one.

"What's your major?" Avery asked, feeling more proud of her than he thought possible.

"You wouldn't believe me if I told you," she said, smirking.

"Try me."

"Computer science," she said proudly. "My ass is smart."

Avery surprised himself and laughed out loud. "I never doubted it for a minute, sweetheart."

Just then, her phone rang, and Lisa went into the kitchen to take the call. Avery waited so that he could say good-bye. Her apartment was small, but nice. It looked like several days' worth of mail was strewn across the coffee table, and the detective-father in him just happened to do a quick inventory of it—mostly junk; a letter from her brother, his son Anthony, who was incarcerated for grand theft auto; the electric and phone bills; and an opened envelope from Thomas, McCarthy, and Engle's Accounting in Centennial. Avery picked it up, peeked at the note inside, and then put it back where he found it.

"Well, I don't mean to throw you out, Avery," Lisa said, emerging from the kitchen. "But I've got shit to do."

It was her way of saying good-bye.

"Mind if I stop by again sometime?" he asked humbly.

"Yeah. I do mind."

He nodded. "Maybe I'll just show up again without calling first," he teased.

Lisa glared at him. "You got lucky this time, Avery. I've had a great day and I'm in a generous mood, which is the only reason I let you in this time. I wouldn't bet on that same kind of compassion next time around. You're liable to get your feelings hurt."

Avery left without saying good-bye, a little wiser than he'd been before she'd answered that door.

TWENTY-EIGHT

"We're not in a relationship, Avery. We've done some things . . . I've done some things that I shouldn't have and that I'm ashamed of."

She'd reluctantly agreed to meet him at a sports bar in west Denver. Reesy hadn't seen or spoken to Avery in almost a week, despite his incessant calling. Lately, it seemed as if she were coming back to her old self again, more focused on her marriage and committed to making her relationship work with Justin. He'd been working so hard to make up for his mistakes and it seemed only fair that she work hard too.

"I don't know what's gotten into me," she said gravely. "Being with you like that was a mistake. Probably the biggest mistake I've ever made in my life."

Of course that's not what he wanted to hear, but it needed to be said. "I love my husband," she said softly. "You may not want to believe it, but it's true."

Avery sat across from her for several minutes without saying a word. Reesy concluded that there really wasn't anything for him to say and that it was best if the two of them simply parted ways.

"I'm sorry I put you through this," she said sincerely, picking up her purse. "I'm sorry if—well. I'm sorry, Avery."

Avery's thoughts did somersaults over each other the whole time she was talking. When a man really wants something, he'll go to any lengths to get it. She had underestimated the effect she'd had on him. Hell, even he hadn't seen it coming, but he'd felt it. Every time he'd held her in his arms, kissed or made love to this woman, he'd surely felt it.

He said it without giving it a second thought. "I'm in love with you, Clarice." There was no taking it back, no second guesses, and no consideration whatsoever for the consequences.

She stared at him, stunned, and sat her purse down next to her.

"And if you think I'm just going to let you walk away from me like nothing ever happened, you're wrong." It was as much a threat as he'd ever made before in his life. Avery felt desperate that he was about to lose someone precious to him. Maybe what he felt for her was love, and maybe it wasn't, but that nauseating feeling swelling in his gut at the thought of never seeing her again was definitely something, even if it didn't have a name.

"You don't mean that," she said softly.

He leaned forward, as close to her as that table between them would allow, and he raised his gaze to hers. "You care for me," he said carefully. "Admit it."

Reesy stared intently at him. "I never said I didn't," she said cautiously. "But I love Justin."

He shrugged. "So, you love Justin. I know you love Justin. You love Justin so fuckin' blindly that you can't see the forest for the goddamned trees."

She frowned. "What's that supposed to mean?"

He came within breaths of telling her about the letter he'd

found in Lisa's apartment from Justin, but decided quickly not to go there—not yet. "It means that you refuse to see how much you mean to me, Reesy. We've been good together," he said, quickly trying to recover from his anger. There were other women in his life. Avery could've had any one of them, but for some reason, she was the only one he wanted.

"We've had sex. We've been friends, but that's all we have between us," she argued.

"No, Reesy," he countered. "Maybe that's all it's been to you, but it's certainly meant more to me than that."

"Avery." She shook her head and stared at him like he was some poor, pitiful, love-struck sap with a broken heart. "I'm sorry if I misled you in any way. I never meant to hurt you or to make you believe that . . ."

Was she fuckin' for real? Reesy sat across from him, gloating over some imaginary notion that she'd been capable of leading him on, when in fact, it had been the other way around since the beginning. Avery had been the one to set the trap for her, and he'd caught her, and now she was struggling to free herself, but that's not how it worked. He could pour vinegar all over her little ego, or he could do the right thing and catch a fly with honey, instead.

"You made me realize that I could have someone special in my life, Reesy, and not fuck it up. You gave me something to look forward to," he explained as sincerely as he possibly could. "I'm a man who's made too many mistakes to count in my life with women, but with you, all I want to do is the right thing, baby. I'm sorry, but I don't want to lose that. I don't want to lose you."

He stood up and leaned close to her. Reesy sat like a statue, frozen in her seat, as his lips met hers, his tongue swept hers, and his eyes locked onto hers.

"I won't apologize for how I feel," he said, standing to leave. "It feels too good."

He was the one who walked out of their meeting first. Avery could be a manipulative sonofabitch when he had to be. He was the master of every excuse in the book at justifying his reason for doing the wrong thing. Reesy was too naïve to play this game well, and he used that to his advantage.

"Avery!" He smiled at the sound of her calling out his name, but it had vanished when he turned to face her.

She hurried over to him, pressed her hands against his chest, raised up on her toes, and kissed him. "I don't know what to do," she said helplessly.

He smiled, but not gallantly. "You just did it."

Reesy drove home convicting herself for agreeing to meet with Avery and for letting herself get pulled into a situation she had no business in. She felt like such an idiot, gullible, and like a carbon-copy of every female she'd ever put down for choosing to do the wrong thing over what was right and as clear as day.

"I love my husband," she whispered as she drove home. And she did love him, but not like she used to. She wanted to love him the way she had before she'd found out about the affair. Justin was making it easy, being his normal, loving, accommodating self. Avery was like a drug habit she couldn't kick. He was new and had a way of making her feel sexy and sensual and desirable. Justin made her feel like a necessity, a piece of a puzzle that needed to be there to complete a picture, and maybe that's how she saw him too. Their family was a unit and it didn't work without all the components in place. She and Justin were terrified of having to deal with a broken unit.

She could admit to herself that she wasn't in love with Avery, but she was in love with how he made her feel, and with the things he said to her, and with the way he looked at her when he said them. Frustration began to wash over her the closer she got to home. Reesy was a wife and a mother, and her family had always been her priority. Now wasn't the time to entertain thoughts of what could have been, or to dwell on the kind of woman she felt like when she was with Avery. That's not who she was. Unfortunately.

TWENTY-NINE

Six months ago, Racine had let the opportunity of a lifetime slip through her fingers. John King had practically been hers for the taking, but she'd fallen for that old adage, "if you love something, set it free," believing in her heart that one day soon, he'd come to the same conclusion she'd come to, that the two of them belonged together, and that he'd come back to Bueller to be with her.

She'd made love to that man with the kind of abandon that only a woman who'd lost her mind over a man could. These long months since he'd been gone had been hell, pure and simple. Racine obsessed over him like an addict, trying not to think about him every second of every day and night, walking around with a smile on her face pretending that she wasn't falling apart inside. Well, now he was back. It didn't matter why. All that mattered was that Racine had this time to make him understand what he meant to her, and what, deep down somewhere inside him, she must've meant to him.

John was a creature of habit and he always stayed at the same motel just off the highway whenever he came to town. Racine pulled into the parking lot, turned off the engine, and sat there for a few moments, taking deep breaths to calm her nerves. It was late, nearly midnight, but she'd made it a point to show up late. Chances were, he was sleeping. She squeezed her eyes shut and imagined him lying naked in bed on his stomach, his strong arms curled around his pillow, with her lying next to him, watching him. He was the most beautiful man in the world, dark, tall, and broad. She couldn't get the taste of him out of her mouth no matter how hard she'd tried.

Racine climbed out of the car and adjusted her coat. It was still seventy degrees out here, and if anybody would've seen her wearing a coat, they'd have thought she looked like a fool. She'd called ahead and found out his room number. Racine found his room on the second floor and braced herself before finally knocking. Her emotions were mixed with excitement and apprehension. She'd never had a problem keeping her cool, but tonight Racine was all out of cool, and filled with a desire for him. She needed him to need her, to reach out to her and to do what came all too naturally.

John finally came to the door, rubbing sleep from his eyes, wearing only his jeans. "Racine?" he asked, sleepily.

She felt like a schoolgirl with a crush. Racine felt more vulnerable than she'd ever felt in her life, and Lord, if he turned her away, her life might as well be over. She quickly gathered her composure and struggled to get her emotions in check.

"You gonna make me stand out here all night?" she asked coolly.

He stepped aside and quietly closed the door behind her. "What's up?"

The question was rhetorical. He knew it as well as she did. Racine untied the belt on her coat and turned to face him. "This is what's up, daddy." She smiled seductively. "Just like you like it. All wrapped up in a pretty bow and on a silver platter. Yours for the taking."

John couldn't help but gawk at Racine standing in the middle of the room wearing a garter belt, black stockings, high-heeled shoes, and a bra with cups barely covering her nipples. He raised his eyebrows and nodded slowly.

She slipped the coat down past her shoulders and let it fall to the floor, pleased by the expression on his face. "Don't act like you don't know what to do with it, John. You know how to make it work better than anybody."

He was flattered. She could see it in his eyes.

Racine took a step toward him and stood close enough to feel his breath on her face. She closed her eyes and inhaled. She could find this man in the dark if she had to. His pheromones filled her lungs like water and she let herself drown in them. "I missed you, baby," she whispered. "Damn. I missed you so much." Her voice trailed off.

"Racine," he whispered.

That's all he had to do—just say her name. She raised herself up onto the tips of her toes, pulled his face to hers, and eased her tongue between his lips until it found his. Racine let out a sigh, he tasted so good.

But suddenly, John surprised her, took hold of her arms, and pulled away from her. "Racine," he said, more sternly.

"What? John?" Tears flooded her eyes. "What is it?" she asked, desperately, fearing the worst. "Baby, what?"

"We can't do this," he said, as tenderly as she'd ever heard him speak.

"Of course we can." She tried to smile. "Baby, we can do this all night long, any way you want it, John. You know me. You know how good it is between us."

He loved her sex. John had always loved the way Racine sexed him because there were no limits or reservations. Together, the two of them were fearless.

He smoothed back her hair, pulled her close, and kissed her forehead. "You don't need to be here," he said, pushing past her.

She turned slowly, confused by what he'd just said. "But . . . you're here. Where else would I be, if I can't be with you?"

There was something about the look on his face that suddenly made her feel uneasy. "You know I got somebody," he said carefully.

"So?" She shrugged. "You got somebody. You've always had somebody, but that never stopped you before."

"It's stopping me now."

Racine couldn't believe what she was hearing. She waited, thinking he was just playing some kind of joke, half-expecting him to start laughing, take her in his arms, and say that he was just kidding. When he stood his ground, anger began to take over where her bruised ego had left off.

"So now all of a sudden you want to be faithful to the bitch?" she asked, appalled. "You come up here and fuck me raw, and now your ass has got a conscience?"

John didn't flinch.

"What am I supposed to do then, John? Am I just supposed to go away quietly and pretend that I don't have feelings for you? Pretend that I'm not in love with you?"

This time, he flinched. "Love?"

Tears began to stream down her face. "Yeah, mothafucka, love," she said, sarcastically. "I'm in love with you, John, and don't stand there like you don't know because we both know you do."

He shrugged. "I had no idea."

She glared at him. "Oh my . . . ! What?" Racine said, stunned, and paced back and forth across the small room. "Look at me, man!" she yelled, stretching out her arms. "Do you think I'd come out of my house dressed like a fuckin' prostitute for a man I didn't love?"

"Racine," he said wearily. "I didn't think . . . I didn't know . . ."

"You didn't think, John King, that's your whole fuckin' problem," she said angrily. "You didn't *think* about how I felt the last time you were here. You didn't *think* about what being with you was doing to me. You don't *think* about anybody but your damn self, and for the life of me I can't figure out what the hell she sees in you!"

John waited quietly, while Racine tried to compose herself. Leave it to him not to argue. Leave it to him to give a woman a silent treatment, let her rant and rave until she could hardly breathe and either give up or leave him standing there.

"I never meant to hurt you."

Racine stopped pacing and stared back at him. "Then love me back, John," she pleaded. "And I promise, I won't be hurt anymore."

"I'm trying real hard to do the right thing for once in my life," he began to explain. "I made a promise and all I want to do is keep it, which ain't easy to do with you standing there looking like that."

Racine almost laughed, but her broken heart stopped her. "Why couldn't you have made me that promise?"

"Different time, different place, Racine, I would've. And," he continued, walking over and taking her hand in his, "I'd have done everything in my power to keep it."

"I love you so much, John." She hiccupped through tears. "You have no idea."

"I have some idea now," he said tenderly. "But you deserve the same kind of promise I made to Connie, Racine. You deserve a man who's willing to make and keep it."

She surprised them both and laughed. "Where the hell am I going to find somebody like that in Bueller?"

John smiled. "You need to move."

She laughed again. "I just want you."

"For now you want me," he said casually. "But you get out of this place, and I guarantee you'll see that I'm a dime a dozen, baby. Men will be falling at your feet and you can pick and choose which one you want."

"How come you keep breaking my heart?" she asked. John helped her on with her coat and walked her to the door.

He shrugged. "'Cause I'm not the right one."

He didn't exactly throw her out, but if John hadn't gotten Racine to leave when he did, all the promises in the world would've been null and void in a matter of minutes. He sat down on the side of the bed and sighed. He had been strong, and he was proud of himself for that. The next time, though, and he hoped there wouldn't be a next time, all bets were off.

THIRTY

Cuba Cuba was her favorite restaurant. Justin had brought her here for the first time on her birthday, three years ago, and he'd had to keep it a surprise or she wouldn't have come. Reesy was a creature of habit, and left to her, they'd eat at the same five restaurants where she always seemed to order one particular item off the menu, usually having something to do with chicken.

The quaint environment of Cuba Cuba was in perfect contrast to its impressive menu. Tonight he'd ordered the seared eight-ounce New York steak topped with sautéed onions, served with yucca fries and mojo. Reesy surprised him and ordered the pan-seared black tiger shrimp with serrano peppers and sofrito served over mashed potatoes, and between the two of them they shared a carafe of Jamaican rum.

The two of them hadn't been out once together since he'd moved home, but tonight Justin had given up waiting on her to give him signs or signals that it was okay for him to make a move. Finally, he took it upon himself to move their relationship forward, and hopefully coax her to come along. He'd made the reservations, dropped off the kids with his mother, and picked Reesy up from the salon, then came straight here.

Their relationship hadn't always been bad. In fact it had always been wonderful, and he counted on those wonderful memories to get his wife to let down her defenses and allow him to be her husband, the way he'd once been.

"Girl." He laughed and shook his head. "When I first saw you wearing them panty shorts, getting ready to run those hurdles, I knew I was in love."

Reesy laughed. How many times had he relived that moment with her, and how many times did she love hearing it? "I was never any good at the hurdles, Justin. I lost every time."

"But you looked fast." He winked. "You had—have—a hurdler's behind, Reesy, so you looked damn fast, baby."

"Well, by that standard, I guess I won them all, huh?"

He stopped eating and stared at her. "As far as I'm concerned, you did."

Justin had been wearing his head clean-shaven for several years now. He'd started losing his hair at the tender age of sixteen, and bald suited him. When she wore heels, he wasn't much taller than she was, and donning a goatee, even she had to admit that he grew more handsome with age. Their boys were spitting images of their father.

"Too bad you got me pregnant," she quipped. "Maybe I could've gotten better at those hurdles."

"I got you pregnant on purpose. I had to get you off that track, by any means necessary."

"Imagine what your son will think when he finds out that his father only got me pregnant with him because he was jealous of a few hurdles." She laughed.

Justin shook his head. "The hurdles weren't the problem, Reese." He sipped some more rum. "It was you prancing around in them damn panty shorts in front of the whole student body. I had to put an end to that."

He wasn't in a hurry to get her home. After dinner Justin drove into downtown Denver and stopped at a little jazz spot he loved in the Pavilions mall. Nelson Rangell was center stage, blowing his heart and soul into his sax. He ordered a beer for himself and a glass of Merlot for Reesy.

The setting was too romantic to ignore, and Justin took full advantage of the ambience. Against mild protests, he coaxed her out onto the floor, pulled her into his arms, and swayed slowly back and forth on the dance floor. She fit him perfectly. Justin inhaled the aroma of her hair, her perfume, and, embedded somewhere between the two, he found her familiar scent. He hadn't held her this close in months, and if he'd had his way, he wouldn't ever let her go.

She nervously cleared her throat. "We shouldn't stay too late," she said softly into his ear. "We'll need to get the kids soon."

"Mom said they could spend the night," he assured her.

It took every ounce of willpower she had not to panic.

Until tonight, the whole time he'd been back home, Justin had been careful and timid with Reesy. He'd acted more like a visiting friend than her husband, and he'd given in to the pace she'd set for their relationship. Tonight, though, he'd made it loud and clear that he had every intention of taking their reunion to the next level. As soon as they walked through the front door of their house, the dreadful feeling she'd been fighting off most of the evening seemed to swallow her whole. Reesy stumbled back into his arms, and he spun her around, pressed her back against the closed door, and covered her mouth with his.

She nearly gagged at the taste of him. But Justin wasn't the problem. Reesy was the problem. More specifically, Reesy with Avery was the problem. Just days ago, it was Avery's tongue she tasted. It was Avery's dick she held in her hands, and it was Avery's dick she'd put in her mouth, despite every warning siren inside her going off about safe sex, and condoms, and breaking commandments. Reesy had gotten drunk on Avery. She'd set herself free all over him in a way she'd never done with Justin. She had bent over the back of his sofa, and begged him to penetrate her in the most savage way. With Justin, there'd always been rules when the two of them made love, unspoken and understood. She'd set them years ago, the first time they made love in his small apartment just outside of the campus, and they'd lived by them. She'd broken every one of those rules with Avery and had become a different woman in the process, one with no boundaries, one without shame or manners, and one without regret—until now.

Justin took her by the hand and led her upstairs to their bedroom. He sat down on the edge of the bed, and slowly began to unbutton her blouse. "We can't wait forever, Reesy," he whispered tenderly. He reached around behind her and unhooked her bra, setting her full breasts free inches away from his face. Justin licked his lips at the sight of them. He pulled her close, and then sensually began to suckle on her nipples, lovingly paying attention to each of them. She closed her eyes, and willed herself to respond. She needed to do this for both their sakes. Reesy had been a fool, playing a silly game of tit for tat, *you cheated on me, so I'm going to cheat on you.* Until this moment, she had never confessed that truth to herself. Avery was her friend, she'd told herself and him. She needed someone who understood her, she'd convinced herself was the reason for having to see him. The wine had gone to her head, she'd told herself the last time they made love. But Justin had fucked a stripper. That was the truth. And in return, she'd fucked someone else too. And that was also the truth.

He pulled her down to the bed by her waist and perched his body over hers. Justin stood up and removed his clothes, then slid Reesy's skirt down her hips and past her ankles. He left her shoes on, though, a move she found subtly surprising. His rigid erection saluted her, and, in one fluid move, he stretched out his body and lay on top of her, sliding himself into the moist folds between her thighs without hesitation and without faltering. Justin knew his way home. No one had to tell him how to get there.

Reesy squeezed her eyes shut, wrapped her arms across his shoulders, her legs around his waist, and tried her best not to re-call that it wasn't that long ago when another man was doing the exact same thing to her, and she had relished it.

THIRTY-ONE

He knocked, then grinned from ear to ear when she answered the door, and stretched open his arms. "Hey baby." He laughed. "Remember me?"

Charlotte fainted.

Damn Your Eyes

THIRTY-TWO

It was hard to miss John's uncle, Moses, when Connie spotted him at the airport. The man was a giant, six-five, six-seven, dark, wearing overalls big enough to house a family of five, easily.

Connie approached him apprehensively, with her baby harnessed to her chest, and dragging a stroller and her luggage behind her. She stopped and stared up at him. "Hi."

His intense gaze gradually shifted from the stratosphere down to where she was standing. "Connie?" If she hadn't just seen his lips move, she'd have sworn that God had just said her name out loud.

"Moses?" she asked meekly. This old man was close to sixty. But he was as big as a bear, and if there were ever a fight between Big John King and Bigger Uncle Moses, she'd have no choice but to put her money on the old dude.

He smiled, and then bent down and took her stroller and suitcase, lifting both off the ground with ease. "Good to see you," he said, before heading out of the airport. Connie followed behind like a small child, taking two and a half steps for every one of his. She'd flown into the nearest airport, which was in Dallas, and from what John's aunt Sara had told her, the drive into Bueller would take about an hour. Connie sighed. It was going to be the longest hour of her life.

John had always been a man of few words, but Moses was a man of even fewer. "How was yo' flight?" he asked, in his low, deep, Southern drawl, as they made their way out onto the highway.

"It was good," she said, perhaps too enthusiastically for a man like him. "I mean . . . fine."

He nodded.

She'd only ever spoken to the man briefly over the phone, like twice.

"Moses," his wife, Sara, would call out to him. "John and Connie are calling. Come say hello?"

"Hey."

And that would be that.

Sara was the one who could talk an ear off. And since John wasn't much better than Moses when it came to maintaining good phone etiquette, it was usually Connie who ended up having to hold up John King's end of the conversation.

Since John had left, Sara had been the one to call Connie to let her know how Adam was doing. Whenever she tried talking to John about it, he usually fired back with his typical one-word responses.

"How's he doing?"

"Same."

"How are you doing?"

"A'right."

"Out of all of them," Sara had explained over the phone, "Adam is the only one who you can get a good conversation from." She laughed. "He'll talk all day when he's in the mood. He can get quiet too, though."

"He's not doing any better?" Connie asked, concerned.

"Naw, girl. And he's not going to. The doctors don't know how he went this long without letting anybody know he was in pain. That's how Adam is, though. He'd sit back there in that little room, listening to them old songs with his mind drifting off to . . . Adam ain't never wanted to be a bother, and he ain't never been one. Me and Moses would do anything for him. But he just kept his pain to himself, until he couldn't no more, but by that time it was too late."

"How is John handling it, Sara?"

She chuckled. "Same way Moses is handling it. Quietly. He may look like his father, but he acts a whole lot like that bull uncle of his. He doesn't say it, but I can see when I look in his eyes that he's lost, Connie. John loves Adam more than I think he knows he loves him, and now that he's about to lose him, I don't think he knows how to let him go. It took him too long to find him, and now this happens."

Connie never even told John she was coming because she knew he'd try to convince her that she didn't need to, but she did need to. He needed her to.

Bueller, Texas, looked like something out of a time warp. Rows of small bungalows lined gravel roads. Some houses looked as if they should've been condemned; others sat on top of cinder blocks lifting them off of the ground. It looked like a place the rest of the world had forgotten. Sara came running out of the house even before Moses had finished parking the car. A pretty, tall, and lean light-skinned woman, her whole face lit up at the sight of Connie, as she laughed and stretched her arms wide to embrace her.

Sara laughed heartily. "Oh my! Oh my goodness!" she exclaimed, hugging Connie tight. "It is so good to finally see your face." Tears filled her eyes. She cradled Connie's face between her hands. "You are more beautiful than your picture. Ain't she, Moses?"

Moses grunted. "Uh . . . huh."

"And where is the baby?" Sara opened the door to the backseat of the car and swooned over Jonathon, who'd mercifully slept the whole way. "Oh, goodness gracious," she said warmly.

Connie unbuckled him from the car seat, lifted him out, and handed him to Sara. "Oh, Moses," she said breathlessly. "Come look."

"I seen him," he said curtly.

"Come look anyway."

He did as he was told, and stood over his wife and great-nephew, gazing down at the boy, trying not to smile. "Yeah," he said proudly.

Sara laughed. "He's got all three of y'all all over him. Ain't that something?"

He managed to laugh. "Yeah."

"John still didn't know you were coming." She looked at Connie. "I never told him."

Connie shrugged. "I never did either."

Sara smiled and winked. "He's at the hospital. Moses, why don't you take her. I'ma stay here with the baby."

The only person Connie had ever trusted with her son was Reesy . . . until now.

Don't know much about a science book
Don't know much about the French I took

John had made sure Sam Cooke stayed on rotation in Adam's room. His old man was in and out of consciousness, but when he did wake up, he'd always managed to smile at the sound of Sam's crooning, and he'd ask the same question each time.

"You here, boy?"

John would respond from across the room. "I'm here."

"Oh," Adam would say before closing his eyes again.

Time between the two of them was drawing to a close, and every single moment counted now. John had always believed that losing his grandmother, Agnes, the woman who'd raised him, had been the hardest loss to take, but he'd been wrong. He'd known his father for two short years and that just hadn't been long enough.

"John?"

Connie stood in the doorway of Adam's room, and if he hadn't known any better, he'd have sworn that he was asleep and that she was a dream. She came over to him, sat in his lap, held his face between her hands, and kissed him. Of course, he'd told her she didn't need to come down here. He didn't need her here for this. Of course he'd been wrong.

John wrapped his arms around her, and held on to her.

THIRTY-THREE

Charlotte's eyes fluttered open, and it took a moment for her to realize that she was on the floor in her living room, staring across the hardwood floor to the space underneath a small table across the room. She made a mental assessment of her extremities, made sure her heart was beating, batted her eyes a few times, and then finally took a deep breath before slowly sitting up. Charlotte lay a few feet from her front door, but for the life of her, she couldn't remember what had happened, except that someone had rang the doorbell, and she'd gotten up to answer it, and when she did, she saw . . . she saw . . . No. No, Charlotte had just gotten dizzy and fallen. That's all. Maybe her blood pressure was up again, or her sugar was out of whack. That's what it was. That's all it was.

She rolled over and managed to get up on all fours, bracing one hand against the wall as she slowly stood up.

"'Bout damn time." His voice boomed through her house and pierced her soul.

Charlotte clutched the front of her robe and fell back against the wall, staring horrified at the man sitting in her living room on her couch. Charlotte's eyes grew wide with fear, her heart raced dangerously fast inside her, and, all of a sudden, she couldn't catch her breath. The devil was alive and in her living room, she thought frightfully, squeezing her eyes shut. "Oh God, no!" she mouthed.

Uncle stood up and laughed. "Girl, if you don't stop acting a fool and get over here and give me a hug!" He held his arms open wide.

Charlotte vehemently shook her head back and forth.

"You know, I woulda been a gentleman and helped you up off the floor, but baby girl, ain't no way I coulda picked your big ass up!" He laughed and winked. "I ain't as young as I used ta be, and you sho' as hell ain't as skinny!" Uncle sat back down, and shook his head. "What happened, girl? You sho' done let yourself go." He frowned. "Come on over here and sit down." He patted the space beside him. "Let's talk about the good old days."

It took several minutes, but Charlotte finally managed to find her voice. "H-hhhow did you find me?" she asked, trembling.

Uncle looked at her like she was crazy. "How the hell you think?"

She couldn't hide her confusion. "Lynn?"

"Damn right, Lynn," he said smugly. "Who else knows where you are?"

Lynn was her friend. Lynn had saved her life. She would've never betrayed Charlotte like this.

Uncle seemed to read her mind. "One word, sweetheart. Arnel. Lynn would fuck an elephant if it meant saving Arnel's ass." Uncle suddenly looked disappointed and shook his head. "You never were a good judge of character, darlin'."

All of a sudden, Charlotte's knees felt weak. She shuffled over to the chair across from him to sit down before she fainted again.

Uncle studied her, scanning Charlotte's body from head to toe. She studied him too, but not so that he'd notice. What was he now? Seventy? He looked at least that old. Gone was the thick, wavy head of hair, and even the freckles on his face looked faded. He had always been a tall man, but Uncle seemed to have shrunken through the years. He'd cut his white hair down to the scalp, and the vivid life that had once fired behind his eyes was gone. He was still Uncle, though, and Charlotte knew instinctively that he was still as evil as they come.

"I remember loving you the first time I ever laid eyes on you," he said introspectively.

Charlotte looked appalled. "Love?" she said, twisting her lip. "You never loved me, Uncle."

He looked hurt. "How can you say that, sugah? Of course I loved you. I loved your ass, your titties, and I sho' 'nuff loved your pussy."

She cringed. The thought that she'd ever let that fool touch her made her sick to her stomach.

"Aw, now don't act like you didn't love me too."

"I didn't!" she blurted out. "I hated you for what you did to me! For what you did to Zoo!"

Uncle leaned forward and stared hard at her. "First of all, I treated you good, damn good, before that night, and you know it," he said in his defense. "I bought you every damn thing you wanted, set you up in a nice place, fed you, paid all your bills. And don't give me none of that bull about what I did to Zoo. You did that to Zoo. You put that boy on the spot like that. Not me."

"You treated me like a prisoner," she argued. "Like I was a piece of property!" Hot tears trailed down her cheeks.

"You were," he said, cavalier. "Hell, girl! You didn't have to do a damn thing but lay up in my bed when I needed you to, or hold on tight to my arm and look pretty in all them nice clothes I bought you when we went out. You had the easy part. Shit."

"Easy," she said softly. "I had it easy? Is that what you think?"

Uncle suddenly looked frustrated. "Obviously, you and me have different opinions of how all that shit went down."

"You wouldn't let me leave, Uncle," she tried to explain. "You kept me like I was your slave."

"There you go exaggerating. How many slaves you know got their goddamned hands out all the time, Charlotte? 'Uncle I need, Uncle I want, Uncle can you get me.' I paid to get your hair done, your nails painted, put you in fur coats, bought you leather purses, gold earrings, and necklaces." He counted on each finger. "How many slaves you know had it like that?"

So, he'd bought her nice things, but Charlotte paid a high price for those nice things too. "You treated me like a prostitute."

Uncle raised both eyebrows. "Nah, girl. I had plenty of hos back then, and I treated you a whole lot better than I ever treated any of them. And you know it."

"What do you want?" she asked bitterly. "Why are you here?"

Uncle leaned back and crossed one long, skinny leg over the other. "I been in prison for twenty-seven years, baby. And every day of those years, I thought about you."

Charlotte looked disgusted. "Why?"

"Hell if I know. I had some good memories of me and you, though. Back then, you were fine, girl. If I didn't love you before they locked me up, I sure as hell fell hard afterward. I fell in love with that pretty little honey-colored sweet thang that used to make my mouth water every time she so much as looked my way. Thoughts like that, especially in prison, can either drive a man crazy or help him to get through that time like nothing else."

She swallowed and shifted uneasily in her seat. "Well, I'm not that girl anymore." Charlotte ran her hand across the scar on the side of her face that Uncle had put there, and looked at him. "You killed that woman, Uncle. You killed her the same way you killed Zoo."

Uncle nodded. "Oh, I killed a whole lot of folks back then, honey." Uncle stared at her until she finally understood what he was saying.

Charlotte sat up. "Sam," she whispered. "You killed . . . Sam?"

Uncle sighed. "That mothafucka was sneaking 'round trying to take what belonged to me," he said defiantly. "Damn right I killed his ass."

Charlotte whimpered.

He stared coldly at her. "What did you think I was gonna do? Just let you walk out on me after all I'd done for you? You was a whole lot of investment, Charlie. And I was a businessman. Sam had no place between us."

Charlotte shuddered uncontrollably. In the back of her mind, she'd always thought Uncle had done something to Sam. Why else hadn't the man showed up to get her like he'd promised? But to hear him actually come out and confess it just proved that Uncle was the devil in the flesh, and he'd tracked her down after twenty-seven years. *Lord have mercy! Lord! Please, have mercy on my soul!*

THIRTY-FOUR

Thomas, McCarthy, and Engle Accounting was one of the top accounting companies in the country, and Justin was a senior accountant, representing some of the business's most prestigious clients. Avery had called Justin, insisting on a meeting. Considering their history, of course he'd expected apprehension, but Justin agreed to meet with him despite any misgivings he may have had.

Denver, Colorado, was a big city with a small-town feel. In any other major metropolis, the odds of a man finding out that his daughter was having an affair with the husband of one of his clients would've been far-fetched, indeed. But not here. Back when Lisa was stripping, and calling herself Cookie, Justin Braxton had been one of her most loyal and generous customers. Avery would never have found out that Justin was banging his little girl had it not been for the fact that Avery was fixated on the idea of banging the man's wife. The irony was enough to make him sick to his stomach.

Avery felt underdressed as the assistant escorted him through posh office space filled with suits and ties, and even stockings. Damn! Did women actually still wear those things?

"Mr. Braxton," the assistant said as she entered Justin's office. "Your one o'clock is here."

Justin stood up and immediately made eye contact with Avery, standing in the doorway.

"Thank you, Tanya. Close the door behind you, please."

Avery actually had photographs of this imbecile, sitting drooling while Lisa worked her magic in his lap. Any good father would've killed this fool, but then again Avery could never be accused of being a good father. Still, the urge was there, and one wrong word from Justin's mouth, and Avery would have no choice but to put his fist through those perfect pearly whites of his.

The two men eyed each other like animals in the wild. Justin was the one who decided to break the silence.

"What in the hell could you possibly have to say to me?"

The man looked like he was worth a billion dollars, standing there in his fancy suit, pricey tie, behind his immaculate desk. But that was just it. He may have looked the part of a big, powerful, corporate baller, but Avery knew that the man had fetishes, and weaknesses, and was hanging on to his marriage by his balls. *I've been fucking your wife,* Avery considered telling him. But telling the truth to Justin would do Avery a grave disservice, at least for now.

"How's Cookie?" Avery smiled when the mere mention of her name seemed to visibly shake the man.

Justin rushed to compose himself, and responded quickly. "How would I know?"

Even though he hadn't been invited, Avery decided to take a seat. Justin apprehensively followed suit. "Why are you here, Stallings?"

Avery was here to assess the situation. That was the truth. He was here to get a feel for the man he was up against when it came to winning Reesy's heart. That was the truth. He was here to find out what was obviously still going on between his daughter, Lisa, and this man, who claimed he was no longer involved with her. And that was the truth. But Justin didn't deserve to know all of the truth.

"You're still seeing her." It wasn't a question.

Justin looked unflustered. "I said I'm not."

"Then why is she getting mail from this firm, Braxton?"

Now, the man was beginning to look a little uncomfortable. Avery smiled.

"Did she tell you that?"

"She didn't have to. I'm a detective, remember? And a father," he said as sincerely as he could.

Justin stared at him, shaking his head and smirking. "You're a fuckin' dick wad, man. And a lousy father."

"I'm not the one cheating on his wife and spending part of the household budget on a stripper, man," Avery said casually. "So, who's the real dick wad here?"

Avery watched as Justin struggled with the internal turmoil churning inside him. Obviously, guilt was a mothafucka. Fortunately for Avery, he'd had more experience with it than perfect and flawless Justin Braxton here, so he'd learned to keep his under wraps years ago.

"I send her money," Justin finally admitted.

"You're still seeing her?" Surprisingly, Avery worried what Justin's response would be. Lisa was still his daughter, after all. He cared, even though he didn't really know how, and even though she never believed he did. The idea that she was still getting paid to fuck around didn't sit well with him.

Justin glared at him. "I'm helping put her through school, Avery. Which is more than you're doing."

His comment was meant to make Avery feel small, and it worked. In less than an instant, his magnanimous ego left the room, leaving him feeling like putty.

"I haven't seen or spoken to Cook . . . Lisa in months, and I have no intention to," he said coolly. "I've only asked that she continue to work on getting her education, and as long as she does, I'll help her out financially, as much as I can, because I believe in her. What about you?"

Desperate men say and do desperate things when they're backed up against the wall and all the fight has been taken away from them. "Does your wife know about your humanitarian efforts?" he asked threateningly.

Justin stared at him with disbelief. "You still trying to go there? Tell me something, Avery." Justin leaned forward and rested his arms on his desk. "Are you worried about Lisa, or are you still after my wife?"

Avery was speechless.

"Reesy may have been clueless, man, but I never was." Justin's expression changed to one of sincerity. "I love my family. I love my wife, my children, and yeah, I've made mistakes, but I'll go down fighting tooth and nail to hold onto what's mine. Reesy's a good woman, a beautiful woman, and believe me, I don't blame you for wanting a woman like that of your own, but don't be stupid. Instead of trying to get at what I got, why don't you try and get in good with your kids? Lisa needs you even if she doesn't act like it. I'm just trying to help her out, the way you should be helping her out. Is that a crime?"

There were a million things that Avery could've said, but didn't. He had his reason for holding back. Avery had a hand to play, and he didn't need to be stupid with it. Justin may very well have played his too hastily, and he'd played it mercilessly.

That shit didn't go down the way he'd planned, and Avery left feeling defeated and ashamed. Justin was still big man on campus and Avery was still trying hard to get out from under his shadow. But despite his own internal admission of how right Justin was, the fact still remained. Avery had fucked his wife, and he'd do it again, and in time, if he switched up his game plan, swallowed his pride, and became the voice of reason, Avery could snatch the rug right out from under that idiot and come away with the game ball when it was all said and done.

THIRTY-FIVE

Cammy's last-minute decision to accompany Reesy on the trip to see Charlotte still resonated as odd to Reesy. Reesy understood that Cammy missed her mother. Reesy missed her too. Both of them were worried about her. But Cammy's behavior when she found out that Reesy was leaving was unprecedentedly frantic.

She showed up at Reesy's house one evening looking disheveled and out of breath, almost as if she'd run to Reesy's house instead of driven.

"I talked to Momma," she said, smiling nervously and running her hands through her hair. "She said you were going to see her?"

Reesy stepped aside and let her in. "Yes. I was going to call you tomorrow about it."

Cammy stared at Reesy, looking as if she would burst into tears at any moment. "I'd like to come too," she said nervously.

"Really." Reesy wasn't surprised, but Cammy's crazed expression raised a lot of questions. "I'm leaving this weekend, Cammy. If I'd have known you were so anxious to come, I'd have planned for a later date."

"No, it's alright. I can make it."

"Don't you have to get permission to take the time off from work?"

"I have time, Reese." She sounded almost angry. "I just need . . . What flight are you taking? So I can make reservations."

She felt like she was home. She should've done this herself, months ago, Cammy concluded quietly to herself as she and Reesy left the airport and climbed into their rental car. It would've been so easy just to hop on a plane, rent a car, and drive home. For some reason, though, the idea never occurred to her. Cammy had stayed put in Denver, because that's where she was told she should be. For a time, that's where she believed she should be. Now, she wasn't so sure anymore.

Reesy wasn't saying much, and Cammy was grateful for the silence between them. She must've looked like a fool to her sister when she insisted on coming along on this trip, but it really didn't matter what Reesy had thought of her. Cammy saw an opportunity and she took it. Reesy could stare at her all she wanted to. Cammy was on her way home, and right now that's all that mattered.

Don't go back, Cammy. That small voice deep inside had been warning her to stay away from this place, from Charlotte, and even from Ty since she'd moved away. It grew louder the moment she found out that Reesy was going to see Charlotte, but Cammy ignored it, packed her bags, and lied and told her boss that she had a personal emergency to tend to back home. *Don't go back!* But why shouldn't she when everything that had ever meant anything to her was back in Murphy: her mother, her man . . . her child. He hadn't been born in Murphy, but he had died there, and part of Cammy had died there too. Maybe that's why she needed to go back so badly. To recover that part of herself left behind. To remember what it felt like to be her again, even the bad parts. To see her mother. Charlotte wasn't a good mother. Cammy knew that now more than ever, but Charlotte was all she had. After losing her own child, she knew what that meant now. She understood that the bond between a mother and a child couldn't ever be broken, not by time or distance, or even death.

"Hello?" Reesy answered her phone. Cammy hadn't even noticed it ringing.

"This isn't a good time," she said abrasively. "I'm not . . . I'm out of town."

In all the time she'd known Reesy, she'd never heard her take that tone with anybody. Reesy cut her eyes quickly to Cammy.

"I don't want . . . Aver . . . I mean, no. There's nothing else to say. Why would you even . . . Fine. If it'll keep you from telling . . . I can't talk now. Later. I'll be home by the end of the week."

She hung up without saying good-bye. Reesy looked visibly upset.

"Was that Justin?" Cammy asked carefully.

Reesy hesitated before finally shaking her head. "No." Her tone made it clear that she wasn't interested in saying another word about that phone call, so Cammy turned her attention back to the view outside her window.

Reesy and Justin had split up for a while. He'd cheated on her and she'd put him out of the house. Cammy hadn't known her sister very long but Reesy never seemed like the type to play those kinds of games. Reesy was the princess, spoiled and smug, and used to getting her way. She'd seen it in the ways Reesy's adoptive parents treated her, in the way Justin had treated her, and even in the ways Charlotte had swooned over her when she first saw her again after all those years. Even Connie treated her delicately, though Connie would never admit it. But unlike everybody else, Connie had a way of keeping Reesy grounded when she got too full of herself.

She studied Reesy as she drove, wondering who had called that could upset her like that. She glanced at her sister, noticing that Reesy was making an effort not to look pissed. She wasn't doing a very good job.

THIRTY-SIX

"So, how long is this tour going to take, exactly?" Connie sat next to John as he slowly drove down the only "highway" in the city, from the motel into town.

"I said I'm gonna give you the fifty-cent tour. Right?"

"Well, how much am I getting for my fifty cents?"

"'Bout half an hour."

She laughed. "Really? It's that small, huh?"

"Small ain't the word, baby girl. But it's home."

John drove past the house he'd grown up in that had belonged to his grandparents. "It doesn't look like much now, but back then, it was a palace," he said with pride. He stopped in front of a dilapidated dwelling with a picket fence that had rotted and fallen to the ground. He stood at the gate and stared at it long and hard, as if he could almost see ghosts.

"Who lived here?" Connie finally asked.

John recalled his fifteen-year-old self, standing outside that gate arguing with the old woman who lived there. She'd hated him, literally, from the moment he was born, and, ironically, she'd been the midwife who'd delivered him too. Roberta was her name, and she cursed John every time she saw him.

"You black-eyed demon! I shoulda kilt you that night! I shoulda put my hands round yo' neck and squeezed 'til you was dead!"

Roberta died with him watching. It was an accident, but he'd always questioned if just maybe it wasn't fate but some fifteen-year-old's notion of wishful thinking that caused that old woman's death.

"John? Who lived in this house?" Connie asked again.

John slowly started to pull away. "Nobody."

Five minutes later, they pulled up in front of another small place, painted a vibrant yellow on the outside, framed at the base by rows of colorful flowers. John honked his horn as he got out of the car. Moments later, a heavyset woman with hips almost too wide for her to squeeze through the doorway came out and stood on the front porch. Her face lit up the moment she saw him, and she grinned from ear to ear. That's when Connie noticed that she didn't have one tooth in her head.

"Boy, is that you?" She laughed hoarsely.

John smiled too. "Girl!" he exclaimed, heading toward her. "Your ass get finer with time, I tell you!"

The two embraced, and Connie was amazed at how animated John had suddenly become. "When you get here?" the woman asked.

"Been here almost a week."

"And you just now gettin' over here to see me?" she scolded.

"Adam's sick," he said solemnly.

The old woman shook her head. "Yeah, that's what I heard." All of a sudden, the woman noticed Connie standing at the bottom of the steps. Her eyes lit up and she gasped. "This her?"

John reached out to take Connie's hand. "It is. Connie, this is my aunt Dot."

"Hello." Connie smiled.

Dot took hold of Connie's hands, pulled her close, and wrapped warm, massive arms around her. "Oh! He talked 'bout you, but I almost didn't believe you was real," Dot said, breathlessly. She pulled away from Connie and stared tenderly back at her, then at John, then back at Connie. "You right, boy. She is so very pretty."

It wasn't the first time Connie had been called pretty, but for some odd reason, this time she blushed like she'd never heard it before. "Thank you, Dot."

They spent the afternoon sitting in Dot's small living room, listening to her tell stories of John's *bad ass* when he was growing up, and Agnes' heartache over losing her daughter Mattie under such tragic circumstances and so young too.

"I s'pose she had to blame somebody, cause she couldn't blame the boy she thought did it."

"Adam?" Connie asked for clarification.

Dot nodded. "Ol' Roberta started all them rumors 'bout him draggin' that girl off and rapin' her and gettin' her pregnant. Her lies damn near got him kilt from what I understand. But Agnes wasn't tryin' to hear the truth fo' a long time after Mattie died."

"She came around though," John added.

"After you was gone," Dot said. "But by then, shoot. You was gone."

"We made our peace, Dot."

"I know you did, baby." She smiled warmly at John. "I think that's what made it okay for her to go on and pass over. She was waitin' on you so she could tell you how sorry she was for how she treated you."

"Better late than never." He shrugged.

"Surely," Dot agreed.

After leaving Dot's, John took Connie out to dinner at Bueller's finest establishment, Jeremiah's BBQ and Grill Eatery, for all-you-can-eat ribs and catfish. Connie stared at the mountain of meat the server had put down between them.

"I know you're not going to eat all that?" she said, frowning.

John started loading up his plate and licking his lips. "Nah, but I'm gonna hurt myself trying."

Connie laughed. "John!"

He'd already taken a bite out of a rib. "Dig in baby," he said, licking his fingers. "Before it gets cold."

"John?"

Shit! At the sound of her voice, he nearly spit out his food. He looked up and into the face of Racine, standing there and staring at Connie.

He swallowed what was in his mouth, then took a drink of his beer and stood up. "Racine," he said, clearing his throat.

Racine managed to take her eyes off of Connie long enough to look at him. "How are you? How's your father?"

He nodded, and cleared his throat again. "Fine." He shrugged. "I mean, as well as can be expected."

He hadn't done anything wrong. Not in months. But he felt as guilty as sin standing there between the two.

Connie reached out her hand for Racine to shake. "I'm Connie." She smiled.

Racine took hold of Connie's fingertips and sort of shook her hand. "Racine. I'm a friend of John's."

Connie's expression changed. Into what, he wasn't sure, but John knew that whatever was churning inside her wasn't good. "Oh," she said coolly. "John's never mentioned you."

Connie's beautiful amber-brown eyes darted quickly in his direction then fixed back on Racine. All of a sudden, he'd lost his appetite.

"We grew up together, and we run into each other from time to time when he's in town."

"Really?" Connie said, coolly.

"Racine?" A man came up to Racine and put his hand around her waist. "We got to go, baby. The movie's starting soon."

Racine smiled radiantly. "Well, it was good meeting you, Connie, and John . . ." Her gaze lingered way too long as far as John was concerned. "My prayers to you and your family."

By the time he sat down again, the ribs were cold, the company was cold, and dinner was over. "I'm not hungry," she said, getting up to leave. John put money on the table, took a rib, and dismally followed her out of the restaurant.

Back in the motel, shit didn't hit the fan right away. They picked up the baby from Moses and Sara's, and went back to the motel room. Connie bathed Jonathon, fed him, put him down for the night, then decided to sling it.

"I'm not going to raise my voice because I don't want to wake up my son," she said frigidly.

John sat there like a bump on a fuckin' log with no idea how to combat her attack.

"Who's Racine, John?"

It was a simple enough question, and maybe if the rest of the night went like this, he'd be alright. "We grew up together," he responded. It was the truth. Plain and simple, he and Racine had known each other since they were kids.

"*Who* is Racine, John?"

Didn't she just ask him that? She had, but in a different way.

"I've known her practically all my life, Connie."

She folded her arms across her chest and stared daggers into him. "Who . . . is . . . Racine? Don't make me ask you again."

John wasn't a liar. He'd never known how to lie, and until this moment, he'd never felt the need to lie. But now more than ever, he wished with all his might that he could.

"We'd broken up, Connie." Shit. Here it comes. "The last time I came down here, you and me were . . ."

Connie's expression glazed over. "You were with her?"

John took a deep breath and blew it out. "I was . . . single, baby."

Connie rolled her eyes, stood up, and threw her arms in the air. The only thing that kept her from going off was that she'd caught sight of Jonathon lying in the other bed, surrounded by pillows.

"Connie." He bolted to his feet. "You and me had decided . . ."

"No, John," she said angrily. "You had decided to call it quits. You didn't want the baby, and you walked out the door because—"

"You put me out," he argued.

"I did no such thing!" she responded, appalled.

"No, Connie. You told me to leave, so I left."

"Left and came down here and fucked the town ho. Great, John. That's just great!"

"I didn't mean . . ."

"For her to slip and fall on your dick?" she said, sarcastically. "So, it was an accident? A terrible mistake?"

Arguing wasn't his thing. Just like lying wasn't his thing. And all of a sudden, something inside him flipped off a switch the moment he realized that no matter what he said, it would be wrong, no matter how much he apologized, he'd still be wrong, and no matter how reasonable he tried to come across, he'd only end up sounding like an idiot.

Connie heard the switch flip as soon as it happened. "So, that's it? You're not willing to talk about this?"

John grabbed his keys. "What for? You already made up your mind that I was wrong."

"Aren't you?"

Yeah. Maybe he'd been wrong for fucking around with Racine the last time he'd come here, but Connie had told him to leave. As far as he was concerned, that meant that he could do whatever and whoever he damn well pleased. The hurt in her eyes convicted him, though. It cut him into a million little pieces and made a mess out of any rational excuse he'd had in his head. John left without saying another word.

THIRTY-SEVEN

Cammy had hardly waited for Reesy to park the car before she jumped out of it and ran up the porch to Charlotte's front door. She frantically rang the doorbell and lunged at Charlotte when she answered.

"Momma," she said passionately, squeezing Charlotte in her arms.

Charlotte remained emotionless and kept her gaze fixed on Reesy as she approached. "Hi, Mom." Reesy smiled.

Charlotte managed to peel Cammy off of her and reached out to hug Reesy, leaving Cammy looking dejected. "I'm glad you came," she muttered to Reesy.

"We missed you, Momma," Cammy added, with tears in her eyes. "We really did."

Cammy quickly fell into a routine that was all too second nature, disappearing into the kitchen and starting to make lunch for everyone. Reesy noticed how uneasy Cammy was around Charlotte, and how hard she worked to try and appease their mother. It was almost as if she'd never even left. Reesy sat on the sofa next to Charlotte, who hadn't smiled once since they'd arrived. She looked a bit shell-shocked to Reesy.

"You look tired, Mom," she said tenderly. "Have you been feeling alright?"

"No," Charlotte replied quietly. "I've just been tired."

Reesy looked concerned. "When was the last time you saw a doctor?"

Charlotte shrugged. She didn't need a doctor. Charlotte needed an exorcist. Uncle had left as suddenly as he'd appeared, but he hadn't said good-bye.

"I'll see you later on, girl," was what he said. He'd be back, but she had no idea when that would be. Charlotte had been sitting and waiting, hardly sleeping, expecting him to show up again at a moment's notice.

"Lunch is ready," Cammy said smiling. "I made sandwiches, Momma."

Cammy stood there grinning like she expected Charlotte to turn flips over a goddamned sandwich.

"Come on." Reesy gently took hold of her elbow and helped Charlotte to her feet. "Let's go get something to eat."

Cammy hugged her again when she sat down at the kitchen table. Charlotte all but pushed her away, and again Cammy looked away wounded. Charlotte hadn't missed having to sit around looking at poked-out lips and teary eyes or walking around on eggshells every time she said the wrong thing to Cammy.

"Where's my lemonade?" Charlotte asked irritably.

Cammy popped up like a jack-in-the-box and hurried to get her mother something to drink. Ten seconds later, she put the glass down next to Charlotte and sat down to eat.

"Straw?" Charlotte said before Cammy could take a bite of her sandwich.

Once again, Cammy jumped up and rummaged through the cabinets to find Charlotte a straw, then sat down again.

"Camille, where is my napkin?" Charlotte scowled.

Cammy started to jump up again, but this time Reesy stopped her.

"Cammy! Sit!"

Cammy stared horrified at Reesy.

"Stop it," Reesy said, trying to sound sympathetic.

Charlotte sighed, defeated, and started to get up to get her own napkin. "Lord have mercy," she muttered under her breath.

"What's wrong with you?" Reesy asked Cammy, who looked like she was on the verge of tears.

Cammy's bottom lip quivered.

"She's a damn fool," Charlotte said, sitting down. "That's what's wrong with her."

"Don't talk like that, Mom," Reesy said sternly.

Charlotte threw her napkin on top of her sandwich. "I ain't hungry."

"Momma, you need to eat," Reesy gently coaxed.

"You should eat, Mom," Cammy said softly.

"You're being ridiculous, Mom," Reesy said.

Charlotte sat sulking. They didn't know what she was going through. Uncle was alive and back in her life again. Charlotte had never in a million years dreamed she'd ever see that man again, but after all this time, he came looking for her. Of all people, why would he want to see her again? Unless he wanted to finish the job he'd started. Uncle was an old man, but he was still the same. And he had shown up again for a reason. Looking at that food made her stomach turn.

"I'ma go lay down," Charlotte said dismally, abruptly leaving her two daughters alone in the kitchen.

———————

As soon as she left, Cammy bolted up from the table and tossed Charlotte's uneaten sandwich in the trash, and then her own.

"Cammy? What's wrong with you?"

"What, Reesy?" Cammy's frustration was showing.

"You're acting like . . ."

"Like what?" Cammy turned angrily.

"Like—I don't even know."

"I'm just glad to see my mother, Reesy."

"I understand that, but you need to chill, girl. You need to relax and stop coming on so damn strong."

"You need to stop trying to tell me how to act," she blurted out. Cammy had never raised her voice to Reesy before, and she never thought she ever would. But Cammy was boiling inside. "I'm a grown woman, Reesy," she said, trying to calm herself. "I don't need you or anybody else telling me what I need to be doing." Cammy was so angry, she was starting to shake.

Reesy stared stunned at her sister. "She's really got a hold on you. Doesn't she?"

Cammy turned away.

"After everything she put you through, Cam, you walked through that front door and fell right back in step, like nothing ever happened."

Reesy had witnessed Charlotte's shitty treatment of Cammy. Charlotte said anything she wanted to Cammy, abusing her emotionally, even physically, and Cammy just took it.

"Do you want to move back here?" Reesy finally asked.

Tears finally escaped from Cammy's face. "This is home, Reesy." She shrugged. "This is where I feel like I belong."

Reesy stared, awed by this girl. "But you're doing so much better now, Cam."

Cammy shook her head. "No. You and Connie think I am, but I'm not. I don't know anything about Denver, or you or Connie."

"We're your family, Cammy."

"You're each other's family," she argued. "Y'all don't know me. People here know me. Momma knows me." Her voice trailed off.

"She knows how to treat you like crap."

Cammy rolled her eyes. "She needs me, though. I know how she is, better than anybody. She says what she wants, but . . . it's only ever been me and her. We need each other, Reesy. Nobody understands that better than me and her."

Until Cammy had come back here, she really hadn't known how true that statement was.

THIRTY-EIGHT

"I'm here to see Adam. Adam Tate." It had taken every ounce of courage for Liz to finally come to this place.

The receptionist smiled. "Are you a family member?"

Liz hesitated for a moment before realizing that nothing mattered more than the truth. "I'm his sister."

She had been so young when her father died, three, maybe four years old, and there were very few memories that she had left of him. But she remembered his face, and she remembered his hands. The image of him was a thousand times more vivid than those she had of her mother. Liz stood at the foot of Adam's bed, mesmerized by the shadowy traits of her father lingering in that old man's fragile flesh. He was dark, like her father. The shape of his mouth reminded her of her father's, and his hands, rugged, strong . . . she wondered if they had been as skilled and yet as gentle as her father's hands had been.

He could've looked like him too, if his face hadn't shown the effects of some form of abuse. Someone had hurt him terribly. The scars told her that.

"You know he had another woman? Had a baby by her too. She found out and that's why he dead. I heard she killed that baby."

"Naw, she didn't kill him. She did try, though."

Adam's eyes fluttered open, and at first he lay still, staring up at the ceiling, until finally he realized someone else was in the room, and his gaze traveled to where she was standing. He smiled, and her heart stopped.

"I . . . know . . . you?" he asked sleepily.

Liz opened her mouth to speak, but the words wouldn't come. He had her father's eyes, dark and piercing. He waited patiently for her to respond, but Liz couldn't. This man was her brother. She had wondered about him practically her whole life, rehearsing the things she'd say to him if she ever got the chance, and now she had the chance, and she was utterly speechless.

The sounds of footsteps behind her caught her attention.

"Hey old man. I got here just in time I see."

Adam smiled broadly. "Hhhhhey . . . son."

The younger man looked at Liz, and she stumbled backward as if she'd just seen a ghost, and she had. This man, Adam's son?

Liz covered her mouth with her hand to stifle a gasp, and hurried out of the room as fast as she could, bumping into John's aunt, Sara, coming through the doorway. Liz stumbled and fell hard to the ground.

Nurses and the woman she'd bumped into hurried to her side. The young man came too, and helped her to her feet.

"I'm fine," she said anxiously, more embarrassed than hurt.

"Are you sure?" someone asked. "Maybe we should get a doctor to take a look."

"I'm fine!" she said again, more adamantly.

Liz looked into the young man's eyes, the one Adam had called son, astonished and awed that two people, so far removed by generations, could look so much alike.

"You look like my father," she blurted out, staring wildly at John.

John looked confused. "I'm sorry, but do I know you?"

"You look just like him," she sobbed, pressing her hand against the side of his face. "Oh, dear Jesus! You could be him!"

"Who's your father?" Sara asked.

Liz turned and stared desperately into Sara's eyes. "My father is Adam's father."

Eventually they managed to convince Liz to take a seat, and someone handed her a glass of water. John knelt on the floor in front of her, and she couldn't take her eyes off of him. He looked as confused as she felt, though, which Liz found oddly comforting. The woman, Sara, excused herself to go check on Adam. She returned a few minutes later after she found him sleeping peacefully.

"What's your name?" Sara asked.

Liz took several deep breaths to compose herself, but she never took her eyes off of him. She couldn't. "Liz. Elizabeth Brooks."

Obviously her name didn't ring a bell to either one of them. But it wasn't important.

"Adam's your brother?" Sara probed.

Liz nodded. "Yes." Her voice cracked.

"I didn't know he had a sister," Sara continued.

"He didn't either. And he has a brother. CJ. Charles Junior." Liz fell in love with her father all over again, but in another man's beautiful face. "You could be him, you look so much like him."

"Charles is your father?" Sara asked.

Liz took another sip of water before responding. "Charles Brooks. He was married to a woman named Roberta."

The name Roberta registered strongly in John and it showed on his face.

"Roberta Brooks was your mother?" He finally spoke up.

She nodded shamefully.

"Didn't she kill . . ." John stopped in midsentence, realizing that he might need more tact than he was capable of.

Liz sobbed again. "She found out about Adam's mother, and Adam. She killed Daddy."

"Oh my God," Sara muttered.

"Roberta hated my guts," John told her.

"Of course she did." Liz let the tears fall again. "You look just like him. And she loved him more than she loved anything or anyone else in the world."

He looked so conflicted, and Liz truly felt sorry for him.

John looked at her. "She loved him so she killed him?"

Liz shrugged. "Imagine the irony, and what she must've felt when she saw you."

"Yeah," he said introspectively. "I guess . . ."

"Had to be a bitch. Don't you think?" Liz said.

"My mother was . . ." Liz didn't have words to describe Roberta. There were moments when she remembered her mother sitting, staring off into space at nothing, mumbling things to herself. Those were the times when Liz felt like she and CJ weren't even real to Roberta. She looked at John. "She was . . ."

John nodded. "Yes. She was."

THIRTY-NINE

Avery had been sending her text messages since she'd left Denver. Cammy had taken Charlotte to the beauty shop, and Reesy finally had the house to herself, so she took the opportunity to use this time to finally call. She shut the bedroom door and dialed his number.

"How many different ways do I have to say it, Avery?" she said, struggling to remain calm. "I can't continue to see you. I want my marriage to work and family to stay together. Period."

"I care about you, Reesy."

"Stop saying that. You keep pulling me in and . . . It's not going to work with you and me, Avery."

"How do you know? Maybe it could if you gave it a chance."

She didn't want to hurt his feelings, but maybe that's what had to happen in order for him to get it. "I love Justin. I don't love you."

"But you want me, Clarice," he said, unfazed. "You've proven that, time and time again. You want me the way I want you."

"Maybe I did, but not anymore. I wanted to get back at Justin, Avery."

"Then he knows?"

"Of course not."

"Of course not. Because that's not what you were doing. You were where you wanted to be, Reesy. It wasn't about Justin. It was—is—about us. If this had anything to do with Justin, then you'd have told him."

"You know what?" Maybe he was right, but it didn't matter. Reesy had made up her mind. "The fact is, I'm not going there with you again. I am committed to my husband, and I'm going to do whatever it takes to make my marriage work. Justin and I have too much at stake to just throw it all away, and if you cared about me as much as you claim to, you'd leave me the hell alone, Avery."

He didn't respond right away. Reesy almost thought he'd hung up on her. "Fine," he said calmly. "I'll back off."

"Thank you," she said, exasperated. Reesy pursed her lips together to keep from crying. She had made such a mess of things, but she sincerely wanted and needed for this to stop now. "I'm sorry if I misled you. I was selfish, Avery, and I never meant for things to go this far."

"I'm here, Reesy," he added. "If you ever need me. I'm here."

Cammy crept out of the house as quietly as she'd come in. Reesy wasn't as together as she wanted everyone to think. She tried to be so high and mighty all the time, but she was cheating on her man, and there wasn't anything high and mighty about all that.

Avery leaned back in the chair in his office and thought about everything she'd just said to him. For once in his life, he had a chance to develop some redeeming qualities, and to step back and do right by the woman he supposedly loved. He hated Justin, even more than he felt he loved Reesy, though. That was the problem.

Justin had gotten off too easily as far as Avery was concerned. He'd gotten away with paying Avery's daughter to fuck him, and he'd somehow managed to get back into his wife's good graces after Avery had proven that the sonofabitch had been unfaithful. And now the magnanimous bastard was shooting for some kind of Good Samaritan award by helping put Lisa through school.

He was in a position to rock that sucker's world in a way he never saw coming. But Reesy would get hurt in the process and that's not something he ever wanted to do. In a perfect life, Avery knew he wasn't her type. Reesy had told the truth. She'd been with him to get back at her husband, but she'd fallen short of really sticking it to her husband and telling him everything. She played her games in her head because when it came down to it, Reesy didn't know how to play any other way.

Avery knew how to play, though, better than anybody. And Justin, despite the cavalier demeanor he put on for his family, wasn't too shabby either. This was a poker match, and a contest of who could out bluff who. Avery knew the game was being played, but Justin didn't, which was to Avery's advantage.

FORTY

The most exciting thing in this whole damn town was this lake. Connie had walked from Moses and Sara's house and stumbled upon it by accident, sat down beside it, and watched it do absolutely nothing. A person could die a slow, quiet, agonizing death in a town like this and nobody would ever even know it. She was miserable, and definitely conflicted. She was here to support John in his time of need, but that was the last thing she wanted to be doing and this was the last place on earth she wanted to be, considering that he'd been screwing around with some broad who was probably his third cousin or something.

Connie didn't remember the chick's name, but she couldn't shake the image of that smug look on her face when she came over to the table the other night at dinner. Women know women, and all women recognize the expression in another woman's eyes that undoubtedly communicates, "I been with your man." She wanted desperately to scream but she'd probably wake the mayor if she did.

How could he do some shit like that, she wondered dismally, running her fingers over her 'fro. Just when things were going so damn good between them, and for them. Connie had finally started to get comfortable being in love, falling headfirst and with reckless abandon into that whole family thing, and John had to go and fuck it up.

The two of them hadn't really spoken to each other in days. They talked around each other, uttering one-word responses and trying hard not to even look at each other, which was hard as hell in that small motel room. Connie wanted to go home, but a sense of obligation kept her here. John probably wanted her to leave too. She could do the single-parent thing. The idea wasn't ideal, but it wasn't impossible. John could become a child-support check and every other weekend-, holiday-, and birthday-type father. A grasshopper suddenly hopped into her lap and Connie jumped and screamed, remembering right then and there that she and nature never did see eye to eye on things.

It took a few moments for her to compose herself, and she stared out across the water, thinking that maybe she did need to just make a reservation and go back to Denver. And John could do John, and what's-her-face, if that's what he wanted. Connie had a son to raise, and a life to live, and she knew deep down that she could do both, even without him.

"No."

"Like, I'm not asking you, John," Connie told him. "I'm going home. If you can't take me to the airport, then I'll ask Moses to do it."

John paced back and forth, while Connie nursed the baby. He stopped and stared at her. "You go back and then what?"

Connie shrugged. "And then whatever."

His expression changed to irritable. "What the hell does that mean?"

"It means . . . whatever," she said, trying to keep her voice down. "You want to end it."

She thought about telling him a lie, but now wasn't the time to be proud. It was time to be real. "No, but I think you ended it when you slept with that woman."

"We weren't even together when that happened, Connie," he explained calmly. "You told me to leave, and I left. And what happened with Racine happened because I thought it was over between you and me."

"Well it wasn't, John," she said bitterly. Sure, she told him to leave, but that didn't mean she was over him. "I just wanted you out of the house."

He looked at her like she'd said something dumb.

"I still loved you, and I thought you still loved me. I mean, hell. You were only gone for a few months. And you figured that it was okay to fuck somebody else in two months?"

He thought about it before responding. "Yeah."

"That's just . . ." She hadn't felt this wounded in a long time. "I just need to go home."

"Well, you'd better start walking then," he said, dismissively. "That airport is a hundred miles away." He finally stopped pacing and sat down.

"Moses will take me," she said, annoyed.

"Nah, Moses won't." He smirked.

"Then I'll ask Sara."

"Sara won't drive anywhere outside of Bueller."

Connie smiled coolly. "I'll take a cab."

"Ain't no cabs."

The two stared silently at each other for several moments. "You can't keep me here," she told him.

"That's exactly what I'm doing, Connie."

"Why? Why would you do this?"

John picked up his car keys and stood up to leave. "You know why I'm doing it." John left without saying another word.

It wasn't that long ago when he'd have driven her to the airport himself, dropped her off, and turned the car back around, driving until he'd finally forgotten what she looked like.

John sat on the front porch next to Moses, both of them staring out at the open space, sipping on beers.

"You did the right thang," Moses said lazily. "She don't need to be going nowhere."

"She's going to ask Sara to drive her to Dallas."

Moses laughed. "And Sara'll ask me, 'cause you know she don't drive outside town."

"I heard that!" Sara shouted from inside the house.

Both men smiled.

"I might need to sleep here tonight," John said.

Moses nodded. "You can sleep in yo' daddy's room, but I wouldn't recommend it. She might just slip out of that room and very well start walking her ass back to Dallas."

John laughed.

"She just mad right now," Moses explained. "Give her some time. She be alright."

"She's going to have to be, Moses. 'Cause I'm not ready to let go."

John and Racine had fucked like fools the last time he'd come to Bueller, but he wasn't about to let sex put an end to what he needed most in the world. He'd never taken a stand on anything in his life, because until now he'd never wanted anything as badly as he wanted Connie. She was pissed, right or wrong. Personally, he felt she was wrong because they weren't even together when he hooked up with Racine, but that was just something neither of them would probably ever see eye to eye on.

Connie had some bad habits that it was time for her to break too. She was too damn quick to toss him out with the trash when his shit started to smell bad. But as funky as it smelled right now, she needed to plug up her nose and ride it out this time. And he needed to stand fast, in that pissy-ass attitude of hers and all, until the dust settled and they could pick up where they'd left off.

FORTY-ONE

"You cut your hair?" Cammy exclaimed as soon as Tyrell answered the door. He looked like a different person without his locks, and even younger than twenty-three years old. Cammy stared stunned until he stepped aside and let her come in.

"Whassup?" he asked coolly, slipping into a T-shirt.

Whassup? wasn't the reaction she was expecting. Ty didn't even look happy to see her, but she decided to smile and to let him know that she was happy to see him. "Wow," she said, trying not to sound as uncomfortable as she felt. Cammy looked around at the small apartment, remembering the times that she'd spent over here with him. "Place still looks the same."

He brushed past her, stretched out on the futon, picked up his game controller, and went back to playing his video game.

Cammy sat down apprehensively and tried to make sense of that game he was playing. It was hard to keep her eyes off of him, though. Tyrell Washington was what was beautiful in Murphy, Kansas. He was what had made her life bearable here. "How've you been?" she asked softly.

He glanced briefly at her then turned his attention back to the television screen. "Maybe if you'd returned any of my calls, you'd know how I been," he said tersely.

His candidness caught her off guard, but he was right. Since she'd moved to Denver, Cammy had hardly spent five minutes on the phone with Ty. She stared in wonder of how young he looked now, like a boy, and not like a grown man. Cammy was four years older than he was, and until now the age difference had never seemed to be an issue. Now, Cammy just felt old inside, like she'd lived a whole lifetime in the span of a few months, and here he was, still living in the same place and playing video games, looking like time had been standing still for him.

"How's business at the garage?"

"It's a'ight."

"You still planning on opening up another one?"

He didn't answer.

Cammy was starting to crumble inside. She'd been back for two days, and seeing Ty again was something she'd been wrestling with since she had made plans to come home again. He was just a reminder of so many things in her life, mostly good things, but lately of bad ones, that it was almost easier to pretend like the two of them had never been together. She'd followed an invisible trail to his place, though. Almost as if she couldn't help herself. Living in the same town as Ty, there would be no way she could resist him. But Cammy realized, sitting here now, that coming here had been a mistake.

"I guess I'll go ahead and let you play your game, Ty," she said dejectedly, getting up to leave.

Ty suddenly tossed his game controller and bolted to his feet. "Why the hell you come over here, Cam?" he asked angrily.

She stopped and slowly turned to face him with fresh tears in her eyes. "I missed you."

He looked as if he didn't believe her. "Right. I been blowing up your phone, trying to get you to talk to me for the last six months, and now all of a sudden you wanna see a brotha. Whassup with that?"

Tyrell was so young. Cammy suddenly felt tired and worn out. How could she explain something to him that she couldn't even explain to herself? "I shouldn't have come," she said softly. Cammy opened the door to leave, but Ty reached over her and slammed it shut, pressed her back against it, and put his arms on either side of her to keep her from leaving.

"I lost a baby too, Cammy," he said hoarsely. "And I lost you, and shit ain't been right in my life since you left."

Cammy was too exhausted to try and hold in her tears or to resist the only person in her life who truly understood her and accepted her. She raised her hands to his hips and slid them underneath his shirt. Ty reluctantly raised his arms and let her slip it past his head and drop it to the floor. He put his hand underneath her chin, raised her mouth to his. She let herself be swept away in this dream, praying that it would never end.

Making love to Ty came naturally and easily and sex had nothing to do with it. Cammy remembered every nuance of his body, mind, and soul. And he knew her better than he knew himself. Ty made love to her with his eyes open, but Cammy couldn't bear to look into them. Too much had happened and there were too many things that she wanted to forget. Staring into his eyes reminded her of every last one of them.

Cammy wrapped her legs around his waist, and held his face to hers. She wanted him close enough to be one and the same.

"I love you, Cammy," he said, kissing her.

"I know," she whispered, hopeful. "Deeper, Ty. Please."

Afterward, he held her in his arms just like he used to do, kissing the side of her neck, dozing in and out of sleep. Murphy, Kansas, wasn't home, she quietly concluded. Tyrell Washington was home. This small bed, in this tiny apartment, being held in his arms, this was home. And for the first time in a long time, Cammy felt like she could finally close her eyes and rest.

"I'm glad you came back to me, Mrs. Washington," he said, half-asleep.

Cammy smiled. "Mrs. Washington. I like the sound of that."

"Me too," he said, sounding like a young and silly boy. "You staying. Right?"

If she'd had any reservations before seeing him again, she certainly didn't have any now. Cammy would be a fool to leave him again. The fact that he was still here, and that he still wanted her, was all she needed to help make up her mind. "I ain't going nowhere, Ty. I belong right here with you."

They'd both drifted off to sleep when Cammy heard her cell phone ringing. "Hello?" she answered groggily. "Oh." She sat up in bed. "Yeah . . . Momma. O . . . Okay. Yeah, I'll be right there. Yes ma'am. Yes."

Cammy started to get out of bed when Ty grabbed hold of her arm. "Cammy," he said, pleading with his eyes. "C'mon now."

"I gotta go, Ty," she said frantically, pulling away from him. Cammy got up and hurried to get dressed.

"You ain't gotta go," he said, sitting up. "Why don't you just get back in bed and let's go back to sleep?"

"Momma needs me." Cammy operated on automatic. Charlotte had called and wanted her to come home, and Cammy needed to get home.

"I need you too, Cammy," he argued.

"I'll call you tomorrow, Ty." She tried to smile.

"So this is how it is?" he said irritably. "Just like how it used to be? What the fuck, Cammy?"

"Don't be like that, Ty," she said, kissing his cheek. "You know how she is."

"Yeah, and I know how you are too, only I thought you had changed."

Cammy stopped and stared back at him. "I . . . I just . . ."

He shook his head. "Go on and run home to your momma, Cammy. And don't bring your ass back here."

She reached out to him. "Don't be like that, baby," she pleaded.

Ty pushed her away. "I ain't doing that shit again, Cammy. We got married, and you supposed to be with me."

"She's my mother. You can't expect me to turn my back on her."

He shrugged. "So I'm supposed to be cool with you always turning your back on me?"

"It ain't like that."

"That's exactly what it's like. What it's always been like, and what it's always going to be like," he said, disappointed. "I love you. You know how much I love you. But if you want things to be like they've always been . . . with you jumping through the roof every time Charlotte tells you to jump, and me putting my life on hold, then you and me don't need to be together."

"You want me to choose you over my own momma?"

Ty didn't say anything.

"Can we talk about this tomorrow?" she asked, dejected.

Ty got up and held the door open for her to leave.

FORTY-TWO

"I don't mean to stare," Liz Brooks said nervously to John. He'd agreed to meet her for coffee, after she'd finally gotten up the courage to ask him. The last time she'd seen him, Liz had made a plumb fool of herself, falling the way she did, but he'd just taken her by surprise. She'd have expected a resemblance like that from Adam, not his son. But Charles Brooks had jumped a generation to appear in that young man. Leave it to her daddy to be so clever.

"Well, if I look as much like . . ." He looked to her for clarification.

"Charles," she said quickly. "That was his name. And yes. You could be his twin."

"Then it's understandable," he said calmly.

She managed to smile.

"I don't remember seeing you in Bueller when I was growing up."

"Oh, I had moved by the time you were born. Gone off to college. I came back a few times, but never stayed too long."

"You never knew Adam?"

She cleared her throat. "No, but I knew of him." The waitress came over to the table to refill her coffee cup, but Liz waved her off. "Growing up, I'd overhear people talking about him, and in the same sentence they would mention my daddy's name, and of course my mother's." She smiled sheepishly. "Kids aren't as dumb as people like to think. Eventually I put it all together," she said proudly.

John smiled. "The rumor mill is alive and well in Bueller, Texas, Miss Brooks. Always has been. Always will be."

"Liz. Please call me Liz."

"Liz."

"I understand that you and Adam have only just connected in recent years?"

"That's right. Like with you, Adam was more of a myth in my life than anything. People said things about him and I bought into it."

"What kinds of things?"

"They said he'd raped my mother, which was how I got here." She looked concerned. "But he didn't."

John shook his head. "No. Mattie was too young for him in years only. If you ask me, she was a little girl with too much time on her hands, blown away by the fact that he loved her enough to do anything for her. Like a kid with a brand-new toy. Being the way he is . . . Adam wasn't capable of rationalizing the situation with Mattie. He just loved her."

"Do you know how he got that way?"

John stared at her. "He was born like that."

"No. He wasn't, John. Momma—Roberta tried to kill him when he was an infant. That's what some people used to say."

"How?"

"Depends on who you ask." She shrugged. "Some say she hit him. Others said she tried to smother him. His mother saw Roberta running away from her house, and when she went inside to check on him in his crib, Adam wasn't breathing."

"You think it's true? You think Roberta would do something like that?" he asked in disbelief.

Liz stared at him, unblinking. "Don't you? She didn't hate you for nothing, John, and she didn't hate you lightly either."

"I just thought she was crazy."

"She was."

John shifted uncomfortably and then suddenly realized something. "So, me and Roberta are related?"

Liz nodded. "I'm your aunt, John. She was my mother, so . . ."

"She used to stare at me with this wild look in her eyes. I was a kid, so I didn't get it."

"I'm sure that when she saw you, she saw my father all over again. She saw what he'd done to her, betraying her by seeing another woman, and she saw the ghost of the man she'd killed. Hating you, and Adam, came as natural as breathing for her."

"How come you don't hate him?"

Liz laughed. "Oh, goodness! I've been too afraid of Adam to hate him."

"Afraid of what?"

"Afraid that Charles loved him more than he loved us," she admitted. "Afraid that if my mother hadn't killed my father, that maybe he'd have left us to be with Adam and that other woman. We were Roberta's children, and I don't believe he ever loved Roberta. And so, did that mean he didn't love my brother and me too? He loved Adam's mother, and so to me that had to mean that he loved Adam."

"I'm sure he loved all of his kids, Liz," he reasoned.

Liz smiled. "I remember moments with my father when I know he loved me. And I remember other moments when he would sit in the room with us, at the kitchen table, and hardly say a word to any of us. I was too young to understand that expression on his face when I was a child, but as I grew older, I recognized it as being a look of discontentment . . . unhappiness. He hated being home, and he was gone a lot."

The two sat quietly for a few moments processing the history flowing between them. They were filling in blank spaces from both of their lives, each of them gradually becoming more complete.

"You should talk to Adam," John finally spoke up. He looked at Liz, who still looked apprehensive at the mention of his name. "He should know about his father, and he should know about you."

"Do you think he'd understand?" she asked nervously.

"Your guess is as good as mine," John said matter-of-factly. "But he should hear it and you should say it before it's too late."

She fidgeted with her napkin. "I shouldn't have waited this long," she said sheepishly. "I should've come sooner. We could've had more time." Liz looked at John.

"I've known my old man for two years and I know better than anybody that every minute counts. Tell Adam who his father was. Tell him that he loved him. Tell him that he has a sister."

"And another brother."

"Let him take it with him. I think he'd like that."

"I'll talk to him tomorrow."

John finished his coffee, put money on the table to pay the bill, and then started to get up from the table.

"Today, Liz. He might not be here tomorrow."

John stood in the doorway of Adam's room, so Liz couldn't turn and run if she wanted to. Liz cautiously approached Adam's bed and quietly pulled up a chair and sat beside him. He looked small and she was awed by the fact that she and this man had a connection decades old. Adam Tate was her family, her brother, and he was dying.

John came into the room and called his name. "Adam."

Adam's eyes fluttered open and he turned his head toward the sound of John's voice. "I was dreamin'."

"Somebody's here to talk to you," John explained. "You need to listen to her."

Adam managed a feeble nod.

Liz reached up and put her hand tenderly on his arm. "Adam?" she said softly.

He turned to look at her, and smiled. "Hi."

"Hi." She chuckled. He had their father's smile. "My name is Liz."

"LLLiz."

"Adam." Liz hesitated and swallowed. "I am your sister."

Adam frowned and thought for a moment. "I . . . I don't hhhhhave no . . . sister."

"Yes. You do," she gently insisted. "We have the same daddy. Charles. Charles was your father and he was mine too."

She could almost see the wheels spinning behind his eyes, trying to make sense of what she'd just said. "My dad . . . dy d . . . d . . . dead."

She looked at John, then back at Adam. "Mine too."

Adam studied her. "I . . . I don't know . . . you."

"We never met before."

Adam grimaced, obviously in pain. Liz started to panic, and she stood up and looked desperately to John. He shook his head, indicating that she should stay.

"We've never met before, Adam, but I am your sister. I was born before you. I'm the oldest. And then there's CJ, and he's your brother."

His eyes grew wide. "He here?"

Liz smiled. "No. He couldn't make it," she lied. CJ didn't know about Adam. But after today, he would.

"I dddddon't . . . know . . . myyyy . . . daddy."

Liz's heart went out to him. None of them had really gotten a chance to know Charles Brooks. She and CJ had a few pictures of their father, but this moment brought the truth home to her in a way she hadn't really thought about before. "He died not long after you were born," she explained. She rubbed her hand over his hair. "You need to know something, though," she said warmly. "You need to know that he loved you."

Adam's confusion seemed to dissipate when he heard those words. Adam was a simple man and only simple things mattered to him. "He did?" he asked hoarsely.

She nodded. "Very, very much. I think he'd want you to know that."

"That's . . . nnnnnnice," he said, sighing. Adam grimaced again, and groaned in pain. John covered Adam's hand with his own, and pushed down on his father's thumb to administer a much needed dose of morphine, and both of them watched as Adam drifted back off to sleep.

FORTY-THREE

Reesy had chosen to stay at a hotel while they visited Charlotte, but Cammy had decided to stay in her old room. Charlotte woke to the smell of bacon and the sound of Cammy humming, probably one of them hip-hop songs she liked so much. If she hadn't known better, Charlotte would've sworn that girl had never left. Camille came here acting the same way she had before moving to Denver, which confused the mess out of Charlotte. The few times she'd spoken to Cammy over the phone after she moved away, the girl sounded like a different person, distant and shady. She was lost, that's what she was. Cammy had no more business living in Denver, Colorado, than a polar bear had living in Africa. She couldn't function on her own. Everybody else might've believed she could, but Charlotte knew better. She knew that girl like nobody else, and without having Charlotte around to tell her what to do, Cammy wouldn't know her ass from that hole in her head.

"Morning, Momma," Cammy said, smiling when Charlotte came into the kitchen and sat down at the table.

Just like she knew would happen, as soon as Charlotte sat down, Cammy sat a plate down in front of her with eggs, bacon, two pieces of buttered toast, and a cup of coffee all ready for Charlotte to drink with just the right amount of cream and sugar already in it.

Charlotte sipped on her coffee. "Reesy ain't here yet?" she asked dryly.

"No," Cammy said, sitting down next to her mother to eat. "She said she'd be here soon, though."

Charlotte glared at her as Cammy shoveled eggs into her mouth. Cammy had been gone for six months and it dawned on Charlotte that she hadn't missed having her around for even one minute in all that time. She'd missed having somebody here to take care of the house, drive her to her doctor's appointments and the beauty shop sometimes, but she hadn't missed Cammy. Her whole life, Camille had been a necessary annoyance and burden. Sitting here looking at her now, Charlotte realized that Cammy was the one who missed being here. She missed her mother and all that ripping and running up and down the streets all the way out in Denver wasn't bound to do anything but to land that fool in all kinds of trouble.

"Couldn't wait to get back here and lay up with that boy again, I see," Charlotte said matter-of-factly. "Keep on fuckin' with him." She sipped from her coffee cup. "You gonna end up pregnant again in no time. Just like before."

Cammy put down her fork and hung her head. "It's not like that, Momma," she said quietly.

"It's not like what? You didn't lay up with him last night before I called? Or did I catch y'all in the middle of doing it?"

There it was. Charlotte almost laughed out loud as the look in Cammy's eyes changed to pitiful as if by magic. Charlotte was a bully where Cammy was concerned. She knew it. She'd always known it. It was easy to back Cammy into a corner, and it was easy to make her cry. *What kind of mother would do that to her own child?* she sometimes wondered. The answer never came to her, though, because Charlotte never looked for it for very long.

"I just needed to see him," she almost whispered.

Charlotte chuckled. "Why? You think he want you back?"

Cammy cut a glance at her mother.

Charlotte put her cup down and leaned close to Cammy. "You really think that boy want you, Cammy?" she asked, curtly. "For what? Pussy? Dumb pussy. What else you got to offer? He out here doing whatever the hell he wanna do, with whoever he wanna do it to. So what makes you think he's sitting up here pining and waiting on you?"

Cammy blinked away tears and pushed her plate away from her. "He loves me," she said, clearing her throat.

Charlotte laughed so hard she nearly fell out of her chair.

"He told me that he loves me! He said it last night when . . ."

"When you had his dick in your mouth, Cammy? Is that when he said it? He loves you about as much as he loves me and we both know he don't give a shit about me," she said, finally composing herself. "You ain't got shit to offer that boy, girl! He know it. You know it. And I certainly know it."

"He's my husband, Momma!" she finally blurted out. "Tyrell and me are married. We got married before I moved away, so I know he loves me! He wouldn't have married me if he didn't."

Charlotte stared at that girl like her head had just lifted off of her shoulders and floated away. "So you did marry him?"

Cammy sat a bit taller in her seat and stared back proudly at Charlotte. "Yes. He married *me*."

"You say that like you happy about it."

Cammy swallowed. "I am happy. I'm very happy."

"Then tell me something, Cammy. If you so proud that you got yourself a little husband, why you sitting here with me, and why did you move your ass all the way to Denver?"

"Good morning, ladies," Reesy said, walking hesitantly into the kitchen. She stared back and forth between the two. "Am I interrupting?"

Cammy pushed back away from the table and started taking up the plates. "Morning, Reesy," she said, avoiding eye contact. "Sit down. Breakfast is ready."

Charlotte slowly stood up to leave. "I'm gonna take my bath," she said, brushing past Reesy.

"Sure, Mom," Reesy said distantly. "You do that."

Lord have mercy! Uncle stumbled back at the sight of that pretty woman answering the door. Damn if she didn't look just like . . .

"Are you alright?" she asked, concerned. "Can I help you?"

He adjusted his shirt, and quickly managed to compose himself. "I'm here to see Miss Charlotte Rodgers."

He glanced over her shoulder and stared in awe at another pretty girl, darker, a bit on the skinny side, but she had Zoo's eyes.

"Are you a friend of hers?" the one at the door asked.

Uncle smiled broadly and winked. "You could say that."

That pretty, heavyset girl invited him inside. Uncle sat down on the sofa, and waited until the other one came back into the room with a glass of lemonade she'd offered him. His eyes darted back and forth between the two, picking out bits and pieces of Charlotte from both of them. If he could've laid those pieces out on the floor, Uncle could've put them together to make Charlotte thirty years younger and fifty pounds lighter.

"I'm Reesy." The one who answered the door sat down next to him and extended her delicate hand to him to shake. All he needed was two pieces of bread and he'd have gobbled that lovely appendage up like a sandwich. "And that's my sister, Cammy."

Cammy. She had Zoo's slimness, the shape of his face, and maybe even a hint of that boy's goofy smile.

"My name is Uncle."

Both girls looked at each other, and then back at him.

The one who called herself Reesy was the bold one, and she didn't have one ounce of hesitation asking for clarification. "That's your real name?"

He nodded. "It most certainly is."

She eyed him suspiciously. "Just Uncle?"

He grinned. "Just Uncle."

"You're a friend of Momma's?" the dark one, Cammy, asked. "I've never seen you before."

"Me and yo' momma go way back. You weren't even a twinkle in that woman's eyes when I knew her." He winked.

"Did you know her from Denver?" Reesy probed.

He looked surprised, and then remembered all those stories Charlotte used to tell about her baby girls back in Colorado. This one here was one of them. "Naw, sugah. From Kansas City." Damn! All this time he'd thought she was lying about those girls. But apparently, that wasn't the case.

"She's never mentioned you," Cammy added.

Uncle shrugged. "It was a long time ago, so I ain't surprised."

Uncle looked up and saw Charlotte standing there, staring at him and clutching the top of her housecoat, looking like a crazy woman about to jump out of her own skin. It was all he could do not to jump up and wrap his arms around that woman.

"Hey, girl!" he said enthusiastically. "How come you didn't tell me you had such beautiful daughters?" He laughed.

"You want some lemonade, Momma?" Cammy had disappeared into the kitchen before Charlotte had even had a chance to respond.

"Are you alright, Mom?" Reesy asked, getting up to help an obviously unprepared Charlotte sit down.

Charlotte looked nervously at Reesy and then back at Uncle. "Yes, baby. I'm, I'm fine."

Uncle sat looking exceptionally pleased with himself. "I was passing by and thought I'd stop in and say hello. Imagine my good fortune," he said smugly. "I never expected that I'd ever get a chance to see yo' babies, Charlotte. Ain't that something?"

"I thought you said you were from Kansas City," Reesy asked suspiciously.

Uncle studied this one. Something about the look in her eyes told him she was the sharp one in this box of pencils. Sharper than that clueless one in the kitchen, and even sharper than her slick-ass momma here. She held his gaze with her own, and he decided right then and there that he liked her smart ass.

"I have family here," he said.

Uncle looked at Charlotte staring back at him, appreciating the small lie he'd just told. "But yo' momma here has always been on my radar."

Cammy came back and handed a glass of lemonade to Charlotte, who finished the whole thing in one gulp.

"You staying for dinner?" Cammy asked innocently.

Uncle slowly stood up to leave. "Naw, baby girl. You ladies probably got better thangs to do than to spend the day hanging out with an old man like me." He looked to each of them, and finally to Charlotte. "Just thought I'd take a chance and stop by to say hello to an old friend. You doing alright, baby?"

Charlotte managed to nod. "It was good seeing you, Uncle." Her voice trailed off.

"As always?"

Uncle waited for her to answer.

"As always." She forced a smile.

FORTY-FOUR

It was the middle of the night when John's uncle, Moses, called his motel room. "We need to get to the hospital," he said gravely.

John rubbed sleep from his eyes, and sighed. "I'll meet you there."

He sat up on the side of the bed and hung his head. This was it. John felt it in his gut and he knew it like he knew he'd take his next breath.

"What is it?" Connie asked groggily.

They hadn't said much to each other lately, and every day that passed that she was still here was a miracle. "Adam," was all he needed to say.

Connie climbed out of bed and headed into the bathroom to wash her face. Ten minutes later, they were in the car and headed to the hospice.

Sara greeted them when they arrived. "The doctors say it won't be much longer," she said, choking up. "Moses is in there with him now."

Connie went into the room, carrying the baby, but John couldn't get his feet to move. She came back over to him, took hold of his hand, and led him to Adam's bedside. John and Moses exchanged glances, and then both stared down at Adam.

Sara leaned down and whispered in Adam's ear. "Your family's here, Adam," she said softly.

Adam slowly opened his eyes and looked first to Moses and feebly squeezed his hand. He saw Sara and tried to smile, and then he saw John with Connie standing in front of him, holding Jonathon.

"Thhhhat yo' girl, son?" he asked weakly.

John nodded. "Yessir."

Adam stared at Connie. "S . . . she pretty . . . l . . . like my girl. I seen you in a picture," he told Connie.

"That's yo' grandson, Adam," Moses said, his voice cracking. "You was asleep before, every time we brought him in."

Adam stared, astonished.

Connie came closer and sat down next to Adam so that he could see the baby.

Adam had tears in his eyes. "He mmmmine?" he asked her.

She smiled. "Of course he is." She blinked and tears started to fall.

Liz quietly walked into the room and stood at the foot of the bed. John had called her on the way to the hospital.

"He look like me?" Adam asked.

John spoke up. "Just like you, old man."

Adam looked over to his son. The two simply stared knowingly at each other until the light slowly faded from Adam's eyes, and the line on the heart monitor flatlined.

Mattie! Mattie! Where you at?

I'm right here, Adam!

He smiled. Me too.

Gradually, everyone began to leave the room. John remained,

standing planted at his father's bedside. Their time together had been short. Too short. To people who didn't know him, Adam was Fool, a name they'd given to a man who had been anything but. To John, Adam had been everything he'd spent a lifetime searching for: love, acceptance. Unassuming and gentle, Adam never had to make a lot of noise to be heard. He never had to be flashy to be seen, or say more than a few words to make an impact. People had felt sorry for him for the way he was, but until this moment, John had never understood that he never needed anybody to feel sorry for him. Adam was perfect, and all any other man could do was to wish he'd been half the man Adam Tate had been.

Connie handed Jonathon to Liz, went back into the room, over to where John stood.

"I uh . . ." he started to speak. He didn't need to.

"I know," she said, wrapping her arms around him. "Me too."

Now was not the time to be jealous. But Racine couldn't take her eyes off of John standing at his father's gravesite. Connie stood next to him the whole time, holding his hand, whispering in his ear, kissing his cheek. Resentment filled Racine, watching this woman who'd never set foot in Bueller, Texas, before, all of a sudden coming to his rescue and being more than loving at his time of need.

John was grieving, so he couldn't see the truth. Connie wasn't the woman for him. She didn't know him, not the way Racine knew him. Racine had been a part of John's life since they were children. She'd been here for him, when Connie had put him out. She'd loved him before he even knew how to be loved. John was a fool and couldn't see it, though, because Connie's blinding light kept the truth hidden from him. The woman was beautiful, and she'd had his kid. Racine had history on her side, and under the right circumstances, John might come to his senses and realize that the best woman for him was the one who'd been under his nose the whole time.

FORTY-FIVE

It was good to be home. Reesy had missed her kids, sleeping in her own bed, and even Justin.

"They act like you've been gone a month, instead of five days," he said, climbing into bed. "Kind of hurts my feelings."

Reesy was already in bed, and she chuckled. "Don't take it personally."

"Yeah, well . . ." It took every ounce of willpower he had not to pounce onto his wife and smother her with lust, love, and everything in between. The kids weren't the only ones who'd missed her. He turned over on his side and put his arm over her waist. Justin kissed her cheek. "So, how was the trip—really?"

Reesy moaned. "Weird."

"How?"

"I don't know. Cammy . . . as soon as she walked through Charlotte's front door she turned into this . . . She started taking care of Charlotte the way she did before she moved away."

He shrugged. "What's weird about that? It's her mother."

"It was unnatural, Justin. She was trying too hard. Her hands were shaking, and she couldn't move fast enough. Charlotte acted like she was fine with it, making demands like she was the queen of Sheba or something. Cammy was trying to appease Charlotte and Charlotte was punishing her for leaving."

"Sounds like a match made in heaven. Cammy spent her whole life with Charlotte and maybe that's just the nature of their relationship."

"Maybe it is, but you'd think Cammy would be sick of it. She hasn't been happy since she moved here. She tries to pretend everything's fine but I can see it in her eyes that it isn't."

"Isn't her boyfriend in Kansas? Maybe she misses him."

"I think she misses all of it. Which I don't get."

"Well, she left her whole life behind in Kansas, Reese. Can't be easy to start over."

"That's just it, Justin. She didn't have a life. She lived and breathed for Charlotte. And the fact that she even had a boyfriend was a miracle. The fact that she was pregnant was a miracle. She lived with Charlotte and only saw the boy when she wasn't waiting hand and foot on the woman. You'd think she'd be relieved to get out from under all that."

"Sounds like Stockholm syndrome."

She looked at him. "What's that?"

"It's when the hostage starts to feel loyalty to the hostage taker."

Reesy laughed.

"Don't laugh. I'm serious."

"Charlotte didn't take that girl hostage, Justin. She gave birth to her."

"Yeah, but she treats her like somebody holding another person hostage. Cammy sounds like she's crippled without her."

Reesy rolled her eyes. "Cammy needs counseling. That's all there is to it."

"Sounds like it."

"Oh, and then there was Uncle." She chuckled.

"Uncle? You've got an uncle?"

"No, the man's name was Uncle."

"Uncle."

"Yes. Some old guy who stopped by the house. I think he was flirting, but it's hard to tell with senior citizens."

"Oh yeah?"

"He kept staring at me and Cammy, looking at us like we were lunch. Honestly, I think he and Charlotte are seeing each other."

"No. Really?"

"Yeah." Reesy smiled. "She looked really shady when she saw him sitting there, like there was something going on between them."

"Maybe that old woman isn't as lonely as she wants everybody to think."

"You should've seen the way he looked at her."

"Like she was lunch?"

"Like she was dessert on the dinner menu." Reesy laughed. "I think I'm going to talk to her, though, about moving out here."

Justin sighed. "If she's seeing somebody, Reese . . ."

"I know. I mean, she might be happy where she is, especially if she's seeing someone," she reasoned. "But I think I ought to mention it." She looked at him. "She's getting older, Justin, and she's not in the best of health."

Justin thought for a moment before responding. Reesy used to believe Charlotte was just misunderstood. She'd taken it pretty hard when she came to terms with her mother's true nature. "You sure you want to do that?" he asked cautiously. "Now that you know what kind of person she really is?"

"Charlotte's got issues," she said reflectively. "She's always had them, and she probably always will. I saw it this last week, watching how she treated Cammy. But she's still my mother. I'd never forgive myself if I left her there all alone, if she didn't want to be there, and something happened."

Of course he understood. "Well, talk to her and see what she says," he said amicably. "If she wants to move back here, then we'll get her a small apartment or something."

She looked relieved. "You mean it?"

"Yeah, sweetheart. We'll do what we can for her."

"Wow," she said jokingly. "Who knew it would be so easy talking you into this?"

Justin squeezed her tighter. "Well, that's the effect you Rodgers women have on men." He kissed her. "Your mother's crazy, Reesy, but there's no denying she's got great genes."

"You're silly."

He expected her to pull away and complain about being tired or not in the mood. But, surprisingly, she did none of those things.

"I missed you, baby," he said, planting soft kisses on her lips.

"I missed you too, Justin," she responded.

Justin rolled over on top of his wife and gently spread her thighs with his knees. He wasn't stupid. The last time the two of them were together, Reesy didn't want him. This time was different. She welcomed his kisses, his touch. She wrapped her arms around him, and held Justin close. Her fingers traveled lightly across his shoulders, down his spine, and followed the curve of his lower back. She raised her knees on either side of him, and let them fall open like butterfly wings.

Justin's rigid penis found its own way to paradise.

The time apart had done them both some good. As tired as she was, Reesy lay awake in bed after Justin had fallen asleep. She curled up behind him, just like old times. She'd savored this intimacy with her husband, like she used to. And Reesy felt blessed to be this man's wife, the way she should've.

FORTY-SIX

Cammy had called Tyrell several times, but he hadn't answered or returned any of her calls. On Tuesday afternoon, she knew he'd be working at the garage, so Cammy took a chance and just showed up.

"We're leaving tomorrow." Ty was bent over an engine, and at first she didn't think he'd heard her. "I said . . ."

He stood up. "I heard you," he said abruptly.

She knew he was angry with her, but Ty had no idea of the kind of pressure Cammy was under. He'd never understood, no matter how many times she'd tried explaining it to him. Ty's people didn't need him the way Charlotte needed Cammy. She loved her mother too much to sit back and watch her suffer. Being away from Charlotte all these months made that clear now more than ever. She'd been wrong to leave her like this, and she'd been wrong to stay gone so long. But she loved him, and coming back here, that had become clear to her too. Given time together, she was convinced they could work through their problems. Ty just needed to be patient a little while longer.

"I'm coming back, Ty," she said nervously. Cammy waited for a re-action but one didn't come. "I'm moving back for good. I'm going to *give my notice at the end of the month, sell my furniture, and then I'll be back here."*

"You moving back in with your momma?" he asked indifferently.

She tried to smile. "Just for a little while."

Ty's impatience showed on his face.

"I just need some time." She tried to explain.

"How many times you gonna tell me that, Cam?" he asked irritably. "And how long am I supposed to wait?"

Cammy's smile faded. "We can make it work, Ty. Momma just needs—"

"She needs. She always needs," he said impatiently. "What about what you need, Cam? What I need?"

Cammy didn't know how to respond to that.

"Yeah, well . . . maybe you can put aside what you need, but I can't. I won't. Not anymore."

"What are you saying?"

"I'm saying that you can come back here if you want to, but don't come back thinking me and you gonna be together. If you can't come back here for me, for us, then I'ma keep it moving."

Isaac had been texting and leaving Cammy messages since she'd been gone, but she hadn't bothered to respond.

"Cammy. I know you getting my messages." He sighed. "Look, just call me or something, baby. I'm worried about you."

Today was her last day off before going back to work. Cammy had been in bed most of the day, with no energy or desire to do anything. The air was different in this city. Walking back into her apartment, Cammy walked right back into that same, sickly residue of despair she'd been living in since she moved here. She felt weighted down and hopeless, burdened by pretending to be someone she wasn't.

Cammy was homesick even before the plane took off. And any chance she had of making her relationship with Ty work was gone. If she went back home, it would be like it was before she'd met him. Ty had been responsible for Cammy's happiness when she was living in Murphy. Before he'd come along, she hadn't known anything else but that house and living with her mother. He'd been the first man to make love to her, and to tell her she was beautiful. He was the only one who'd ever wanted her.

"It's me again," Isaac said. "Baby, please. Just lemme know you alright."

Cammy waited for several minutes before finally calling Isaac back.

"Hey," she said, wearily.

"Hey girl! Where you been?"

"Outta town. I went to see my momma."

"I called."

"I accidently left my phone at home," she lied.

"You shoulda told me you were leaving, Cam. You had me worried, girl."

"I didn't know I was leaving, Isaac. It was a last-minute thing."

"Well, is she alright? It wasn't nothing serious, was it?"

"No. She's fine."

"I wanna see you," he said quickly. "I miss you, baby girl. Got a brotha over here trippin'."

She didn't want to think about anything anymore. Cammy had spent all day thinking about what she'd lost, and about how her life had become something she just didn't understand anymore.

"You home?" Isaac asked.

"I'm home, Isaac," she said quietly.

"I'm on my way."

Isaac didn't appreciate Cammy taking off like she did, even if it was to see her mother. And that shit she said about forgetting her phone was a mothafuckin' lie. But it was all good. He fucked that pussy nice and slow, marking that shit and making it his. He had the afternoon and all damn night, and he planned on taking full advantage of the situation.

He smoothed his hands over the heart-shaped ass spread out in front of him, slapped it, and then soothed the place where he'd hit it.

"Shhhhit, baby! Fuck! Fuck me, girl!"

He pushed inside her as deep as his nine inches could go. Any mothafucka putting it to this pussy was going to know without a doubt that he'd been all up in this shit. Isaac was writing his name on it, with every stroke.

"Not so deep, Isaac," she protested over her shoulder.

"Shhhhh . . . girl! Lemme do this."

Isaac lay awake next to Cammy, who was sound asleep. This was the last time she was pulling this shit. Momma or no momma, Cammy's ass wasn't taking off like this again, and she sure as hell wasn't leaving without taking her damn phone. She had a lot to learn about being with him. But that was cool. He'd just have to make sure she knew how to act going forward. That's all.

FORTY-SEVEN

John didn't bother telling anyone he was leaving the house. He did what came naturally. John started up his car and just drove, but to nowhere in particular. Bueller hadn't grown much since he was a kid. The old store where he used to steal candy with his buddy Lewis had fallen to the ground and been hauled away decades ago. Weeds had grown up around the house he'd grown up in. He'd been paying some dude to keep them under control since his grandmother, Agnes, had passed away. Obviously, he was wasting his money.

In the grand scheme of things, Adam wasn't much: a broken man, mentally incapable of taking care of himself, and too far out of touch with reality to matter, but hell. He was all that John had left. He'd been the only connection between John and Mattie, his only connection to the version of the truth about his parents that John had grown up with, and the other version, which played out to be vastly kinder. Adam was just good people, despite the bad things that had happened to him, and John doubted that the old man knew how to be anything else.

Whenever he came around Adam, John would just sit with him, sometimes neither one of them saying a word, or with Adam going on and on incoherently about shit that only mattered to him. He'd find himself basking in the goodness coming from Adam, filling the air, thinking that maybe he could get enough of it to land on him, to somehow make himself a better man. Each time, though, John would leave as the same man who'd shown up, and he'd just have to accept that he was as good as he was ever going to get. Without Adam around anymore, there was no mistaking the sizeable hole in him now, left behind by the only man he'd ever really loved.

"I had a feeling you'd end up here tonight," Racine said, over his shoulder.

John had been drawn to that dive like a magnet and back to his same seat at the bar that he sat in every time he came here.

"You know me too well." He motioned to the bartender, who responded with gin and a beer.

She slid onto the stool next to him. "I take pride in that." She chuckled. The magician bartender sat a rum and Coke down in front of her. "Besides, where else you gonna go in Bueller for a drink this time of night?"

He didn't want company, but he knew instinctively that telling her that wouldn't do him any good.

"You miss him?"

He didn't respond. John didn't want conversation.

Racine was a mind reader, especially where he was concerned. "We don't need to talk, John. We can just drink."

And that's what they did, which was fine with him.

He measured the time passing by how many drinks he'd had, and John had put down way too much alcohol. So much, in fact, that he never even saw Connie coming into the bar.

"John."

He wasn't the smartest man in the world, and he was drunk off of his ass, but even in his condition, John knew that this wasn't a good situation to be in. The first thought that came to his mind was to try and stand up and get his big ass out of the line of fire. The next thought was to sit here and finish his beer and hope that Connie would at least be considerate enough to wait until he was done to kill him.

Racine could've done the right thing and left quietly and without incident. He glanced at her, and it was pretty obvious that she had no plans to go anywhere.

"John," Connie said sternly, planting herself on the side of him that didn't have Racine on it. "It's late. You need to come home."

John didn't budge, and he didn't say a word, but he didn't need to. Racine decided to speak up on his behalf.

"Can't you see that the man's having a drink," she said snidely. "He just lost his father, for God's sake."

Connie had always been the cool type. In the two and half years he'd known her, she'd never let another female get under her skin. Nobody except for that sister of hers, every now and then—the middle one. It was the calm, cool collectedness of Connie that he always admired. The shit was sexy, and reminded him a lot of himself. Drama was not in her vocabulary, he figured, and that, like him, she'd lived enough of it to last a lifetime.

"I'm not talking to you," she said coolly. "Come on." She took the beer bottle from his hand and set it on the bar. "Let's go."

Racine sprung up from that bar stool, planted her hand on her hip, and took a fighter's stance behind John, who managed to spin around before the two could meet in the middle. "Did it ever occur to you that maybe he's not ready to leave yet?"

Connie sighed irritably. "I said, I'm not talking to you." It was hard for him not to feel proud. Baby girl was maintaining that cool.

Out of the corner of his eye, John thought he noticed a neck swirl coming from Racine's direction.

"Well, I'm talking to you, bitch. He's not ready to leave, so maybe you should."

Connie kept it steady, but he felt it, that tension building and emanating from the human body moments before it's about to spring. And damn if she didn't. In one quick motion, Connie leapt up from where she was sitting and lunged full body toward Racine, who stumbled back as surprised by the motion as anybody, but John managed to straighten his arm and stop her before she landed on Racine's face.

John laughed. "Whoa!"

Connie glared at him, her amber eyes on fire and burning holes into his. Then she fixed her steely gaze on Racine.

Connie never raised her voice. She didn't have to. "I did not come all the way down here to have to put my foot up your country ass, but if it has to go down like that, then I don't have a problem with it."

Racine twisted and twirled her neck some more. "And I ain't got no problem fuckin' you up!"

"Good luck with that," she warned. "But if you want to fuck something, I suggest you go stumble your bubble ass out there into one of those pastures and find your own goddamned bull. Leave mine alone."

John furrowed his brows, wondering if that was a compliment or if she'd just dogged him too. He was going to have to ask her about that, later on, when he sobered up.

"Too late," Racine said smugly. "I've fucked your bull every which way but loose, so, if anything, I'd say that maybe you're the one who should be trying to find a replacement."

Damn! He felt like meat.

Color flushed from Connie's cheeks, but she didn't miss a beat. "Then savor it, bitch," she said again—calmly. "Because you won't get it again. See, the difference between you and me is—" she poked the space between John's eyes. "He loves me. Maybe he did fuck you, but I'd bet my right leg you've never heard him say he loved you." Connie poked him in the chest. "I'm in here. And come hell or high water, can't you or any other broad in this world *ever* take my place there." Then she poked him hard in his groin. "The closest you can get is here." Connie pressed hard enough to cause some serious pain. John grimaced. "Dick ain't hard to get. All you had to do was give up your dignity and spread that fat ass of yours for dick that don't give a damn about you. A goddamned monkey can do that."

Racine's bottom lip quivered. "He cares about me," she argued weakly.

Connie smirked. "He cares about a football game. He cares about German chocolate cake. He cares about that new power drill I bought him for his birthday. So, yeah . . . bitch. Maybe you can lump yourself in with the rest of that shit. You do that if it helps you sleep at night."

Racine stared at John almost as if she were seeing him for the first time. Connie could've just let it end there, because obviously she'd won. But no. She had to go in for the kill.

"See, I have worked too hard for this shit right here." She poked her finger hard in his chest. "I have been through hell and back for this right here," she said, emphatically, poking him even harder. "And I will be damned if I let you, or any other broad, saddle up next to this and think you're is a bad enough bitch to walk out that door with my goddamned man."

He'd never seen that side of her. Hell, he didn't even know there was that side of her. "Connie," he started to say.

"Hush!" she commanded, then turned her attention back to Racine. "I feel sorry for you. You want what you can't have and you've put your whole self on the line for nothing. What did you get out of this, besides embarrassed?" Connie grabbed a handful of John's shirt, and then pulled him to his feet. She glared at Racine. "Swing if you want to," she threatened. "But I'm pissed, and I will lay your wide ass out on the floor then step on your dusty behind on my way out the door, and I promise you, I'm taking him with me."

She never raised her voice. Racine never swung. And John left with the woman he loved.

She'd calmed down by the time she pulled the car into the parking lot of the motel. They sat there for several minutes in silence, before John finally spoke up.

"Does this mean that you forgive me?" he asked sluggishly.

Connie refused to look at him. "That's not what this means, John," she said quietly.

"Then what's it mean?"

"It means I love you. That's all it means."

"That's not enough?"

She shrugged and started to get out of the car. "I don't know anymore."

FORTY-EIGHT

For the last few days since she'd been back home, Reesy had been mentally preparing herself for the conversation she'd promised Connie they would have with Jade.

"You should be there too, Justin," she'd told her husband.

Justin shook his head. "Nope. This is a conversation that should be between the three of you, Clarice. That's all she needs to make her understand. I'd just be in the way."

He was right. The three of them would sit down together and tell that little girl the truth about her life. Reesy had dreaded this truth for long enough, for reasons even she didn't understand. On one hand, she was afraid that Jade would just end up confused and uncertain about where she fit in with her family. But Reesy had also been afraid that telling that child the truth would leave Reesy feeling just as uncertain about where she fit in to her daughter's world. What if Jade decided she wanted to be with Connie? Justin had tried to reassure her that that would never happen, but, deep down, her greatest fear had been that she would lose her baby.

"How's John?" Reesy asked Connie over the phone.

"Coping," Connie replied simply. "We should be home in a few days."

"We'll see you when you get back, then."

"*Ciao*, baby," Connie replied.

Reesy had been so disappointed in Connie when she asked her and Justin to take care of Jade "for a while." Reesy had tried to maintain her faith in Connie, and she'd truly wanted to believe that Connie would get her act together and would be standing at Reesy and Justin's door a few months later to claim her little girl, but that never happened. By the time she did have a change of heart, though, Jade was six, and it was too late.

Jade had overheard Connie and Reesy arguing in the kitchen several months ago, when Connie blurted out that it was time for them to tell Jade the truth. How much she'd heard had never been determined, and how much she understood of what she'd heard had never been addressed. Jade was her baby. She was as much Reesy and Justin's child as the two Reesy had actually given birth to, and Reesy'd always been fiercely protective of that fact. She'd die for that little girl, and she'd kill to protect her, like any mother would for their child. And the truth was, if it ever came down to Reesy having to choose between Connie and Jade, well, she'd miss her sister terribly.

Not long after Reesy hung up the phone from speaking to Connie, Jade appeared in the living room and sat down next to Reesy on the sofa holding something in her hand.

"What's that?" Reesy asked, taking a photograph from Jade.

"I found it," she said sweetly.

Reesy stared at the photograph of Jade holding Jonathon at the hospital the day after he was born.

"He looks like Uncle John," Jade volunteered.

Reesy nodded. "Yes, he does."

"And he looks like Aunt Connie too, a little bit."

"He does, a little bit," she agreed.

"And . . ." Jade bit down on her bottom lip, then glanced apprehensively at her mother. "He looks like me a little bit too."

This wasn't the way she'd expected it to come. Jade was only eight, but she was bright and inquisitive and as nosey as any little eight-year-old girl. Jade knew *something*. At eight, Reesy guessed that that was as far as it went.

"Yes, Jade," Reesy said quietly. "He does look kind of like you too."

Jade stared at her mother, looking to her for answers because she trusted that only her mother could explain something in a way that would make sense. Reesy took a deep breath and saw this moment for what it was—opportunity. No, it wasn't going to be like she'd planned, but this was real life, and real life seldom showed up looking the way you'd like.

"When you were a baby," she said softly, "you had a different mommy."

Jade's eyes grew wide with anticipation, but she didn't say a word and Reesy didn't expect her to. She just needed to hear what she probably already suspected she knew.

Reesy smiled at her pretty, brilliant girl. "Aunt Connie was your mommy," Reesy went on to explain.

Jade's chin dropped.

Reesy's expression remained soft and easy, open. "She wasn't very happy back then."

"She was sad?" Jade asked, concerned.

Reesy nodded. "Very sad."

Jade thought for a moment. "About me?"

"Oh, no, baby. She wasn't sad about you. She was sad about

things that had happened to her long before you were born, and she couldn't stop being sad, no matter how hard she tried. So, when you were born, she didn't want to be sad in front of you, so she asked me and Daddy to take you until she got over being sad."

Jade was speechless, but only for a moment. "But she didn't stop being sad?"

Reesy kissed her head. "She did. But by that time you were older and we had all decided that you should be our little girl. Connie thought so too. She didn't want you to be confused or afraid, and she saw that you were happy with us. She wanted you to be happy." She smoothed back Jade's hair. "We loved you more and more every day that you lived with us, and Aunt Connie saw that happening and we decided you should stay here with us."

She blinked and stared at Reesy. "Does she remember that she had me?"

"Of course," she said thoughtfully. "She's very proud of you."

"Did Uncle John make her stop being sad?"

Reesy laughed. "I guess he helped."

"Did Jonathon stop making her sad too?" she asked, staring down at the baby in the picture.

"Yes. I think Connie wanted to be a mom after she let you stay with us. I think she deserved to be a mom. Don't you?"

Jade was quiet for several minutes before finally responding. "She's a good mommy."

"Yeah, baby," she said thoughtfully. "She is a good mommy now."

"Do I have to go live with Aunt Connie and Uncle John now?"

Jade's response shocked Reesy more than anything in the world could have. "Do you want to?" she asked quietly. Lord! What would she ever do without her little girl? She'd asked the question because she needed to know, and because Jade needed to know too.

The little girl quickly shook her head. "I want to stay with you and Daddy."

Reesy gathered her daughter up in her arms, and squeezed her tight. "I want you to stay with me and Daddy too, baby. I don't ever want you to leave." She'd started to cry. "I love you so much."

"I love you too, Mommy," Jade said, muffled. "And I love Aunt Connie too, and Jonathon, and Uncle John. But I like my room."

FORTY-NINE

Alice had been kind enough to ride out to the cemetery with Liz. Her mother's gravesite had a simple headstone that said her name, Roberta Brooks, and the years of her lifespan, 1926–1978. Liz laid roses on top of her mother's resting place.

"Growing up, and even after I left and came back, I'd see her sometimes," she said solemnly.

Alice looped her arm with Liz's. "That woman was crazy." She curled the corners of her mouth.

Liz smiled. "I never said nothing to her. She didn't know who I was."

"You believe that?" Alice asked, astonished.

Liz looked at her. "I absolutely do. Don't you?"

"She knew who you were, Liz. She knew who CJ was too. Momma said she used to see her lurking around behind the stands in the stadium when he played football."

Liz looked shocked. "How come you never told me that?"

She shrugged. "I thought you knew. I'd see the way you looked at her when we passed her in town, and I just figured y'all knew who each other was."

"She never looked at me, though."

"After you passed by her she would. I'd see her doing it, and I thought you saw her too. I just thought she was crazy and you didn't want any kind of association with a crazy woman."

They stood quietly next to each other for a few minutes.

"I think she's the reason I never got married."

"You think so?"

"I remember her crying all the time when daddy was gone. She'd sit off somewhere away from me and CJ, and she'd look so sad."

"She knew about that other woman," Alice said matter-of-factly.

"Maybe. Eventually she did. The only time I ever remember her being happy, though, was when she heard his truck pull up in front of the house. All of a sudden, like magic, the tears would stop, and she'd jump up from the floor smiling like it was Christmas. Of course, I don't remember him smiling. Sometimes he would with me, or when he held CJ, but he never looked happy when she was around."

"He didn't want to be with her."

"I never wanted to be married like that," she said introspectively.

"Not everybody's marriage is like that, though, Liz."

"He was absolutely everything to her." She looked at Alice. "Her joy hinged on him. Period. How could you put everything into another human being like that? I never wanted to be like that, dependent on somebody else to make me happy or miserable. There was no gray with Momma and her feelings for Daddy. It was either black or white. Good or bad."

"My marriage ain't like that," Alice argued. "CJ's marriage ain't like that either."

"But for some reason I was always afraid that mine would be," she stressed.

"You sound just like her. Like it's all or nothing."

"Exactly. I saw love through my mother's eyes. I was old enough to learn what she knew about love. CJ was just a baby."

"You know better, though, Liz. You're a smart woman, a writer, and you ain't Roberta."

Liz stared down at her mother's grave. Charles Brooks had been Roberta's whole world when they were married, and Roberta had been Liz's world when she was that small child watching her mother fall apart the minute that man left the house.

"I live my life through the stories I write, Alice," she said softly. "Because I can control what goes on, and I can decide how it ends. But that's the only place I've ever truly lived."

Alice put her arms around Liz and squeezed.

"Daddy's buried over there." She pointed. "Adam's buried at his feet. And Adam's son is the spitting image of the man she loved, and he has a son."

"What are you trying to say?" Alice asked, confused.

"Just that this woman is probably turning over in her grave right now."

Alice laughed. "Child, you know she is."

Liz pulled out her cell phone and dialed CJ's number.

"Hey," she said, smiling. "Did I wake you up?"

"You certainly did," he replied. "But what else is new?"

"I want you to check your e-mail sometime today."

"Okay. Whatchu send me?"

"I sent you some pictures."

"Of who?"

"Call me when you see them. And we'll talk about it then." She sighed.

"Alright, then. You'll be hearing from me."

"I love you."

"Shit. Now you got me worried."

Liz smiled. "Don't you dare be worried, little brother. Don't you know I always take care of you?"

He laughed. "You always did, sister."

"And I always will."

FIFTY

"I spoke to Justin, Mom, and, well, we wanted to know how you'd feel about moving back here to Denver."

Charlotte got tears in her eyes when Reesy called her. "What? Moving back?"

"I know it would be a huge change to uproot your life and come here, but I personally think that it would be for the best. We'd get you your own apartment, something small but nice, and you could be closer to family, Mom. I don't expect you to make a decision right away, but . . ."

"Oh!" Charlotte exclaimed. "I'd love to, Reesy! You have no idea how much it would mean to me to be closer to my family!"

Reesy laughed. "I was hoping you'd feel that way. Look, there's a lot to do to get you ready to come here. I think that either Cammy or I will have to make another trip to Murphy to help get the house in order. Of course, we'll have to put it up for sale."

"I rent this old place, Reesy," Charlotte told her. "I don't own nothing here, except for that car outside."

"Well, even better. We'll have to get the house packed up, then. Justin and I will start looking for a place here for you, and we'll go from there."

This was her dream coming true right here and now. Charlotte was going home again, to stay this time. Deep down she always knew that Reesy would be the one. Reesy came through for her momma in a way those other two never would.

"I love you so much for this, baby," Charlotte said with tears in her eyes.

"Oh, Mom. This is where you belong. It'll all work out, and you'll be home before you know it."

Charlotte had been dancing through her house all morning since she'd gotten off the phone with Reesy, going from room to room, making a mental inventory of what she'd take with her and what she'd throw in the trash. She didn't need that much. Most of what she owned was junk anyway, and the last thing she wanted to do was to move trash into a new apartment.

She finally sat down, exhausted and relishing the idea of what it meant to go home again after all these years. Charlotte had left years ago, thinking she could find a better life someplace else. But it didn't take long for her to realize that the grass wasn't as green as she'd thought it would be on the other side. She had made plenty of mistakes in her life and in her girls' lives, but Charlotte was being given a second chance now. God must've heard her prayers and seen her tears, because her prayers were finally being answered. And just in time too. Her thoughts turned dark and drifted to Uncle.

She hadn't seen or heard from him since the day he'd shown up and met Cammy and Reesy. She felt him, though; his presence lingered in her house like mildew, and her gut instinct warned her that he was still in Murphy. Uncle hadn't said what he wanted. He hadn't told her why he was here, except to pretend he was just catching up with an old friend. She and Uncle weren't friends. The man had tried to kill her. He'd had his so-called associates rape and beat her within inches of her life. He must've known the impact his presence still had on her. Even after all these years, Uncle couldn't have believed that time had been enough to heal the rift between them. More and more, Charlotte was beginning to think that the man was here to finish business he hadn't been able to finish back then. Of course, it didn't make sense. Uncle was an old man now and Charlotte wasn't the beauty queen she'd been back then. But the thought that he'd spent all this time sitting in prison planning for the day when he could see her again sent a shudder through her body. Uncle wasn't like most men. He didn't think the way normal people thought, and she'd be a fool to believe that there was anything normal about him paying her a visit.

"You told him where to find me."

Charlotte hadn't bothered to say hello to Lynn when she called. Lynn had betrayed her; after all these years, Lynn had put Charlotte back in the same line of fire that she'd helped her escape from.

"You know how Uncle is, Charlotte," Lynn responded sheepishly. "I didn't have no choice."

"Why is he here?" Charlotte demanded.

"If you don't know, then how am I supposed to know?"

"I thought you were my friend, Lynn."

"Charlotte," Lynn said irritably. "I don't know what I am to you."

"I told you everything. Everything, Lynn, I . . ." All of a sudden, pieces started to fall into place. "And you told him. Didn't you?"

Lynn didn't say anything.

"That's how he found out about me and Zoo, and about Sam coming back into town. Ain't it!"

"He'd have hurt Arnel if I didn't say nothing!" Lynn shouted. "My God, Charlotte! Do you know the kinds of things he did to Arnel? His own brother? What he woulda done to me?"

Charlotte couldn't believe it. The whole time she was running her mouth to Lynn, thinking that woman was her friend, Lynn was going back and telling Uncle every goddamned thing.

"You set me up," Charlotte said dismally.

"He set us both up. He told me to keep an eye on you. So, that's what I did. I did what I had to do."

Charlotte didn't give a damn what her reasons were. The truth was staring her in the face now, and Lynn was a fuckin' liar. "You almost got me killed," she said in disbelief.

"I saved your life. If I hadn't come through when I did . . ."

"You wouldn't have had to save my life, Lynn, if you hadn't put it out there in the first place! And now you doing it again! You told that fool how to find me after all these years? He ain't threatening Arnel's sorry ass now, Lynn!"

"You don't know that!"

"Arnel's nasty ass is laying up over there with the AIDS! Uncle don't want nothing to do with him now!"

"You know what—"

"Naw, bitch! Do you know what? You putting my ass on the line now because you want to. Ain't that right? You told that niggah where to find me 'cause he asked. This ain't got nothing to do with Arnel, Lynn! This is about you and me! Tell me I'm wrong!"

Lynn didn't respond right away.

"Uncle asked me where you were," she said quietly. "So, I told him."

She and Lynn had a lot of years between them. Truth be known, Lynn had always been Charlotte's only real friend, until now.

"Well, you tell that old mothafucka this, next time you talk to him," Charlotte said indignantly. "You tell him that my baby girl is sending me a ticket and I'm leaving this fuckin' town. You tell him that he ain't never gonna find me again. I don't give a damn how long and how hard he looks. You tell him that he can go to hell, and that he can take your pitiful ass with him when he does."

"Fuck you, Charlotte!"

"Oh, both of y'all already did that, Lynn. You can't hurt me no more and neither can Uncle," she said smugly. "I'm going home, and you, Arnel, and Uncle can kiss my yellow ass when I do."

Charlotte hung up the phone, satisfied, and without so much as a good-bye.

FIFTY-ONE

Reesy had agreed to meet Avery at his office to talk. She sat across from him, looking gorgeous without even trying, and Avery couldn't help but feel enamored.

"After today, you and I will never see each other again, Avery," she said convincingly. "I never meant to lead you on in any way, but it's over. If you want the truth, then I can admit it. I used you to get back at Justin. I'm not proud of that, but that's what this was about for me. And I'm sorry."

If she had meant to hurt his feelings, she'd failed miserably. *Keep on using me until you use me up.* The words to that old Bill Withers song rang loud and clear in his head, and, honestly, Avery could live with being an instrument for revenge.

"I love Justin," she softly admitted. "He and I have reconnected, and for the sake of our children, our marriage, we both want to work through our problems to get our lives back on track. That's just how it is."

She sat patiently, waiting for him to respond. For a moment, he gave some thought to letting her walk out of that door to get back to her life without saying another word. Half the time he couldn't decide if he loved Reesy or just wanted to own and keep her like a trophy, but he cared for her. He'd always cared for her. She was as lovely a woman as he'd ever met, classy, beautiful, and sincere. Avery had come to the conclusion a long time ago that a woman like her was far too good for a cad like him, and even if he did manage to steal her away from her husband, it would only be a matter of time before he fucked up and made a mess of the relationship. She would never be more than a fantasy to Avery, and he'd prop her up on that pedestal he'd built for her and love her from his lowly place on the ground.

Reesy picked up her purse and prepared to leave. "Don't call me anymore, Avery. Please. Just leave us alone."

Something wicked sprung up inside him, and Avery just couldn't let her walk out of that door believing that Justin was the better man. Lisa thought it, and Reesy bought into it, but Avery didn't have it in him to let it go.

"What if I were to tell you that your husband was still involved with the stripper, Reesy?" He chose his words carefully. Justin and Lisa might not have been seeing each other intimately anymore, but they were still involved. From the look he saw on her face, knowing that Justin was still in touch with the woman was more than enough.

"You're doing this to get back at me for ending this relationship, aren't you?" she asked uneasily.

The hurt he saw in her eyes was almost unbearable for Avery, but he'd already crossed the line and turning back now was impossible.

"He sends her money. From what I can see, that's all he's doing." There. He'd told the truth, but that truth hadn't softened the impact of the situation. *Your old man isn't fucking her anymore, Reesy, but he's still giving her money.* "I can prove it."

Reesy didn't ask to see proof. He hadn't expected that she'd need to see any.

"You are good at this," she said, almost smiling. "Aren't you, Avery? Turning my world upside down, almost like it's a game to you."

"It's not a game," he said gravely. "I just think you should know that Justin isn't all that you think he is."

"Neither are you," she said, staring sadly at him.

Reesy left without saying good-bye, and Avery resigned himself to the fact that it really was over between them.

She hadn't said much to him when he came home from work, but Justin just figured that Reesy had had a rough day juggling three rambunctious kids. He helped to get dinner on the table, got the kids off the television long enough to finish homework and get their showers taken, and shuffled them all off to bed with as little chaos as possible. By the time he stepped out of the shower to get ready to go down for the night, Reesy was sitting on the side of the bed, waiting for him, and it was obvious that she'd had more on her mind than the three kids.

"What have we done to ourselves, Justin?" she asked, quietly.

He had no idea what she was talking about, and he smiled and shrugged. "I don't know, Reese," he said jokingly. "What?"

Reesy didn't find it funny, and he soon realized that something was seriously wrong. He sat down on the bed next to her, and as soon as he did, Reesy got up and sat in the chair across the room.

"What's going on, Reesy?" he asked seriously.

Avery was a prick for what he'd done, and despite how gullible he must have thought she was, she knew exactly why he'd done it. And that made him lower than the scum on the bottom of her shoes. But it didn't negate the fact that she and her husband were living a lie.

"You're still seeing her," Reesy stated softly.

Justin was confused at first, but only for a moment. His expression went blank, and his mouth fell open, but words were nowhere to be found.

"I know you are, so don't waste your time lying," she said calmly.

"I wasn't going to lie," he admitted. "I'm not seeing her, Reesy."

"Then what do you want to call it?"

He hadn't laid eyes on Cookie in months. He hadn't wanted to, and only fleetingly did the woman ever even cross his mind, but, from the look on her face, Justin knew that Reesy wouldn't believe him even if he told her that.

"It's not what you think."

She sat quietly, unable to take her eyes off of his, and unwilling to argue or to make a fuss. "You have no idea what I think."

Justin came over to where she was sitting and got down on one knee in front of her. "I made the biggest mistake of my life with her," he explained earnestly. "Nobody knows that better than me."

"No, Justin," she said, leaning forward. "We all know it. Me and the kids, believe me—we most definitely know it."

"But I'm not seeing her now, Reesy. I love you, and I want you, and I'm not putting that at risk again."

"You send her money," she blurted out.

He didn't know how to answer that. He'd sent her money to help her with college. But explaining that to Reesy would only fall on deaf ears, because of course she didn't want to hear that, and she certainly wouldn't be empathetic to the girl's plight, or to his noble efforts. He was sending money to a woman he'd cheated with. It made no difference why.

"It's not what you think," he repeated again, helplessly.

"You know what I think?" she asked. "I think that this fairy tale we've been living is over."

Justin shook his head. "Nah! Reese. No!"

"I think we've spent too much time lying to each other, and pretending to be something that we aren't, Justin."

"I'm sorry," he said desperately. "Reesy. It's not—I just, I wanted to help her." He sounded ridiculous and he knew it. And the way she looked at him confirmed it. "It was money to help her pay for books at college. That's it. That's all it is. I haven't seen or spoken to her at all, Reesy. I swear to God, I haven't."

"I've been having an affair too, Justin." Her voice trailed off. Justin looked like he'd just been kicked in the gut. "You're not the only one who's been betraying our marriage vows." Tears flooded her eyes. "We both have."

Justin sat speechless and confused at her feet.

"I thought it would've been hard, but it wasn't. I thought I'd feel guilty, or that you'd look at me and be able to tell that I'd been cheating on you, but I didn't feel guilty, and it wasn't obvious to you." Justin rose to his feet, studying her, hoping to see some hint that she was only saying this to try and get back at him.

Reesy stood up too.

"Don't do this," he pleaded. "We're back on track here, Reese. We're back to the way we used to be."

"We've pretended to be back on track," she said, forcing a weak smile. "I think we both wanted things to be back to the way they were, but how could they, Justin? How could they when we've both been lying to each other?"

"With who?" he asked desperately. "Who've you been . . ."

She swallowed hard. "I think you know."

Justin backed up and collapsed in the chair behind him. "Avery?"

"Punishment," she said, through tears. "I wanted to punish you, to hurt you, the way you'd hurt me."

Justin stared helplessly at his wife, looking like all the fight had been taken out of him. "Avery."

Reesy shrugged. "It backfired, Justin," she sobbed. "I, I ended up punishing both of us."

Neither of them said another word to the other for the rest of the night. Justin eventually disappeared into the guest room to sleep. But Reesy couldn't sleep. She'd told Justin about Avery out of spite, thinking it would hurt him the way her finding out about his mistress had hurt her. Obviously, it had. What she hadn't counted on was how much it had hurt her to cause him that kind of pain. Her marriage was all but over, and the emptiness left in its place left her feeling cold and lonelier than she'd ever thought it was possible to feel.

FIFTY-TWO

He hadn't seen her for two days, and Cammy was trying to be cute and not return his calls. The last message he left her gave no room for any kind of misinterpretation.

"I don't know why you tripping, Cammy, but uh . . . I ain't the one to be tripping on, baby. We together, right? I'm supposed to be your man? I don't know what's going on with you, but uh . . . I'ma keep it real, C. I ain't into playing games. I call you, and you either answer or call me back. That's what's up."

Isaac couldn't help falling for her the way he did. Cammy was the one, and he knew it, even if she didn't. He was old school when it came to shit like that. Once a man found his woman, he claimed her and he made her his, and he kept her his too. That's just how the shit went down. He'd been through a ton of chicken heads in his life, but Cammy was better than all of them put together. He'd be a fool to let her go. If she wanted him to prove himself to her, to fight for her, then he didn't have a problem with that. Some women had that mentality. They played hard because they wanted you to play harder. Cammy was running because she wanted him to chase her. And Isaac would catch up with her too. Hell yeah, he would.

Isaac had gotten off from work early, drove to Cammy's apartment building, and waited outside in the parking lot. That girl was the skittish type, but he knew a good thing when he saw it. She was the quiet type, knowing when to listen to a man, instead of running her mouth all the damn time. Cammy was gentle and sweet, too damn sweet for a thug like him, but he dug that about her.

Isaac leaned back in his seat and closed his eyes, thinking about the way she smiled, and the softness in her voice. Cammy moved like she was floating through water, gliding smooth and easy and graceful. The night they first met, he'd seen the way other brothas were checking her out, and Isaac made his move before any of them had a chance to. Mothafuckas here were too damn timid, but that played to his advantage. Isaac saw what he wanted and made his move, and before the night was over, he'd won the prize.

He was getting impatient, and Isaac decided to text her this time.

GIRL WHERE U AT?

"Man, why you be sweatin' that bitch?" One of his boys had asked him. *"Females is plentiful, playa. She ain't nothin' but a blade of grass. Got plenty more where she came from."*

That fool had no idea what he was talking about. Cammy wasn't just any female. And Isaac wasn't down for the foolishness anymore. He'd fucked around long enough, and now he was ready to do that husband thing, find a nice woman and start a family. He laughed out loud at the thought. Never in a million years did he ever think he'd find himself thinking like that, but hell . . . that's what he wanted, and he wanted it with her.

The sound of her voice caught his attention. Isaac sat up and saw Cammy getting out of her car, carrying a bag of groceries with that damn phone to her ear. She obviously wasn't talking to him, so who the hell was she running her mouth to?

"Can't we just talk about this?" she asked, sounding upset. "Ty! Tyrell, I know . . ."

Cammy stopped walking. Isaac stopped behind her.

"You know what I've been going through," she said. "I know, but seeing you again . . . It made me realize how much you mean to me, and how lonely I am without you."

Isaac eased closer to her.

"We can work through that. I know I keep saying that but I mean it. I believe in us, Ty. I have to, 'cause what else do I have? I love you."

She wasn't talking to Isaac. Rage engulfed him and the next thing he knew, he had a handful of that woman's hair in one hand and was snatching the phone from her ear with the other.

"Who the fuck you talking to, C?" Isaac put the phone to his ear. "Who the fuck is this?"

"Who the fuck is this?" Ty answered angrily. "Where's Cammy? Put her on the phone!"

"Fuck you!" Isaac dropped the phone to the ground and stomped it under his feet.

"Isaac!" Cammy sobbed.

He dragged her across the parking lot to a more secluded place next to the building, and slammed her back up against the wall.

"I been calling your ass and you on the fuckin' phone with some other mothafucka?" he said, gritting his teeth. Isaac put almost all his weight against her, squeezing the air out of her.

"Isaac," she mouthed. "Stop it!"

"Naw, bitch!" He glared at her. "You stop it! What the fuck you think you doing? Huh? You think I'm playing? You think I'm bullshitting with you?"

Cammy's eyes grew wide with fear. "Let me go, Isaac," she demanded, trying to compose herself.

"Naw, C. I ain't letting you go. I ain't ever letting you go. And next time that mothafucka calls you, you be sure to let him know that."

He pulled her by the collar of her jacket into the building, dragging her to her apartment. "Open the goddamned door!" he said angrily in her ear.

Cammy shook her head. "Let me go, or I'll scream," she threatened.

Isaac put his hand around her neck and squeezed. "Scream, C," he said matter-of-factly.

Cammy couldn't breathe. She scratched at his hand to get him to let go, but Isaac only tightened his grip.

"Open the fuckin' door or I swear I'll put your ass down right here."

He released his grip long enough for her to unlock the door, and then Isaac pushed her inside and locked it behind them.

FIFTY-THREE

"Is Cammy coming?" Connie asked Reesy as she followed her into Reesy's kitchen.

"She said she's not feeling well," Reesy responded.

Connie wasn't surprised, and Reesy didn't sound as if she was either. Sister-meeting rule number one: don't expect Cammy to show up if she can find an excuse to get out of it.

"It's okay, though." Reesy poured Connie a glass of iced tea.

"Decaf?" Connie asked.

"Decaf."

The kids were at school, and Justin was at the office. Jonathon was sound asleep in the baby carrier.

"How was your trip?" Connie decided to ask.

Reesy looked at her with a funny expression on her face. "I know you did not just ask me that."

"What?" Connie said, taking a bite out of a cookie. "I'm curious."

"Why? You hate your mother."

"No. I hate your mother. Charlotte was just the vessel I had to pass through to get to this planet. That's all."

Reesy shook her head. "It was fine. You know. We're talking

about Charlotte, after all. And Cammy, who did a one-eighty the minute she set foot inside the house."

"Meaning?"

"Meaning she reverted back into being Charlotte's go-to girl, foot soldier, handmaiden. Whatever you want to call it."

"Really?"

"Yeah. She couldn't do enough for the woman," Reesy said, concerned. "If Charlotte had told her to bend over backward and kiss the ground, I think she would've tried it."

Connie wasn't surprised by that either. "Cammy's confused, Reese." She sighed.

"That's an understatement. I kept waiting for her to snap out of this trance she seems to be in, and when she did finally show some enthusiasm, it happened there. In the very same environment she couldn't wait to get out of."

"Cammy never said she wanted to leave Kansas," Connie said casually.

Reesy stared at her. "Of course she wanted to leave. She needed to leave."

Connie shrugged. "Maybe."

"You think it was wrong to move her out here?"

"I think that we should've asked if she wanted to move out here."

"But if she'd stayed, Connie, she'd still be waiting on Charlotte like a slave with no life and no prospects for one."

"I don't know. I'm just saying, she doesn't seem like she wants to be here. She doesn't seem like she wants to be here with us. She's not trying to make a life for herself."

"Sounds like somebody's talking from experience," Reesy responded.

"Don't trip," Connie said, picking up another cookie. "My life is fine."

"Yeah, now. But you were as lost as she was at one point."

"True. Wallowing in self-pity can become addictive, but I'm so not there anymore. And you know it." She dared Reesy to argue.

Reesy threw her hands up in surrender. "I know. I know."

Connie had come a long way in the years since she and Reesy had reunited after being separated when they were children. She'd fought tooth and nail to get over the tragedy that had once been her life and she had no intention of ever going back to that dark place again. Cammy still had a long way to go before she saw the light, and there was no guarantee that she ever would.

"Hey, Connie." Justin surprised them both and was home early. He came over and kissed her on the cheek.

"Hey." She smiled.

Reesy had a strange look on her face. "What are you doing home so early?"

He barely even glanced in her direction. "I came back to get something." Justin headed out of the kitchen.

Reesy had a look of disappointment in her eyes that Connie hadn't seen since she'd told her that there was no Santa Claus.

"What's wrong?"

Reesy forced a smile. "Nothing."

Connie wasn't buying it and it didn't take long for Reesy to figure that out.

"We're separating," she quietly confessed.

"What?" Connie asked, shocked. "I thought the two of you were doing okay."

"We were."

"Were? What's going on?"

Reesy hesitated, searching her thoughts for where to begin. "I found out that he's still in contact with the woman he had the affair with," she explained.

Disappointment washed over Connie's face. "Oh no! Reesy?"

Lord! What was it with men and their dicks? John and the country bumpkin in Texas and Justin and the stripper . . .

Connie thought about telling her tale of woe to Reesy about John's escapades in Texas, but decided that this was not a time to try and one-up anybody. Justin had walked on water in everybody's eyes and now he was sinking like a rock, straight to the bottom, and deservedly so.

Reesy sighed, and reluctantly continued. "I cheated on him, Connie," she admitted.

Connie nearly threw up the cookies she'd eaten. "You what?"

Reesy couldn't bring herself to repeat it, but Connie had heard her loud and clear the first time.

Reesy had cheated on Justin? What did that mean? Connie struggled to compute her sister's confession. Reesy didn't do things like that. She was perfect and incapable of doing something as lowly as being unfaithful in her marriage. Everyone who knew Reesy had put her up on a pedestal that reached heaven because she was the good one. The perfect one. The one without flaw or blemish. Connie and Cammy might've been messes, but not Reesy, and she'd never failed to remind them of that fact.

"Why?" Connie asked, astounded.

Reesy jumped at the sound of the front door slamming shut. Justin had left without saying good-bye.

"Why is he still sending her money?" Reesy said, choking back sobs.

"He's sending . . ."

"He says it's to help pay her way through school." Her voice cracked. "That's bullshit."

Even the word "bullshit" sounded odd coming from Reesy.

"Why would he do that?"

"Oh, you know Justin," she said sarcastically. "He's just a swell guy."

"And that's why you cheated on him?"

"No, Connie. I cheated on him because . . ."

Connie waited for Reesy to find her answer to the question.

"I just did," she said sadly.

"With who?"

She glared at her sister. "It doesn't matter."

"That detective."

"I said it doesn't matter!"

"Reesy," Connie said, sounding hopeless. If Justin and Reesy couldn't make their relationship work, then what hope was there for everybody else?

"I told Jade that you were her birth mother," Reesy suddenly blurted out.

Connie was beyond stunned. If Reesy wanted to change the subject, then she'd just done one hell of a job. "What?" she whispered.

Reesy started pacing back and forth in the kitchen. "I had to."

Connie had no idea what to say next. They'd agreed to talk to Jade together. She'd been rehearsing her part for months now and the last thing she'd expected was for Reesy to take it upon herself to . . .

"I can't believe you did that," Connie replied in disbelief. All of a sudden, she began to feel sick to her stomach. "This is all too much," Connie said, slowly swaying in her seat. Justin cheated, and now Reesy had admitted to cheating, and Jade, her little girl, knew the whole truth.

Reesy stopped and looked at her. "I would've waited, Connie, but she came to me, and she just looked like she . . . like she knew, but didn't. Like she had questions and needed me to give her the answers."

"We were supposed to do it together, Reese," Connie said austerely.

"The opportunity was there, Connie. It was wide open and right and . . ." She shrugged. "I did what I felt I had to do."

Connie swallowed and took a sip of her drink. She stood up and gathered her diaper bag and son. "I, uh . . . How did she . . ." She looked desperately to Reesy. "Does she hate me?"

"No, sweetie," she said tenderly. "She doesn't hate you."

Connie stared pitifully at Reesy. "She probably hates me, Reese."

Reesy rushed over to her. "No, Connie! No, she doesn't."

Connie felt unsteady on her feet for a moment, and then hurried out of the kitchen without saying another word.

"Connie!"

FIFTY-FOUR

It hadn't been that long ago that Charlotte would've seen Reesy's number come up on her caller ID and avoided it like the plague, but these days when her baby girl called, she couldn't get to the phone fast enough.

Charlotte had started cleaning out closets and packing ever since Reesy had told her that she was sending for her to come home. It had been years since she'd had something to look forward to, and now her greatest dream was about to become a reality and she could hardly contain herself.

"Hello, Love Bug," she said warmly when she picked up the phone.

"Hey, Momma. How are you?"

Charlotte hadn't been able to be anything but happy since she found out she was moving back home. "Wonderful. I'm just wonderful, baby. How are you?"

Charlotte was so consumed by her own joy that she failed to notice the hesitation coming from Reesy.

"Mom, I'm calling because, well . . . We're going to have to hold off on moving you out here for a while."

Hold off? What the hell did she mean, hold off? Charlotte sat down, thinking she must have misunderstood her. "What do you mean, Clarice?" Charlotte asked apprehensively.

Reesy cleared her throat. "Justin and I are, well, we have some issues that we need to try and work through and this just wouldn't be a good time for you to make such a big move."

Charlotte struggled to maintain her composure. She and Justin had issues? What did that have to do with moving her to Denver?

"Mom? Are you there?"

"I don't understand, Reesy," Charlotte said, nearly choking on her anger. "Why can't I come?"

"We're having problems," she said wearily. "I don't know if Justin and I will stay married."

"But what does that have to do with me, Clarice?"

Reesy was quiet on the other end of the phone for longer than Charlotte was comfortable with. "Reesy?" she called her daughter's name sternly. "Answer me."

"I have to go, Charlotte," Reesy suddenly said. "We'll talk about it later."

Charlotte listened as Reesy hung up the phone, a sound that resonated like the world crashing down around her. All of her hopes and dreams had gone up in smoke, just like that. And Reesy had played such a terrible trick on her. Charlotte had been a fool, almost believing that, for once, things were going her way and that she could finally be free of this tomb called Murphy once and for all. Lord! Why? Why had she been led to believe that goodness was finally coming her way? She should've known better than to believe it, though. Depression weighed down on top of her, and Charlotte felt like she was being buried alive.

———

She had no idea how much time had passed when she heard the doorbell ring. Charlotte managed to drag her heavy frame across the room to answer it, without bothering to ask who it was.

"Just to be close to you, girl . . ." Uncle sang the old Commodores tune as soon as he laid eyes on Charlotte when she answered the door, and then he laughed. "And I'll bet you never thought you'd ever see me again."

He didn't wait to be invited in. Uncle suspected that he was about as welcome as a hemorrhoid, but what difference did it make? He was here, and she was here, and all was right with the mean old world again.

Charlotte stood in the doorway, so stunned she couldn't move, not even to close the door behind him. Fear left her frozen where she stood. Uncle reached over her and pushed the door shut.

"Close your mouth, baby. You giving me ideas." He winked.

Uncle slowly walked into the living room and surveyed the humble surroundings. Everything about this broad was raggedy now, he thought to himself. But then again, it always had been. Back in the day, though, she had been too damn fine for him to notice or care.

He sat down in the middle of the sofa and stared back up at Charlotte, who was still gawking at him from across the small room. "Sit your ass down, girl," he insisted. "You gonna give me a crick in my neck standing all the way over there."

Charlotte moved slowly, robotically, as she was told, and sat down in the floral armchair across from him. She never once took her eyes off of him.

"You as glad to see me again as I am to see you?" he asked mischievously, his eyes twinkling. "Tell the truth."

"No," she mouthed.

"I didn't think so," he responded. "I messed you up good.

Didn't I?" He pointed to her face, and then drew an invisible line from the corner of his mouth to his ear along his jawbone. "Damn! I didn't think I hit you that hard. That's fucked up, baby. I apologize for that," he said sincerely. "I really do."

Charlotte shivered at the nonexistent chill filling the room. She couldn't take her eyes off the man.

"You too damn good to me, Uncle," she'd told him once. *"Ain't nobody ever been as good to me as you. Whatchu want, daddy? I'm here to serve."*

He gave her whatever she asked for, and, in return, all she ever had to do was fuck him.

"I know you never wanted to see me again," he explained carefully, unwilling to take his eyes off hers. "But I could've told you, darlin'—you can't trust Lynn's pitiful ass as far as you can throw her." He chuckled.

Charlotte finally found the courage to speak. "L-Lynn told you how to find me."

Uncle smiled. "She told me where she put you not long after she got back to Kansas City," he admitted. "I'd have paid you a visit back then but—well, let's just say I had some business to take care of first."

Charlotte swallowed hard, and then worked up the courage to ask the question. "You here to kill me, Uncle?" Her voice quivered.

"Why?" he asked, grinning. "You think I should?"

She didn't respond.

"I been rehabilitated, baby," Uncle confessed. "The last time I killed anybody was the night you left," he said coolly. "You recall that?"

He knew she did. Uncle had put a gun to Zoo's head and shot that boy, right in front of Charlotte's eyes.

"It hurt me to have to do it. I really liked that boy," he said fondly. "But I let my temper get the best of me that night, and I paid dearly for it."

Charlotte had paid for it too. She'd lived with the scars of what he'd done to her, inside and out, for close to thirty years, and the fear that one day he'd find her and finish what he started. Why else would he be here?

"I sure am thirsty, baby," he said casually. "Why don't you go get me something to drink." Uncle smiled broadly, knowing he wouldn't have to ask twice. "I promise, I'll be here when you get back. We got a whole lot of catching up to do before it's over, girl."

Charlotte got up and headed for the kitchen.

"And what's for supper?" Uncle called behind her. "I got a taste for some fried chicken. You always did make the best friend chicken."

FIFTY-FIVE

Justin burst into Avery's office without bothering to knock.

"I gotta go," Avery told the person on the phone. He hurried and hung up.

"You're dead!" Justin yelled. He came around the desk, and Avery managed to get to his feet just in time to receive a right hook from Justin.

Avery swung back, but missed, and Justin hit him again. Avery spit blood on the floor near his desk, and then luckily managed to block another punch coming from Justin.

"She had a right to know!" Avery shouted as he moved quickly and managed to push Justin back across the room until his back was pressed up against the wall. "I'm not your problem, man! You are," Avery said, out of breath. "You are!"

"You want her." Justin said, out of breath. He twisted his body until he was free from Avery's grip, and grabbed him by the collar, then pushed him so hard that Avery fell backward, toppling over a chair. "That's what this is about!" Justin stalked him. "You want my fuckin' wife, man? You've been sleeping with my wife?"

Avery looked stunned that he knew.

Justin nodded. "Yeah! She told me. She told me every god-damned thing!"

"I told her the truth," he said, standing to his feet. "She should know the truth!"

Justin stared at Avery like the man had lost his fucking mind. "You don't give a damn about truth, Avery. This is about Reesy. You've always wanted her, and the only reason you told her this shit was to get her to come to you!"

"You're the one who fucked around on his wife, Justin!" Avery yelled. "Reesy's too blinded by your fuckin' light to see that you're not who you pretend to be."

"So this is about me, then," Justin said, finally seeing the truth. "You trying to get back at me. For fucking your daughter, Avery, or for caring more about her than you ever did?"

"I love my kid."

"Yeah," Justin said sarcastically. "You damn near sounded like you meant it, man."

Justin shook his head in awe at this sonofabitch who had the nerve to sit in judgment of Justin after all the shit he'd pulled. Avery Stallings was a sonofabitch playing games with people's lives, pretending to care for Reesy, when it was clear as day that the only person his ass cared about was himself. "Reesy ain't go-ing nowhere, man," Justin said with confidence. "She might not want me anymore, but I guarantee you, she definitely won't be running to your ass for solace."

"She did once," Avery said through his bloody smile. "She'll do it again."

"Tell me something, Avery. Did you ever tell her who that woman was in the photograph? Did you ever tell her that Cookie is your daughter?"

"What difference would that make?"

"Truth, man. You're so fuckin' driven by making sure my wife knows the truth. But you only want to make sure she knows your version of it."

"Pictures don't lie, Justin. You were getting it on with another woman, and that's the truth. And as far as appearances go, you still are. Look, if turning this shit around on me is going to make you feel better, Justin, that's fine. You had an affair with another woman. That's fact. You're still in contact with this other woman. Another fact. What the hell do you think your wife is supposed to think?"

Talking to Avery wasn't getting him anywhere. But everything Avery Stallings had done to Justin had all been by design, and it had all been done to accomplish one thing. "Reesy's going to think whatever she wants to think, man," he said wearily.

He and Reesy hadn't spoken to each other in days, since he'd found out about her affair. They put up appearances for the sake of the kids, but the truth was their marriage was probably over, and maybe that was as it should be. The trust was gone. The commitment was shattered. And they were fast becoming strangers to each other. "But she's not dumb. I guarantee you that whatever bullshit persona you wear when she's around is rice-paper thin, and it won't take her long to see right through it, and you too."

Avery leaned back confidently. "Your wife came to me before, Justin," he said calmly. "I was there for her in ways you don't want to imagine, man. And I'll be there for her again."

Justin bolted to his feet, crossed the room, and lunged at Avery, knocking him backward in his chair to the floor.

"Justin!" Reesy called out his name from the door.

Justin's fist stopped inches away from Avery's face.

"Stop it, Justin," she said to him. "He's not worth it." She wouldn't even look at Avery. "Come with me and let's go home."

Justin slowly stepped back away from Avery, and finally turned to Reesy.

He shrugged and shook his head. "Go home to what, Reese?" he asked, defeated. "What the hell do I have to come home to?"

She'd punished him for his transgression, tortured him for betraying her trust and their marriage, and then she'd turned around and done the same exact thing.

Reesy's eyes filled with tears. "Beating him up isn't going to help matters. The damage is done, Justin. Now it's time for us to figure out our next move," she said softly.

Justin stared back at her. "Obviously, family doesn't mean as much to either of us as we thought, Clarice."

"That's not true." Reesy's voice cracked. "That's not true and you know it."

Avery made it to his feet and stood behind Justin, staring longingly at Reesy. "Nothing's changed, Clarice," he said. "I care so much about you."

She looked at Avery. "Shut up!"

"You came to me," Avery argued. "When you needed someone, you came to me."

Reesy turned her attention to Justin. "I was angry with you, and I couldn't forgive you for what you did. And I made I mistake, Justin. Just like you, I made a terrible mistake."

"You don't make mistakes, Reesy," Justin said sadly. "Everybody else does, but not you. You're righteous. Remember? You're always on point, and everybody else is wrong. I cheated on you." He shrugged. "My sin was unforgivable. But you cheat on me, and you want to talk things through? What? Like I'm supposed to turn the other cheek and forgive you, like I wanted you to forgive me?"

Reesy didn't know how to respond. He was right. Reesy had lived her life in excellence, being careful to raise the perfect kids, be the perfect wife and daughter. She'd stood atop her pedestal, looking down her nose at anyone who'd lived short of her expectations, knowing that no one, not Justin or Connie, or even Cammy, could point at her and condemn her for anything. She'd let go of her ideals to be with Avery. And she'd used Justin as her excuse.

"I've messed up, Justin," she said quietly. "I'm sorry. That's all I can say. I am so sorry."

"We're all fuckin' sorry, Reesy." Justin turned to Avery. "Almost all of us." He turned back to Reesy. "I tried, baby. I tried to make it up to you the only way I knew how, and it wasn't enough."

Reesy walked over to him. "What do you want me to say?" She stared deeply into his eyes. Yes, they'd both made mistakes, and yes, they'd both done things to put their relationship in jeopardy, but for the first time in a very long time, she had more faith in her marriage, in him, than she'd ever had in all the years she'd known him. "I have you," she whispered. "And I want to make this work, Justin."

Justin nodded reluctantly. He loved her. Reesy was everything to him, and living without her was something he could never fathom. "Now, I'm the one who needs time, Reesy."

He brushed past her and left the room.

"He's still wrong, Reesy," Avery argued. "He's still involved with the same woman he cheated on you with."

"Your daughter. Right, Avery?"

He stared blankly at her.

"I heard."

Reesy never said good-bye. In the depths of his heart, he willed for her to someday come knocking on his door again, needing someone to listen and be her friend again. He savored the day she'd be back in his arms, and in his bed. But deep down inside, Avery knew that those things would never happen.

FIFTY-SIX

It was late when John finally made it home. Since coming back from Texas, he seemed to have more work than he could handle, and even with hiring half a dozen new guys in the last week, there was still more work than bodies. Connie was sitting in the living room, feeding Jonathon, when he walked in. John grunted something that was supposed to sound like hello, went into the kitchen, and pulled out a beer. He finished it without coming up for air and then reached for another, which he planned on enjoying this time.

"Sara called," Connie said, coming into the kitchen.

John closed the refrigerator door and sat down at the table. *Sara called.* That was the longest sentence Connie had said to him since Adam's funeral.

"She wanted to know how you were doing."

He was too tired to even respond.

Connie set a plate down in front of him, and then sat down at the table too. Instinctively, he knew what was coming next. John started eating, hoping that chewing would drown out the words about to come out of her mouth.

"We need to talk, John."

"Not now, Connie," he said between bites.

"You always say that."

John nodded, and continued shoveling mashed potatoes into his mouth.

"I can't just act like it didn't happen and you can't just make it go away."

When he wouldn't stop eating, she did the unthinkable and pulled his plate out from under him.

"Can I eat?" he said irritably. "Can I just eat?"

"Talk to me!"

"About what?"

Connie stared at him like he'd lost his damn mind. "You know about what. About Racine."

John looked at his food. "Give me back my plate, Connie," he demanded.

Reluctantly, she slid it back over to him. "I need to know what happened."

John went back to eating. "You know what happened."

"Then I need to know why."

This time, he looked at her like she was the crazy one.

"I know we were having problems, John, but why would you do something like that?"

That must've been one of those trick questions women know how to ask better than men know how to answer. It was a trap, and no matter what he said, it would be dead-ass wrong and loaded with all the ammunition she'd need to do whatever it was she had already made up her mind she wanted to do. He didn't tell her, but internally, John was pleading the fifth.

"I'd always believed our love was stronger than that," she said softly. Connie studied him, waiting for a response, but of course none came. "I can't live with it, John. I can't let it go."

He stopped eating and stared back at her. "It didn't mean any-thing, Connie."

"It did to me."

The food was starting to feel like lead in his belly, and John put down his fork and pushed his plate away from him. Connie was too good at this shit, and whether she wanted to admit to it or not, she always had a way of making it too damn easy for him. She had this thing about pushing a brotha away whenever she thought things were getting tough. John had this thing about leaving when things started to get too tough. He'd been working hard to change his old habits, but, once again, she was sitting here, getting ready to tell him that he needed to walk.

"I think that we should—"

He'd already wrapped his mind around what she was about to say when the sound of the doorbell ringing and banging on the door interrupted her.

"Connie! Connie! Let me in!"

John got up and swung open the door and a terrified Cammy bolted past him and ran into the house, crying hysterically.

"Oh, God! Oh!"

Connie hurried to her. "Cammy? What's wrong? What's hap-pening?"

John watched a black Chrysler pull up behind Cammy's car in front of the house. Some young cat jumped out, looking crazy. He stopped short when he saw John coming out of the house.

"Yo, man! I'm looking for Cammy!"

John stood on the front steps sizing this dude up. "She's in-side," he said calmly.

"Go get her, man! I need to talk to her."

John glared at him.

"I ain't playing, man!" The young dude paced back and forth

like a leopard in the front yard. "Send her out here! I need to talk to her."

John didn't know what was going on, but he knew he didn't want this nonsense happening at his house. "Why don't you just leave? Cammy obviously doesn't want to talk and we don't need no trouble here."

The dude stepped closer to John. "This ain't got nothing to do with you, brotha. Just send Cammy out here, and we'll be on our way."

"I said no, man."

The next thing John knew, this fool reached behind him and pulled out a 9mm. He didn't point it at John, but he might as well have.

"Send her on out here, brotha," he demanded nervously.

This was a worse ending to a bad day, and John had had enough. He walked down the steps toward this fool, who decided to do the wrong thing and actually point that thing in John's direction.

"John! No!" He heard Connie's voice come from inside the house.

"You gonna shoot me, mothafucka?" he asked, stalking the man.

"Man, don't make me!" he said, backing up toward the street.

Rage surged through his veins and pumped like drums in his chest. John hadn't felt this angry in years, and if that mothafucka was lucky, he'd get off a shot before John put his hands on him.

"I'm a moose, man, and for your sake, you'd better have plenty of bullets in that bitch if you plan on taking me down, 'cause you gonna need 'em!"

John's knees ached from installing hardwood floors all day, but he'd chase this bitch down if he didn't put that piece back in his pants.

"John!" Connie shouted again.

"Isaac! Put the gun down!" Cammy shouted. "Isaac, please!"

Isaac crossed to the other side of the street, and John continued to stalk him. He'd fired a fool today, leaving John to have to pick up the slack. One of his suppliers had ordered the wrong fuckin' windows, causing a job to have to be pushed back another two weeks. Somehow, somebody had gotten his number and had been blowing up his phone all damn day about a leaky roof, and a god-damned garage door had come off the hinges and needed to be put back on. John didn't do garage doors! And to top it all off, Connie was still holding on tough to this Racine thing like a pit bull, and was ready to send his ass packing over shit that happened when they weren't even together. This fool picked the wrong damn day to show up at John's door.

"Back off, man!" Isaac shouted.

John felt like a beast ready to tear the flesh off this fool with his bare hands.

He must've looked like one too, because the next thing he knew, Isaac had dropped the gun and took off running. He made a huge loop around John, then jumped into his car and hauled ass down the street.

"What's going on, Cammy?" Connie turned to her. "Who the hell was that?"

Cammy had tears streaming down her cheeks, and she reeked of alcohol. She shakily sat down on the sofa. "He's just . . . somebody I know."

"What the hell is wrong with you?" Connie asked, appalled. "My God, Cammy! That fool had a gun!"

Cammy stared pathetically at her. "I didn't know," she whispered.

Connie composed herself and sat down next to her. Cammy was a mess, and not just now, but she'd been a mess for far too long, and it was only getting worse with time. Cammy turned away from Connie ashamedly, but Connie put a hand underneath her sister's chin and made Cammy face her.

"Cammy," she said tenderly. "Baby, I don't know what you're going through, but you're going to have to deal with it."

"I'm fine, Connie," she protested weakly.

"No. Cammy, you're not fine. I don't think you've ever been fine." Cammy bravely looked into Connie's eyes.

"You need help. Reesy and I can't help you, unless you tell us what's going on."

Cammy's lip quivered. "I don't know, Connie," she sobbed. "I don't know what's wrong with me."

Connie could guess some of the things happening to Cammy. She'd lost her baby in that car wreck, and some of what she was dealing with probably had a lot to do with that. She'd been uprooted from the only home and life she'd ever known and then thrust out here into a world totally foreign to her, with no type of preparation whatsoever for how to deal with the world on her own. Everyone just assumed that a woman her age should know, but how could she, when she'd been told what to do her whole life by someone else?

Connie put her arms around her and held her. "I want you to stay here tonight," she said gently. "Will you do that for me? And tomorrow, you and me can talk. I mean really talk, Cammy. Can you do that?"

Cammy nodded meekly.

John came in a few minutes after Cammy went upstairs to the spare bedroom, looking like something wild and ferocious off of the National Geographic channel.

Connie rushed over to him and punched him hard in the chest. "What the hell is wrong with you!" she shouted.

He stared blankly at her.

Connie pummeled him some more. "He could've shot you, John!" she said, beating him in the arms, chest, and she even managed to get a blow in to his stomach.

"He wasn't going to shoot nobody," he said indifferently, heading back into the kitchen. John hadn't finished eating and he hoped his food hadn't gotten cold.

Connie sat across from him, glaring at him like he was evil. "What if he'd have pulled the trigger?"

He shrugged. "He wasn't going to."

"What if he had!"

"Then you and me wouldn't be having this conversation right now," he said, annoyed. "Would we?"

Connie struggled with all of her might not to laugh, but she failed. "You are a moron!"

FIFTY-SEVEN

Justin hadn't seen Cookie, Lisa, in months. Back then, she'd looked like a stripper, but now she looked just like a college student. She'd called his office asking if it would be alright to come by. Given the circumstances, Justin agreed. His life had gone to shit, so seeing his ex-mistress couldn't do any more harm.

She came into his office and sat down across from him. She smiled and looked even younger. "Fancy digs," she said, scanning his office.

It was still hard for him not to have a crush on a gorgeous woman like Lisa. The first time he'd seen her at the club, she came out dressed in white see-through chiffon. Justin couldn't take his eyes off of her, and watching her had been an out-of-body experience.

"Thanks for agreeing to see me, Justin."

"How've you been?" he asked warmly.

She rolled her eyes and sighed. "Busy. School ain't no joke. If I'm not reading, I'm writing papers, or taking tests. It's crazy."

"You'll be fine," he said reassuringly. "I've got faith in you."

She stared sincerely at him. "Yeah. And I appreciate you for it."

Sitting across from this woman, Justin felt like an old man, weary and drained. He had no business recalling any of the memories he had of the two of them together, but it was almost impossible not to. He'd been a fool back then, caught up in the fantasy that she wasn't with him for the money. Justin must've spent a couple grand on Cookie, Lisa, back then. For him, though, it hadn't been about the money. He'd needed her company, and to feel like he was needed by somebody other than the kids. Reesy had been so caught up in finding her mother that Justin seemed to be more of an annoyance to his wife than anything else. He'd paid Lisa to fill a void, and, right or wrong, it's what he thought he needed back then more than anything.

"I wanted to talk to you because I think Avery might be up to something," she quietly explained. "Lately, I've been hearing from him more than I have my entire life, and he's been asking questions."

"You came to warn me?" He almost smiled.

"He may be trying to stir up trouble, Justin. He keeps asking me if I'm still seeing you, and I just tell him it's none of his goddamned business, but like always, he's not listening to me."

"Avery's beaten you to the punch, Lisa," Justin said calmly.

Her eyes widened. "Have you spoken to him?"

"In a matter of speaking. Yes. We've talked."

"Justin." She suddenly got defensive. "Believe me, I haven't said anything to him about you and me. There is no you and me, so whatever he's done . . ."

"It's alright," he said, trying to calm her down. "Whatever damage that was left to do to my marriage has been done, Lisa. And I take full responsibility for all of it. I don't blame you."

"What happened, Justin?" she asked solemnly.

Justin wrestled internally with telling her the whole truth. The bottom line was that Lisa and her father were at the center of all of the troubles he and Reesy were having. These two people had been the reason that everything he'd ever valued was damaged irreparably. And Justin suddenly wished he'd never laid eyes on either one of them.

"I think you should leave, Lisa," he said as gently as he could.

She looked concerned. "Justin?"

He cleared his throat. "Really. You should go."

She hated seeing him hurt like this. Lisa cared about Justin. She'd even go as far as to say she was in love with him, but she knew better than to ever tell him that. She stood up to leave, stopped short of walking through the door, and turned to him.

"I'm really sorry."

"So am I."

Justin made it a point to stay away from the house as often as he could these days. By the time he made it home, the kids were in bed, and Reesy was just coming out of the shower. Justin sat on the side of the bed, pulling off his shoes.

Conversation between them was practically nonexistent, the air between them strained. She crawled into bed and turned off the light on the nightstand. Justin disappeared into the bathroom to shower, hoping that by the time he came out, she'd at least pretend to be asleep.

Justin had been standing under the water long after he'd bathed himself. It was easier to believe he could flap his wings and fly than it was to believe that Reesy would sleep with somebody else. Justin could admit that he'd been wrong about continuing any kind of relationship with Lisa. No matter how many ways he found to justify it, the truth was he should've cut his ties and left them that way.

Reesy had lied when she told him that she wanted to try to put their marriage back on track. That's the part he couldn't understand. Justin had been moved out of the house for nearly six months when she agreed to let him move home again.

"We've been together too long, have too much at stake, to let our marriage fall apart over this, Reesy," he'd argued. "I love you and my kids, and I made a mistake. But in all the years we've been together, I've worked—we've worked—hard to build a family that we both can be proud of. Please. Don't throw it all away over this."

Justin had begged for a second chance, because Reesy was worth it. But then, that's what she wanted him and everybody around her to think. She was the victim, and everything wrong in their marriage had been his fault. Never mind the fact that she had become so obsessed with tracking down her long-lost mother that she'd practically turned her back on him completely. Justin was a nuisance, inconsiderate and impatient, unable to sympathize with her plight. He was the selfish one. And as usual, she was blameless. Now, she was as guilty as he was, but even now she still had a way of making him feel that her infidelity was his fault.

He came out of the shower and climbed into bed next to her. She wasn't asleep, but Reesy had her back turned to him, giving him the message that she wasn't in the mood for any type of conversation.

"I found a place," he said quietly.

He didn't expect a response, and he didn't get one.

"I'll be moving out in a few weeks."

She waited a few minutes before finally responding. "We'll need to explain it to the kids."

He sighed. "Yeah."

"What should we do about the house?" she asked softly.

"What do you mean?"

She finally turned over on her back and stared up at the ceiling. "I'm not going to be able to afford to keep it on my own, Justin. The kids and I—"

"Will be fine," he interrupted. "Don't worry about the house."

Reesy swallowed. "This is really happening. Isn't it? I don't think I ever believed it before, but . . . it's really over."

"I guess it is, Reese." Justin felt himself start to choke up. He'd loved this woman since he first laid eyes on her in college, and he couldn't remember a moment when he didn't love her.

"We could've done better," she sobbed.

"Maybe we did the best we could."

Reesy shook her head. "No. We could've done so much better." She turned and looked at him. "I didn't love him."

"I know, Reesy. I never loved her."

She smiled weakly. "Then our marriage ended over absolutely nothing, Justin. And that's too bad." Reesy turned her back to him again, and cried quietly until she eventually fell asleep.

FIFTY-EIGHT

He called it "seasoning the beef" when he found an inexperienced girl he'd planned on putting on the streets. Uncle had parties for events like this, celebrating a girl's transition into woman-hood. Usually, the girl wasn't a virgin, but she was young and had been swept off her feet by somebody working for Uncle who'd convinced her that he loved her and made her fall in love with him, before putting her to work for Uncle.

Charlotte hated those parties, but for some reason he insisted on bringing her anyway, despite her protests.

"Sit down, honey girl," he commanded, patting the seat next to him. "Gerard! You bring the liquor?"

"Got it right here, Uncle!" Gerard laughed. "What's yo' pleasure?"

Johnnie Taylor records spun continuously on the record player. A thick layer of marijuana smoke permeated the entire apartment, couples danced in the middle of the room, and chips, dip, fried chicken, and potato salad were always on the menu. Every now and then, if you listened hard enough through the ruckus, you could hear a young girl crying and pleading, begging to be let loose.

"Where that Black Velvet?" Uncle shouted back. "And bring a beer for my baby here!" He laughed and squeezed Charlotte close.

Uncle was like a proud papa at these parties, smoking cigars and pounding on his chest, slapping fives, and strutting around the room like he'd just won an Olympic medal.

"Can somebody take me home, Uncle?" Charlotte asked quietly.

Uncle didn't answer.

"You know I don't like these parties," she explained. "I just wanna go home."

Uncle got up and disappeared into the bedroom. Ten minutes later he emerged zipping up his pants and slapping more fives.

"That one there is gone be alright," he said confidently.

Charlotte stared disgustedly at him.

He smiled wickedly. "Young and sweet," he said, sitting down next to her. "Almost as sweet as you, darlin'."

Charlotte bolted to her feet, and started to slap him across the face, but Uncle caught her hand in midair. "Nasty!" She blurted out. "You . . . nasty mothafucka!"

Suddenly, the whole room became quiet, except for the sounds coming from the bedroom. The music had stopped and everyone stared at what was happening between the two of them.

Uncle pulled her down until Charlotte was on her knees in front of him. He grabbed her by her upper arms, and dug his fingers into them so deeply, she knew she'd be bruised later.

"I own that in there," he said about the girl in the room. "Just like I own you."

Charlotte grimaced. "You don't own me! You ain't never owned me!"

"One word! One goddamned word and you and that girl in there can trade places. You don't believe me?" Uncle softly kissed her lips. "Try me, and sons of bitches will pull a train on yo' pretty ass 'til the sun come up. I swear."

Charlotte sold her soul to the devil when she became Uncle's woman. Back then, she'd been so caught up in all the things he could do for her: buying her nice clothes, putting her up in that apartment, parading her around town in fur coats and diamonds. She'd never had it like that before Uncle came along and she honestly never thought that she ever would.

That night she'd left, he'd planned on killing her. No matter what he told her now, Charlotte knew that if Lynn hadn't showed up when she did, Charlotte wouldn't be sitting here in this old house now. Months passed before she was able to sleep through the night again without waking up screaming because she saw his face in her nightmares. There were times when she didn't think she'd ever get over what he'd done to her, and Charlotte had thought about taking her own life just to find some peace. It wasn't until Cammy was born that she finally had something to live for. Reesy had turned her back on Charlotte, and Connie had never given a damn about her, but Cammy had always been there for her momma. She'd always been the one Charlotte could count on in her time of need. Charlotte sometimes took Cammy's love and devotion for granted, but that girl proved the last time Charlotte saw her that she was still her baby girl, willing to do any and everything for her momma.

"Cammy," Charlotte whispered into the phone. "Cammy, you awake?"

"Momma?" Cammy responded groggily. "What time is it?"

Charlotte lay in her bed, staring terrified at the door to her bedroom, which was closed. She looked at the clock. It was after midnight.

"Cammy," her voice trembled. "Baby, I miss you."

"I miss you too. Momma, what's wrong?"

She wanted to tell her that Uncle was stalking around again, hinting that he might do her harm. But Charlotte didn't know how to say it. Cammy didn't know who Uncle was. She just thought he was someone her mother knew, but she didn't know the whole truth about that man, and about the things he'd done to Charlotte. She wouldn't have understood.

"When you coming home, Cammy?" Charlotte swallowed and fought to compose herself.

"What?"

"Don't be dumb, Cammy," she said, frustrated. "You heard me."

"I . . . I don't know, Momma," Cammy said quietly.

"I need you here," Charlotte stressed. "You know this old house makes noises at night."

"I know."

"You know how they scare me sometimes."

"It's just the house settling, Momma. It's nothing."

Maybe it was nothing. Maybe . . . it was him. Charlotte was too terrified to get up to see for herself.

"I'm a old man now, girl. I ain't gonna do nothing to you."

Uncle was a liar and a murderer. He hadn't changed either. He'd gotten old, but he was still an evil man with evil intentions. Why else would he have found her after all these years? She could've gotten away from him if Reesy had kept her word and sent for her. Charlotte would've been free of him once and for all, and he'd have never found her. But now he knew where she was, and he knew that she was alone, and there was nothing she could do to stop him from killing her.

"You need to come on home now," she said sternly. "I need your help around here, Cammy. I need . . . I need you to come home and help me."

Charlotte waited for Cammy to respond, but she didn't.

"You hear me?" she asked nervously. "Don't play with me, girl. I know you hear me."

"I . . . I can't . . . come right now, Momma," Cammy responded softly. "I need some help too."

Charlotte could hardly believe her ears. Cammy was talking crazy, no doubt, full of ideas from those two sisters of hers. "You need to bring your ass home, Camille," she demanded. "Now, I don't know what you got going on out there, but—"

"You'll be fine, Momma. It's just that old house settling," she repeated, almost as if she couldn't remember that she'd already said that.

"I want you home with me!" Charlotte sat up in bed. "Camille! I need you here! I need you to get here as soon as you can, or I'll . . ."

"You'll what?" Cammy asked, surprising her.

Charlotte was suddenly speechless.

"What can you do to me that you haven't already done, Momma?"

"I haven't done anything to you," she responded, appalled. "I'm your momma, Camille." She swallowed. "I've raised you, and I've taken care of you."

"Is that what you call it?" she asked listlessly.

Charlotte suddenly became angry and defensive. "What the hell is wrong with you?" she asked coldly. "You sound like you've lost your fuckin' mind. You don't talk to me like that," she threatened. "You don't ever talk to me like that, little girl! You wouldn't be a damn thing without me! You know it, just like I know it!"

"I know it, Momma. I'm tired, and it's late, and I'm going back to sleep now."

"Don't you hang up this phone, Camille!"

"Good night, Momma. And don't worry about the noises. They ain't nothing but that old house settling."

FIFTY-NINE

"So," John moaned satisfactorily as Connie rolled off of him. "Does this mean we straight now?"

She rolled her eyes. "Please."

He looked at her. "You make love to me like that and you're still pissed?"

Connie sighed. "I made love to you like that for sentimental reasons," she explained rationally. "You could've been shot. It kind of got me to thinking what if you had been, then I would've felt bad."

He looked confused. "So, you made love to me because I didn't get shot?"

Connie hesitated before responding. "I made love to you because you could've. He could've killed you, John. I didn't like the thought."

"Well, he wasn't going to shoot me."

"You don't know that."

"But if the threat of me getting shot is going to make you wanna make love to me like you just did, hell, I'll put a damn bull's-eye on my back."

"I'm still not happy," she admitted dismally.

"I am."

"You were with somebody else, John. You cheated on me. Now how would you feel if it were the other way around? What if I'd been the one who'd stepped out on you, even under those circumstances? Yes, we had split up—briefly. But in my heart, it was too soon for either one of us to do something like that."

"I didn't know there was a time limit, Connie," he said dryly.

"You think this is a joke?"

He sighed deeply. After the kind of sex she'd just doled out to him, all John wanted to do was to turn over, hold her close, and then drift off into a sex-induced sleep, the kind that left drool on the pillow. But she wasn't going to let it go. That much was obvious.

"Alright, let's just put it out there. We both agree that I was wrong. Right?"

Of course she'd say it was right, but, deep down, he wasn't convinced. By all accounts Connie had told him that their relationship was over, and as far as he knew it was.

"Right. But don't just say it's right because you think it's what I want to hear. You have to know you were wrong, John, or else it doesn't mean anything."

"Of course I'm going to say you're right. I was wrong."

"Because I think you were wrong?"

"No." Yes. "Because it makes sense to say I was wrong," he argued, trying to play by the rules of engagement that she'd set for this match up without confusing himself. In the end, it was just easier to agree than it was to disagree. "We weren't together, but we hadn't been apart that long."

Connie quietly rationalized what he'd just said, and surprisingly bought into it. "Alright," she said reluctantly.

"And let's both agree that you're unhappy about what I did. Correct?"

"You know I am."

"Which makes me unhappy, too. Can you get with that?"

"Sure."

"Alright." He was starting to feel pretty good about where this conversation was headed. And as long as he didn't say anything stupid, it could turn out even better than he'd hoped. "So, it happened, Connie. I mean, it's a done deal, baby. There's no going back. There's no changing it. There's nothing I can do to erase it. Can we agree on that?"

She rolled her eyes again. "John . . ."

"Yes or no?"

"Yes, but—"

"That's it. There are no buts. It is what it is. The damage has been done. Period."

"It's done and it's something I can't live with."

"Then you want to live without me?" Booyah! The look in her eyes spoke volumes at that moment. Connie hadn't even seen that one coming.

"I can," she said quietly. "And you know it."

Damn! That hurt. John quickly recovered, because this was one match he wasn't willing to walk away from so easily. In the past, he'd been the champ at throwing up his hands and walking away, especially where women were concerned. There had always been another one waiting around the corner. But he was determined to stand his ground and see this one through until the last round.

"Look at how far we've come, Connie," he reasoned. "From where we started two and a half years ago, look at where we are now."

She didn't have anything to say to that. John was starting to feel pumped up again.

"Leaving me would be easy. That's your MO, baby. You're quick to put a brotha out."

"And you're quick to leave."

"Exactly," he countered. He turned over on his side to face her. "I fucked up, Connie. I fucked up because I hurt you. I didn't plan on it, but I did it."

"How am I supposed to trust that it won't happen again?" she asked softly. "You cheated once."

"Once," he held up a finger. "Connie, we have to agree that both of us are doing the best we know how. We have to agree that we've both surprised ourselves in this relationship and have done better than either of us ever expected we could do. If I wanted somebody else, I could've had somebody else."

He didn't have to say Racine's name for her to know who he was talking about.

"I came back here for you. And you let me come back, for me."

Tears filled her eyes. "The odds have been against us from the beginning."

"Hell yeah, they have. But shit . . . after everything we've been through, I'd put some money down on us."

She smiled. "You mean that?"

"I do." He kissed her.

Connie curled up in his arms and sighed. "Don't you ever go to Texas without me again."

He laughed. "No problem."

"Racine's too fuckin' desperate."

He was about to make a joke about the effect his good loving had had on that woman, but John decided not to take a chance and ruin the truce. The best thing he could do would be to never mention Racine's name again.

She got quiet and John thought that she'd fallen asleep. Connie was his life's blood. He realized that every time the thought crossed his mind that he would have to live without her. So, what was stopping him from taking this thing to a whole other level?

"Connie?" he whispered.

"Hmmm," she said, sleepily.

He'd been thinking about it off and on for a while. John had been making progress since he'd met the woman. He'd become the kind of man he'd never believed he could, never even knew he wanted to be, until she came into his life. So, it was only natural that he'd want to complete the evolution of John King and take it to the next level.

"We uh . . . we oughta get married or something."

When she didn't answer right away, John wished he could take back what he'd just said.

"Okay."

He kissed her head. Now he could sleep. Yeah. Now he was cool.

SIXTY

"Arnel passed away, Uncle." Lynn had called him, crying. "He died last night."

Arnel wasn't much, but he was family.

"When's the funeral?" Uncle asked resignedly.

"Saturday at four. Mount Zion."

Of course he had to be there. It was time to go home anyway. Uncle had been here long enough. He made his way through the narrow streets of Murphy and headed to Charlotte's for one last visit.

"C'mon now, Charlotte," he said from outside her front door. "You ain't foolin' nobody. The car's right out front, so I know you home. Let me in." He tapped again with his walking stick.

Uncle was starting to get irritated by Charlotte's dumb games. Uncle rang the doorbell and knocked harder this time. "Answer the goddamned door, Charlie! You don't want me to break the fuckin' window! You know I will!"

Moments later she opened the door, looking a hot mess, as usual. Uncle opened the screen door and let himself in.

He stopped in front of her and looked her up and down, then shook his head. "You really let yo'self go, girl," he muttered.

Uncle sat down for what would probably be the last time. Uncle wasn't coming back to this sorry-ass town and he'd had his fill of this sorry-ass woman too. The Charlotte he'd known wasn't no part of this woman anymore.

"I have to say." He stared disappointedly at her. "This new you ain't even close to being how I pictured you."

Charlotte stared down at her feet, willing them to move as she made her way over to that old, dingy chair she always sat in.

"I didn't expect you to look the same. Hell, we both got years on us and nothing can change that, but you look as old as me, girl, and you what? Ten, twelve years younger?"

"Why did you come here, Uncle?" she finally had the nerve to ask. "What do you want with me?"

The familiar darkness filled Uncle's eyes. "To reconnect, darlin'," he said calmly. "Me and you go way back. And I ain't never let you stray too far away from my thoughts."

The sound of his voice reached deep into her soul and touched parts of her that Charlotte had forgotten were there. There were times when she couldn't get enough of him, that he'd leave her weak and moaning and longing. There were times when he sent shivers down her spine and was at the center of all her nightmares. Uncle had given her everything she could want, and had come within inches of taking her life. She stared at him, knowing that he was right. They were connected. They would always be connected, and no matter how far away she was from him, there was no escaping the impact he had had on her life.

"I lied," he continued coolly. "I hadn't planned on letting you live that night, sugah."

Charlotte shuddered.

"I got loose with my thinking and I made a mistake. I took off to get rid of Zoo. I left 'cause I had a hard time thinking about killing you. I needed to think and get my head right."

Charlotte blinked and tears fell down her cheeks. "You were going to come back and kill me?" she asked hesitantly.

Uncle chuckled. "We got pulled over." He looked at her. "God was on your side that night, baby girl. Ain't that something?"

Her darkest fears had come true. Charlotte was sitting three feet away from the man who wanted her dead, and she was more alone than she'd ever been in her life. Her children had all turned their backs on her. The only friend she'd ever had, Lynn, had betrayed her, and the only two people left in the world in that moment were Charlotte and Uncle.

He stared unemotionally at her. "I'm thirsty, darling," he said menacingly. "Why don't you go get me something cool to drink?"

SIXTY-ONE

Uncle had told them to rape her. He made Zoo watch while they did it. Charlotte shuffled through the kitchen, getting a glass from the cupboard, and then going to the refrigerator and pulling out a pitcher of iced tea. Charlotte had spent years trying to ignore the memories from that night, of the things they'd done to her. She squeezed her eyes shut whenever the image of Uncle putting that gun to that boy's head and pulling the trigger came into view.

He'd intended on killing her that night but the police had gotten to him before he had a chance to.

"Cammy?" She thought she saw that girl, but . . . no. Cammy wasn't here anymore.

"I own you, girl. I ain't never gonna let you go, honey."

Goodness gracious! Where in the hell was that girl? Cammy needed to make more iced tea. The pitcher was almost empty. A lump swelled in her throat thinking about her baby girl. Cammy had been her rock and her reason for getting through each day. She needed Cammy. Right now, she needed Cammy more than she had ever needed anyone.

"Fill every nook and cranny! Let that bitch know what it feels like to be fucked for real."

Fuckin' Reesy! Charlotte was so angry, she felt herself beginning to hyperventilate. If she'd have done what she said she'd do . . . Reesy let her down. She betrayed her in the worst way, and Charlotte would never forgive Reesy for leaving her alone.

"Where's my drink, Charlotte?"

The sound of his voice startled her, and Charlotte nearly spilled it all over the counter. Before she realized it, Uncle was upon her, standing close enough for her to feel his breath on the side of her face. Charlotte didn't dare look up at him. He reached in front of her and took the glass from the counter.

"C'mon back in the living room," he commanded coolly. "Keep me company."

Uncle turned and started to head out of the kitchen. Charlotte would never recall picking up that knife, but she would remember until the day she died how relieved she felt as she drove it into his bony back.

Godammit! That fool put a knife in him. Uncle grunted, and dropped slowly to one knee, shaking his head and trying to catch his breath. "Whatchu . . ." He gasped. "What the hell you do that for, sugah?" He coughed, and then laughed. Oh! That shit hurt. He dropped even farther to the floor, bracing himself on his fists. Blood, warm and thick, trailed down his sides, and all of a sudden, he realized firsthand what it felt like to die.

He stared at a cheap table across the room. Uncle blinked. His vision blurred, sweat beaded on his face, and trying to catch his breath sent shockwaves of pain through his torso. "I . . . c . . . came . . . to get a word . . . girl." He grimaced. His arms trembled, too weak to hold him up any longer. He hadn't seen her in a while. Too long, and look at what had happened to the two of them. Their asses went and got old. He squeezed his eyes shut and remembered how fine she'd been back in the day. Fine. Pretty, light-skinned woman—fine. That girl was . . .

Lord, he felt heavy. All the air in the world seemed to press down on top of him, crushing him. Uncle sank to the floor, lying on his side, fighting for just a bit of air, but his lungs couldn't seem to get full. He almost laughed at them ugly-ass house shoes she had on. When she first answered the door, he had to blink twice, and adjust his glasses. Uncle was nearly seventy, and he knew he had bad eyes, but, hell, they weren't that bad. She looked a mess. What happened to that pretty woman he'd have given his last dollar for?

"Damn, girl!" he exclaimed, struggling to focus on Charlotte standing across the room. "You went and got fat on me," and then he laughed. She didn't, though. Once again, he'd gone and said too much too fast, letting the first thing that came to his head fall out of his mouth. But then, hadn't that always been his way?

Ain't we a pair, he remembered thinking when he saw her again after all these years. If he thought it, he probably said it. And they were. Even now, with his life slowly slipping away from him on that woman's kitchen floor, and her standing across from him wearing them ugly house shoes, they certainly were—a pair.

Uncle lay on her floor, bleeding all over it, and all Charlotte Rodgers could do was stand there and stare. It dawned on her that she'd been holding her breath, and she made the conscious effort to inhale—deeply, and then slowly, exhale all that blood-tainted air from her lungs. She was crying too, but didn't know why. It wasn't for him. Charlotte cried because she'd killed a man. She cried because she'd killed this man, and because killing him meant that she could stop being afraid. She could lay down to sleep at night now, and not have to suffer through the glimpse of a memory or the threat that one day she'd run into him again—that he'd show up out of the blue, just like he'd done today.

She willed her legs to move and stepped over him, trembling. Her knees felt as if they'd buckle underneath her if she took one more step, but Charlotte had to step over him to get into the living room to her chair so that she could sit down before she fainted. She started to call out to Cammy to come get her a beer, but then she remembered that Cammy was gone. Cammy was in Denver, Colorado, with her sisters. There was nobody in that house she could call, and Charlotte would just have to suffer without a beer until she could get herself together to go and get one.

Her good knife stuck out of his back. It was the sharpest one in the house and could cut through anything. Part of her hated the thought of losing that knife, and for a moment she thought about retrieving it, but then cringed at the thought. Charlotte covered her mouth with her hand and stifled a bitter sob.

"Why'd you have to come here?" she screamed, knowing full well that he wasn't going to answer.

Uncle was such an evil man; it wasn't hard for her to figure out what he wanted. Her memories of Uncle were frozen in time, and in her memories he was still that young, ugly, piss-yellow version of himself, dressed sharp and to the nines. But the old man in her kitchen was a shadow of the man she'd known. She never thought it was possible for him to get even skinnier, but he'd managed somehow. Tall, willowy, slumped slightly by age, the evil reigned supreme in those eyes of his, and he still spat venom as good as any poisonous snake from his vile mouth.

He was a fool too, if he thought she was going to let him walk right into her own house and let him finish her off. Uncle was feeble in the head and he deserved that knife in the back. And now, Charlotte was finally free.

SIXTY-TWO

"Nothing I do seems to be right," Cammy admitted openly to Connie. She'd spent several nights at Connie and John's after Isaac had followed her there. Cammy had come on instinct, hoping that John would be home, and thankfully he was. But she could've gotten him killed.

"If anything would've happened to him, Connie," she said with tears filling her eyes.

"It would've been his own damn fault, Cammy. Nobody told that idiot to stand toe-to-toe with a man with a gun."

"If it hadn't been for him, though, Isaac . . ." her voice trailed off.

Connie had made them hot cups of tea. Sandlewood incense wafted through the house and something jazzy played from the speakers. Jonathon was asleep, John had gone to work, and the two of them sat curled up on the sofa.

"Who is Isaac?" Connie asked.

Cammy pursed her lips, unsure of what to say. "I just met him out one night." She sounded embarrassed. "I don't know, Connie," she finally admitted. "I don't know who he is."

Cammy looked and sounded so defeated and weary. Connie

couldn't help but feel sorry for this poor woman. She'd been through so much, and had put on a brave front, to the point that it was obviously tearing her apart.

"Reesy said that you were thinking about moving back home?"

Cammy nodded.

"Why?"

She shrugged.

"Why, Cammy?" Connie asked, more determined this time.

"It was just easier being home," she said, so softly that Connie could barely hear her.

"Easier? How?"

Cammy shrugged again.

"You keep shrugging your shoulders like that and your neck's going to disappear."

Cammy stared at her, perplexed and nearly smiling.

"Come on. Let's keep it real. How would moving home be easier?"

She thought for several minutes before answering. "I know what to do when I'm home. How to act. How to feel. What to do."

"You don't know those things here, though?"

Cammy shook her head. "I know that y'all think I should be happy being here. I thought I would be. It's nice here."

"But it's not home?"

"No."

"You miss Charlotte?"

Cammy looked confused by the question. "I miss . . ."

Connie waited for her to finish her statement, but it became obvious that Cammy couldn't finish it.

"What about the baby, Cammy?" Connie asked carefully. Tears immediately welled up in the girl's eyes. "You never talk about the baby."

"I can't." Her voice quivered. "Besides." She swallowed. "Talking about him won't bring him back."

"No," Connie said sympathetically. "But maybe talking about him will help you to heal."

She shook her head. "No. No, it won't."

"He was real, Cam. He was part of you and maybe talking about him and how you feel, even if it's bad, will somehow help you to honor him."

Cammy didn't respond right away. Connie could see the wheels turning behind her eyes, though. She was at least processing some things now, and Connie was certain that that was something Cammy had never done, perhaps because she didn't know how.

"I miss my baby, Connie," she sobbed.

"I know you do. And you should miss him."

"He wasn't even born yet, and I . . ."

"He was in your body, Cam. He was as real as you and me. Of course you miss him."

Cammy looked desperately into Connie's eyes. "Everybody thinks I should be over it."

Connie shook her head. "That's not true, Cam. You put on a good face, girl. And you tried to make us all think you were over it, but we never thought it would be that easy."

"I just don't know how to be happy, Connie. I don't think I ever knew."

Connie put her arms around Cammy and hugged her. "And that's the bottom line. Isn't it, Cammy?" Cammy was coming from a place that Connie understood all too well. Happiness wasn't a given. It was a skill that most people just took for granted, one that didn't come so easily to the Cammys and Connies of the world.

"You can't buy that shit at the drugstore," Connie joked.

"Nobody can tell you how to be happy either. And you don't wake up one morning and have it sitting there waiting for you next to your coffee. But you deserve it as much as the next person, sweetie. And I promise you, it's not as far away as you might think. You just have to know what it looks like, and go get yourself some."

The last man on earth she expected to see standing at the door of her apartment was Tyrell. Cammy stared at him numbly, unfazed by seeing him here. He stood there, almost as if he expected her to run and jump into his arms or something, but Cammy didn't have the energy to desperately be in love with him anymore. They didn't exchange hugs or formalities. He just looked at her and asked, "You okay?"

Cammy stepped aside to let him in.

"I got here as soon as I could."

The last time she'd spoken to Ty was almost four days ago when Isaac had broken her phone. "I tried calling but didn't get no answer."

She nervously cleared her throat. "My phone was turned off. I haven't been in the mood to talk."

The two of them stood silently in the middle of the room for several minutes before she motioned for him to sit down.

"What's going on, Cam?" he asked, concerned. "Who was that fool on the phone that night?"

She shrugged wearily. "Just someone I know, Ty."

"He hurt you?"

Cammy shook her head, but Ty didn't look like he believed her. Cammy hadn't seen or heard from Isaac for days, since he'd followed her to Connie and John's, and she hoped that she'd never see him again.

Cammy walked past him and sat down on the couch. Ty sat next to her.

"You didn't need to come out here," she said indifferently.

He looked stunned that she'd make a comment like that. "Yes I did. Especially after I heard that idiot on the phone, and then you didn't answer my calls or nothing. What else was I supposed to do?"

"I'm fine, Ty."

"Are you? 'Cause you don't act fine, Cam. You don't look fine, either. You look like you ain't been sleeping."

That's all she'd been doing lately. Cammy managed to get to work and do her job, but it was all very robotic. When she wasn't working, she was sleeping. Talking to Connie had done something to her, although she wasn't sure what. But Connie had told her that she needed to talk to a professional, and that she would help find her a counselor. Cammy wasn't sure she wanted to talk to a total stranger about anything, but Connie insisted and, like with most things, Cammy went along without argument.

"I was just worried about you, Cam," Ty said sincerely. "I thought something bad had happened."

"But that's just it," Cammy suddenly said. "Something bad has happened, and it's been happening for most of my life, Ty."

He looked confused.

"What did you ever see in me?"

"What?"

"Think about it. When we were together, we weren't really together."

"That's because you were always stuck up under your mom."

"So, why did you want me?"

"I love you, Cam! Dang! Ain't it obvious?"

"But why? I never gave you nothing. I was never there for you the way you needed me to be. What did you love about me?"

"You!"

"And who am I?"

Ty was suddenly frustrated. "Now you just talking crazy."

"No. Who am I, Tyrell?"

When he didn't answer, Cammy had her answer. "See? You don't even know. And how could you know when I don't even know?"

"Cammy." He sighed. "You're not making any sense."

But she was. For the first time in her whole life Cammy felt like she was making more sense than she'd ever made before. Tyrell couldn't understand because he was as confused as she had been.

"All I've ever been was Charlotte's Cammy, Ty. Or your Cam. I've been what everybody wanted me to be, and done what everybody else thought I should do."

Now he looked offended. "All I wanted was for you to be my wife, and my baby's momma."

Cammy shook her head. "And all Charlotte wanted was for me to be her little girl who never left her side. But nobody ever thought about what I wanted."

"I thought you wanted me," he said, sounding wounded.

"I wanted you for all the wrong reasons, Tyrell. I wanted you to fill in the blanks where I couldn't fill them in myself."

"There you go talking crazy again."

"I wanted you to tell me who to be," she explained earnestly. "'Cause I really don't know."

"You're the woman I married. You're the woman I fell in love with."

"No, Ty. I don't know who you fell in love with, but I don't think it was me. Not the real me."

"Well, who is the real you, then? Maybe I can convince her that we need to be together."

Cammy thought for a moment, and then stood up and crossed the room. She turned to face him. "See, that's what I have to figure out. I'd have ended up being the same thing for you that I've been to my momma and anybody else who came into my life who thinks they know what I should be doing better than I do."

"So . . . you telling me that I need to turn my ass around and get back to Murphy?"

Cammy nodded. "I'm telling you that's exactly what you should do, because right now . . . ain't nothing here for you."

"I'm not waiting on you, Cammy."

"And you shouldn't, Ty. It's time for both of us to move on."

Cammy went to bed after he left with all sorts of thoughts running through her mind, but that dreadful feeling that had been sleeping in the bed with her wasn't there. He might not believe it, but she knew with certainty that she wasn't ready for a relationship with Ty or any man. Cammy needed help. She needed to find out who she was and what she wanted. Part of her was afraid that she'd never find it, but there was another part that desperately needed to.

"It won't happen overnight," Connie had told her. "It took me a long time to understand that I deserved to be happy just like everybody else. But you gotta want it, Cammy. You can give up or you can be strong and fight through your doubts and depression. Believe me, giving up is much, much harder."

SIXTY-THREE

"You should've worn white," Reesy fussed, helping Connie get into her dress.

Connie looked at Reesy's reflection in the mirror. "You're kidding. Right?"

Connie's dress was a 1950s-style pink Belle Wiggle dress with black accents that hugged every curve of her enviable figure.

"How you can have a kid at your age and be able to get away with wearing something like this is beyond me," Reesy said, zipping her into the dress.

"I like it," Cammy said admiringly, fluffing Connie's 'fro.

Connie winked at Cammy.

When they had put her all together, the three women stood in front of the mirror admiring their creation. Connie looked breathtaking, in her own eclectic way.

Three months ago, John sort of asked her to marry him, and on a whim, they sort of picked a day, Connie sort of made the arrangements with her sisters' help, and John had promised to show up on time.

"You look pretty, Aunt Connie!" Jade rushed into the room and wrapped both arms around Connie's hips.

"You think so?" Connie quipped.

Jade stood back to assess her again. "Yeah." She nodded. "Yeah, I like that dress."

Both of Connie's kids were here on her wedding day. How cool was that? Connie and Jade had come to terms with each other months ago, and she was back to being Aunt Connie again, but with a twist.

She'd sat down with Jade in her room not long after getting back from Texas with John. Connie had been afraid to touch her, and she had no idea how to explain what her mind-set had been like back then. How do you tell an eight-year-old that you were fucked up in the head without using the F word and still make an impact?

"So, you know about me . . . and you?" she asked Jade hesitantly. Jade stared wide-eyed at Connie, looking for answers that Connie had never been able to truly embrace herself.

"You're my first mommy?"

Tears stung her eyes and Connie nodded. "Yeah. That's what I am."

Out of the mouths of babes. Wow.

Jade thought for a few minutes before continuing. "Mommy said that you were sad and that's why you gave me to her and Daddy."

"I was very sad, Jade," Connie confessed. "But not about you. I was sad about some bad things that had happened to me in my life and I didn't know how to stop being sad. And I didn't want my sadness to rub off on you," she added. "I am so sorry, baby."

Jade stood up and put her arms around Connie. "It's okay," she said, tenderly. "It's okay, Aunt Connie."

Jade had a mommy and a daddy who would die for her and a first mommy/favorite aunt who would do the same. She seemed to relish the novelty of that.

The small and quaint ceremony was being held in Reesy's back-yard with just a handful of people in attendance.

"You should've invited more people, Connie," Reesy had complained.

Connie sighed irritably. "John and I have virtually no friends, Reese. We've invited everybody we know."

Reesy laughed. "That's so sad."

Connie laughed too. "I know. Right."

Reesy was the maid of honor, and Cammy was the official babysitter for Jonathon. There was a time when she couldn't go near that boy without getting all teary, but lately she'd gotten better. Cammy was seeing a counselor who was helping her to find herself and cope with the loss of her baby. That poor girl had a host of emotional issues that had plagued her her whole life, but at least now she was dealing with them.

"I might be in therapy for the rest of my life," she admitted once to her sisters.

"Damn, I hope not," Reesy responded.

"For real," Connie agreed.

The three of them all burst out laughing.

"Did you pick this day on purpose?" Reesy had been wanting to ask Connie this question for weeks now.

Connie's introspective expression confirmed what she'd suspected. "Yeah. I think so."

Charlotte was going to be arraigned today on murder charges. Connie couldn't resist the irony.

"Other than the birth of my son, Reese, this is the happiest day of my life—if John shows up," she added. "What better way to pay homage to the woman who made the first half of my life miserable?"

"We shouldn't have just left her alone at a time like this," Cammy added dismally.

Connie stared at her. "How many times has she left you alone, Cammy?"

Reesy and Justin had been separated for the last three months. The kids were taking it hard, but everyone was trying to make the most of a bad situation. Both of them were committed to their children, though, and to making this transition as painless for them as they possibly could.

Justin was John's best man, which everyone found weird when they found out.

"I didn't think John liked you," Reesy said when she heard the news.

Justin smiled. "No, he doesn't like you, Reese," he said, almost apologetically. "I think he's cool with me."

She couldn't help but laugh when he said it, because it was the truth. There had never been any love lost between John and Reesy. As far as she was concerned, John had never been good enough for her sister, and as far as he was concerned, Connie deserved a much better sister. But in recent months, and on some distant level, they had both started to warm up to each other, maybe.

Justin and Reesy had come together today for John and Connie. It was hard to ignore how quickly both of them fell into place, however, when Justin walked through that door. The children became the obedient little soldiers that they could sometimes be. Justin helped arrange and organize and set up, knowing exactly where to find things, just like he'd never left.

Reesy watched him, impressed by his ability to fall into step so effortlessly. She missed them, and in the few short months since he'd been gone, she'd come to realize that replacing a man like Justin might not ever happen.

"You okay?" he asked, passing by her on his way to the back-yard.

She nodded and smiled. "Yeah. Thanks for asking."

He hesitated, and Reesy caught the faint hint of a smile. "I think we're all set back here," he said, before disappearing out back.

John was fifteen minutes late. Reesy was fuming. "See this is why—"

"Reese!" Connie stopped her short. "He'll be here."

Reesy rolled her eyes.

Cammy stood at the window, staring down the street, anxiously waiting to see him come speeding into the cul-de-sac.

Connie was the only one who didn't seem flustered.

"Call him, Connie," Reesy demanded.

Connie ignored her.

"He's here!" Cammy shouted.

The three women sprang into action, putting the finishing touches on the bride. Connie suddenly froze. "Oh God!" she said frantically.

"What?" Reesy and Cammy questioned in unison.

Connie's eyes widened, and suddenly every cool thing about her dissipated.

"Connie?" Reesy asked, concerned. "What is it?"

Connie stared fearfully at her. "I don't think I can do this, Reese," she said, panicked. "I . . . can't . . ."

Reesy was beyond agitated. "Oh, you're doing it! Cammy, get the bouquet!" Reesy took a firm hold of Connie's elbow and practically dragged her out of the room, down the stairs, through the living room, and finally propped her up in front of the door leading to the backyard.

"Reesy!" she said, breathless. "Please. Don't make me."

Reesy laughed. "Too late, girlfriend. He's waiting." She slid open the door and practically booted Connie out onto the lanai to everyone's amazement.

When Reesy finally noticed John, all she could do was groan. That idiot still had on his tool belt.

Hours later, the kids were in bed, the guests had left, Connie was a married woman, and Justin had stayed behind to help clean up.

"I put away all the chairs," he said, coming in from the garage. "You need help with anything else?"

Reesy had just finished wiping down the counters. "No. Thanks." She smiled warmly.

"I'll uh . . . come get the kids around nine on Saturday. Bring them back Sunday night?"

She nodded. "Sure, Justin. That's fine."

"Good night, Reese."

"Night."

The loneliest sound in the world for Reesy was the sound that her front door made when he closed it behind him. The two of them had created such a beautiful world together and they'd made the mistake of allowing their egos to take control and ruin everything. Reesy's pride had been her biggest mistake. She'd let it lead her to do terrible things all because she wouldn't allow herself to forgive Justin for the hurt he'd caused her.

Reason would argue that she was right to feel the way she did. But her heart took issue with reason. Reason finished up, turned off the light, and decided to head upstairs to bed.

"Reese," he said, standing near the door.

She turned, startled by the fact that he was still there. "Justin," she whispered.

He shuffled from one foot to the other. "Would uh . . . Would you mind if . . ."

He didn't even need to finish saying it. Reesy held out her hand. "Actually." She smiled. "I wouldn't mind at all."

He took hold of her hand and followed her upstairs to their bedroom.

EPILOGUE

"You killed a man in cold blood, Miss Rodgers," the district attorney had told her. *"We're going for the maximum, life."*

Cammy came to visit when she could. Charlotte kept demanding that she move closer so that she could see her mother more often, but Charlotte might as well have asked Cammy to be locked up with her. And that's really what her mother wanted. She was a prisoner, and maybe she'd always been. She'd made Cammy a prisoner too.

Cammy sat on the other side of the glass partition talking to her mother through a phone receiver, listening to Charlotte go on and on about the injustices of this place and about how unsafe she felt.

"I don't belong in a place like this, Camille," she said, almost as if Cammy had been the one to put her there. Charlotte glared angrily at her. "I need you to talk to my lawyer again and see what he's doing with getting me outta here. It's been too damn long."

"I spoke to him, Momma," Cammy said softly. "He can't do anything else."

"That's a lie!" she said bitterly. "I was afraid for my life," she said, emphatically pointing her own finger hard into her chest. "I had to protect myself."

They'd found no weapon on the old man. Charlotte had stabbed him when his back was to her, and he was seventy years old. If he had been a threat to Charlotte, it had only been in her mind.

"Reesy wanted me to ask you if you got the package she sent."

Charlotte rolled her eyes. "I got it. But when's she bringing her ass down to see me? Reesy is good about sending shit that don't mean a damn thing in a place like this, but she can't get on a plane to come see me?"

"She said she'd try and come soon."

"Soon," Charlotte said belligerently. "Tell Reesy to kiss my goddamned ass! Soon!"

Cammy visited because that's what a good daughter, who loved her mother, would do. Nothing or no one could ever make her stop loving her mother. Nothing could make her turn her back on her completely. But Cammy was coming to terms with the kind of woman her mother was: selfish, manipulative, maybe even evil on some level. She had mistreated Cammy her whole life, taking advantage of the love a child has for her mother and twisting it into something that only benefitted her. Charlotte never gave a damn about any of her daughters. It was as if someone had pried open Cammy's eyes and forced her to see the truth.

"Why'd you kill that man, Momma?" Cammy asked, looking for one more piece of the puzzle to help put her mother into perspective.

Charlotte stopped complaining and stared hard at Cammy. "I told you why."

By all accounts, he'd been defenseless.

"Because he was gonna kill me."

That cell was too damn small, the food was bad, and that bed was hell on her back. Charlotte had tried to tell them people the truth, but they wouldn't believe it. Uncle had come to kill her. He'd have done it too, if she hadn't gotten to him first.

"You think I just stab people with no reason?" she'd argued to that police officer in that small room. "Look at his record! Uncle had a record. He'd been in and out of jail, he'd killed people, raped, stole! And you wanna put me in jail for taking that menace out of society! Hmpf!" She sat back and folded her hands in her lap. "Y'all should be giving me a fuckin' medal."